DEATH AMONG RUBIES

ALSO AVAILABLE BY R. J. KORETO:

Death on the Sapphire

DEATH AMONG RUBIES

A LADY FRANCES FFOLKES MYSTERY

R. J. Koreto

CROOKED
LANE

NEW YORK

Copyright © 2016 by R. J. Koreto

Published in the United States by Crooked Lane Books, an imprint of The Quick Brown Fox & Company LLC.

Crooked Lane Books and its logo are trademarks of The Quick Brown Fox & Company LLC.

Library of Congress Catalog-in-Publication data available upon request.

ISBN (hardcover): 978-1-62953-776-4
ISBN (paperback): 978-1-62953-816-7
ISBN (ePub): 978-1-62953-817-4
ISBN (Kindle): 978-1-62953-818-1
ISBN (ePub): 978-1-62953-819-8

Cover design by Andy Ruggirello
Book design by Jennifer Canzone

Printed in the United States.

www.crookedlanebooks.com

Crooked Lane Books
34 West 27th St., 10th Floor
New York, NY 10001

First Edition: October 2016

10 9 8 7 6 5 4 3 2 1

To my wife, Elizabeth,
truly a woman far above rubies

CHAPTER 1

Hal took a step back to contemplate the flesh tones on the canvas, the lovely pinks and peaches of his model's skin, the copper sheen of her hair lit to flame by the afternoon sun as it poured over the white robe that left one shoulder tantalizingly bare. He smiled in satisfaction and resumed painting.

"I know we're going for a classical ideal, not historical accuracy," she said. "But as I've said before, it's hard to believe anyone thought ancient Greek shepherdesses would dress like this."

"I agree. And speaking of ideals, Greek shepherdesses had modest, doe eyes—not your disconcertingly frank ones, my dear Franny, to say nothing of your impudent smile." He grinned at her and she grinned back.

"My friends like you," she said.

"Really?" he asked. She looked at him, his pale green eyes, the slightly ruffled hair that was usually slicked back to perfection, the wrinkled shirt splattered with paint.

"Yes, really," she said. "You sound surprised."

"I guess I am surprised. I didn't expect . . ." He searched for words. "They are artists and poets and musicians. I didn't expect them to like me—or for me to like them."

"You're an artist too," she said.

Hal didn't say anything for a while, but Franny didn't mind. She had become used to the way Hal carefully thought about what he was going to say. On most days he was Henry Whea-ton, Esq. Dressed in a black coat and gold-rimmed spectacles, he managed the legal and financial lives of some of the most distinguished men in London—including Frances's brother Charles, the Marquess of Seaforth.

But on days like today, when she could lure him away for a short holiday, he was an artist—and a most devoted suitor.

"I'm not a real artist, Franny, although it's sweet of you to say so," he eventually said. "I'm a solicitor who dabbles. And my successes are due to a most lovely muse."

"Flatterer," she said. "But as a solicitor, aren't you worried about what your fellow members of the Law Society would say if they heard you were painting Lady Frances Ffolkes—sister of a noble client—practically undressed?" She gave him a challenging look, but he didn't get upset.

"Not at all, my dear. They'd slap me on the back and take turns buying me drinks."

"You're a beast. All men are beasts."

"But you're a very good model. And in a little while I'll be done."

"Can I see it then?" she asked, full of excitement.

"Of course." He painted in silence for about another fifteen minutes, then stepped back. It was as good as he could make it.

"Come, Franny. Have a look." She jumped off her perch, adjusted her shepherdess dress, and quickly padded over on bare feet to see what Hal had created.

"Oh!" she said, then fell silent as she stared. Hal smiled. Franny robbed of speech was a rare occurrence.

"What do you think?" he asked.

"Is that what I really look like? It's just . . . marvelous. I'm . . ." She said no more, but gave him a kiss.

"It's what you look like to me—as much as my poor skills can make it. I'm not quite at the level of Sir Joshua Reynolds." He was the great portraitist of a previous generation, whom Hal much admired.

"Oh Hal, never mind Reynolds. I met the most unusual artist when I was last in Paris, a Spaniard, and I saw some of his creations. His way of painting—it took my breath away. I can't even describe it. A completely fresh way of looking at people. His name was Picasso. Pablo Picasso."

"I shall keep an eye open for his work in London and someday we shall travel to Paris and see his paintings together."

"Of course," said Frances, laying a hand on his arm. "But my point was not about following Reynolds or Picasso. I think you're wonderful just as Hal."

A second kiss was interrupted as the door flew open and a man entered the makeshift studio. As opposed to Hal, the visitor was very well dressed, even to the point of flamboyance.

"Sorry to interrupt you two," he said with a mocking tone. Hal blushed.

"I was giving the hardest working artist here a congratulatory kiss for finishing my portrait."

"You finished it? Good show, Wheaton. You must've been working on it before you came here."

"I was posing for Hal in his home studio in London these past weeks," said Frances.

"Really? I continually find you more outré than I expect, Wheaton."

"I assume that's a compliment," said Hal.

"Gerry, stop teasing Hal. He's been working today, which is more than you have. Anyway, what are you wearing? You look like Oscar Wilde. And that's not a compliment."

Gerry just laughed. "Well said, Franny. Anyway, we decided to go for a walk, build ourselves an appetite. Coming?"

"That sounds delightful," said Frances. "I'll just run up and change and give Hal a chance to clean up." She skipped out of the room, and Hal watched her retreat. In the Greek-style dress, with her unbound red hair flowing behind her, she really did look like some forest sprite.

Hal began cleaning his brushes as Gerry continued to study the canvas.

"You really caught our Franny," said Gerry. "You're a man of many parts."

Hal just shrugged. The other guests, men and women, came by in a motley collection of outfits. They looked with curiosity at both the portrait and the man who painted it, while doling out compliments tinged with surprise.

But they all turned to stare when Frances came back.

"Well, how do I look?" she said. Hal and the rest of the company were astonished. Franny was wearing a pair of corduroy trousers, hiking boots, a man's tailored buttoned-up shirt, suspenders, and a wide-brimmed hat. A rough hunting jacket, to keep her warm against the English autumn, completed the ensemble. She was just over five feet tall, so only her nicely rounded figure kept her from being mistaken for a young farmhand.

"So Wheaton," said Gerry. "What do you think of your lady fair?"

"I think she looks far more fetching than she has a right to in that getup." That provoked laughter from everyone.

"It is unbelievably comfortable and practical. I am deeply envious of you men for keeping such clothes to yourselves. I'm going to suggest clothes like this at our next women's suffrage meeting."

Hal laughed as she took his arm, and the company walked out the door and onto the hills. Franny liked the way the breeze ruffled his unruly black hair, which was usually slicked to perfection. In his office, he looked so . . . correct. Reading spectacles hid his liquid green eyes and made him look older, especially when he hunched his tall, lean form over his desk. Out here the years fell away, especially when a wide grin broke onto his fair face.

After about half a mile, their fellow house party members stretched into a long line, and so the two were mostly alone.

"Where did you even get an outfit like that?" Hal asked, as Frances walked boldly over the rough ground without worrying about full skirts and elegant boots more suitable for London streets.

"I came across donated boys' clothes when sorting them for the poor box, and it occurred to me one could buy these new somewhere in London. My maid Mallow did the necessary tailoring. I told her that ladies were now wearing such clothes for country rambles, but she did not approve."

"And speaking of clothes, does Mallow know you posed for me as a classical Greek shepherdess?"

"No," said Frances, with a rueful smile. That would've been too much. "Oh Hal, look at me. Years of behavior that upset my mother, infuriated my father, horrified a slew of governesses, ruined any chance my family had of making an aristocratic match for me—and here I am afraid of offending my maid."

Hal laughed. "Well, she is a wonderful and unusual maid. With a rather wonderful and unusual mistress. And I want you to know that there is a lovely room for Mallow in my house if her mistress were to become my wife." Now he stopped and looked at her.

"Hal, if I don't marry you, I will never marry. But there are a few things I still have to do before I take that step. Just a little patience."

He said nothing for a few moments, and Frances was suddenly afraid she had pushed his patience too far. But then he smiled at her.

"Oh very well, there's nothing I can deny you. I will wait. Now let's walk briskly and work up an appetite, then we'll cook some dinner. In this servant-free bohemian household, I understand you and I have been assigned to the kitchen detail tonight."

Frances made a face. "It'll be a disappointing evening. London solicitors and daughters of peers of the realm aren't trained to cook."

"You do yourself an injustice. I've seen you at work." He had come once to the grim corner of London's East End where Frances helped run a soup kitchen, slicing carrots and turnips and wrestling vats almost as big as she was. And when a pair of local toughs showed up to make trouble, before Hal could even intervene, she chased them off with language he couldn't believe she knew.

"Ah, but our fellow guests will be expecting something better than a cauldron of stew."

"Our efforts can't be worse than the chicken Gerry and Nora cooked last night. Anyway, you'll get your reward next week when you travel to Kestrel's Eyrie. I hear it's one of the greatest houses in England, and I don't see the guests of Sir Calleford taking turns cooking."

"That would be something to see. But no, everything will be just so there, I'm sure. However, this will be a working visit for us. Sir Calleford's daughter Gwendolyn is making a visit home, so her great friend Thomasina and I are going with her, and we plan to find some quiet time to work on various suffrage projects."

"Excellent. And Thomasina—that would be Thomasina Calvin, the young woman you call Tommie? I've noticed you never mention Tommie without Gwen or Gwen without Tommie, like salt and pepper."

Frances studied Hal's face to see if she could find understanding there. "They are like two puzzle pieces that fit only with each other. They love each other very much."

"Like sisters?"

"No. They love each other . . . like Gwen and Tommie."

Hal nodded, and Frances saw that he did, in fact, understand. "How remarkable you are, Franny. Suffragist, muse, fashion pioneer—" she laughed at that "—and now, I see, philosopher as well." They walked a while more and then Hal chuckled. "But I hope you can stay away from investigating another murder. The constables in rural districts tend to be conservative, and they may have less patience with the Lady Sherlock than Scotland Yard does."

"Are you making fun of me?" she asked, peering from under her hat.

"Of course not. I was, and am, immensely proud of you. I just want you to be safe."

"Is that advice coming from my solicitor, or my suitor?"

"Let's say your suitor. If it was from your solicitor, I'd have to charge you a shilling. Now we'll have to head back soon, to see if a distinguished man of law and a lady of the proud House of Seaforth can somehow figure out how to fry sausages and boil potatoes."

Charles, Marquess of Seaforth and Undersecretary for European Affairs, slipped into his wife's dressing room as Mallow was putting the finishing touches on his wife's dress and making adjustments to her hair.

"You look lovely, Mary. Mallow, I daresay her ladyship's maid Garritty would not have done better."

Mallow blushed. There was little doubt in her mind that Lady Frances's brother was one of the greatest men in England.

"Thank you, my lord."

He watched his sister's young maid work. She was helping out this week while Garritty was away assisting her niece with a new baby, since Frances had said she would be spending a few days with some "bohemian" friends in in the country and wouldn't need a maid anyway.

This was a good opportunity. He knew that those soft brown eyes and face with a childlike prettiness hid detailed knowledge of everything his sister was up to. A lady's maid knew all her mistress's secrets. But how to pry them out of her?

"Mr. Henry Wheaton—you know, the family solicitor— dined here recently, Mallow. Lady Frances must see him quite a bit too, doesn't she? I know they are friends. Do you know if he's part of the house party Lady Frances is attending?"

Mallow didn't turn a hair. She smoothed the pleats on Mary's dress and then turned those quiet eyes onto his lordship.

"I'm sure I couldn't say, my lord."

"But then again, she's probably been too busy with her political meetings to socialize much—women's suffrage and all that." He slipped into a jovial tone.

"I'm sure I couldn't say, my lord." Not the slightest trace of rebuke. Delivered as smoothly as if she had said it for the first time. He tried another tack.

"Lady Seaforth and I are patrons of the police widows and orphans fund. The commissioner of police will be dining here next week, Mallow. I know Lady Frances often has dealings with the police and I'll give him her regards—if she's been wandering the halls of Scotland Yard recently."

"I'm sure I couldn't say, my lord."

At that point, Mary, admiring the results in her mirror, thanked Mallow warmly for her excellent work, and told her she could return to the servants' hall until it was time to get her ready for bed at the evening's end.

"Very good, my lady—and good evening to you, my lord." Mallow curtsied and slipped out. Maybe it was his imagination, but Charles could swear there was a spring in her step and that she was holding her chin up—just the way Franny did when she had done something to make herself proud.

Anyway, as the door closed, Mary started to laugh.

"What's so funny?"

"You! I just watched one of highest ranking diplomats in England stymied by his sister's maid. You attempted to pump her about Franny's romantic life, political activities, and police involvement and got precisely nowhere."

"God knows what my sister is up to," he muttered. "All I know is that she's a most talented little liar and has taught all her skills to that maid of hers. When Franny still lived at home and our mother was alive, Mallow helped Franny sneak around a dozen rules. Mother knew but couldn't prove anything against either of them."

"I know—the most delightful mistress-and-maid pair in London. Stop fretting. Franny has always been able to take care of herself, and Mallow is always by her side. But never mind Franny, who I'm sure is fine. Have you had word from Kestrel's Eyrie?"

At that, he brightened. "Yes. Sir Calleford sent a coded cable to my office this morning and a confidential clerk dropped it off earlier. Everything has been going smoothly."

Mary arched one of her elegant eyebrows. She was a political wife and knew what was happening, what was at stake. Mary was also aware that there were things her husband couldn't tell her, though he could give her hints.

"Calleford said everyone is being very cooperative. It bodes well for future plans."

"I'm glad to hear that." She glanced at the clock. "We should go down. The Kaiser's ambassador is due soon. You know Germans are never late." And arm in arm they headed downstairs.

<hr />

Gwendolyn Kestrel loved Evensong, and her great friend Thomasina "Tommie" Calvin was pleased enough to go with her to St. Paul's Cathedral. Gwen came particularly for the music and participated fully, while Tommie's enjoyment came from contemplating the cathedral's visual beauty. She also liked seeing how happy Gwen was. It took very little to make Gwen happy: Evensong, an occasional evening of theater, spending time with the dogs and horses at her father's estate.

After service, they planned as usual for dinner at a quiet café nearby. Those were the times Tommie most cherished. There were so few places, so few situations, where she didn't feel judged: wearing the wrong clothes, saying the wrong thing, enduring comments about when she'd get married. If only the whole of London could be like their suffragist meetings—probably the only group where Tommie felt comfortable.

"That was so lovely," said Gwen. "The choir was in particularly good form. Can we stop for a few moments and tell the rector how much we liked it?"

Tommie smiled indulgently. "Of course. How about this—you tell him how much you enjoyed the music, then I'll meet you out front. I'm going to go into the chapel and light a candle for my father." It was one of Tommie's last remnants of any religious observance.

She had the chapel to herself, but as she was finishing, she heard footsteps and turned around to see who it was. The light was dim, but she could see he was dressed like a gentleman. A man of middle years. Rather serious looking, clean-shaven with a roman nose and a high-domed head. She stepped away from the candles to give him room, but he turned to her.

"Miss Calvin? Miss Thomasina Calvin?"

She blinked. This man didn't look at all familiar.

"Yes . . ." she said hesitatingly.

"I find it rather odd to see you and Miss Kestrel attending a sacred service in one of the greatest cathedrals in England. Your relationship is an affront to all decent Christian behavior."

The words flowed out of him without any menace, as casually as if they were discussing the weather. She tried to speak, but nothing came out.

"You may not care. But Miss Kestrel's father, Sir Calleford, is a wealthy and powerful man. I suggest you cease your corruption of Miss Kestrel while there is still time to save her. And if you cannot curb your base lusts, at least turn your attentions to a less well-connected young woman and don't plan any visits to Kestrel's Eyrie. Good day, Miss Calvin."

He turned and disappeared as quickly as he came.

For a few moments, Tommie felt as if she couldn't breathe—the horrible, disgusting accusations degrading her feelings for the person she loved best in all the world. Her legs started trembling, and feeling sick, she sat on the cold stone floor. Air finally came in great gulps. How could he—how could anyone . . .

She might've stayed like that for an hour or more, but the thought of Gwen made her pull herself together. If Gwen found her like this, there would be no explaining what happened or what the man had said. Gwen was incapable of understanding the baser emotions.

She took a deep breath and made a halfhearted attempt at straightening her clothes. *Stop wallowing and think*, she told herself. *Who was that man?* He definitely wasn't familiar. So perhaps he was an agent sent by someone to frighten and intimidate her. How could someone hate her and Gwen so much? True, they were in the suffragist group, which had its vocal detractors to be sure, but even so, that wouldn't explain that particular accusation. And men usually harangued them when they were speaking in the park, not by cornering them in churches.

Feeling a little steadier, she made her way back to the entrance, where Gwen was waiting for her.

"I'm so glad I stopped to talk to the rector. He seemed very pleased with my compliments. But Tommie—are you unwell?" It was one of the things Tommie loved best about Gwen: no one was more sensitive to the pain in those she loved—and she did love Tommie.

"I was a little overcome for a moment, thinking about my father. But I'm all right now, really. I think I'd just like some strong tea with sugar with our dinner."

"You need to get away. I'm so glad you'll be coming with me to Kestrel's Eyrie—you and Franny."

Of course, their upcoming trip came rushing back to her. She had been looking forward to it—and now that man had been very specific that she shouldn't visit the Eyrie. But she wasn't going to let Gwen go there alone.

And Franny was coming. She was absolutely trustworthy—Tommie could tell her what had happened. Franny would know what to do; Franny was well educated and so clever.

Franny was fearless.

———◦•••◦———

Cheer and laughter dominated the drawing room at Kestrel's Eyrie. Phoebe Blake had ordered a fire, which chased the autumn chill from the large, old-fashioned room. Despite the cool weather, the guests slipped out briefly for some fresh air and a glimpse of a particularly beautiful moon.

Everyone had an after-dinner drink: brandy for the men and cordials for the women. Mrs. Blake had understood that Mr. Mehmet's religion prohibited intoxicating beverages, but he had taken a little wine at dinner to make a toast, and now sipped some sweet sherry.

"I thank you for catering to my needs, Mrs. Blake," he had said earlier. "But some believe that Allah permits small amounts of the fermented grape. It is drunken behavior only that offends him."

Mrs. Blake had no interest in the fine points of Islamic theology, so she just said something noncommittal and moved on. She spoke briefly to the doctor and his wife. Sir Calleford thought it was kind to invite them to these events, and they always accepted, even though they were completely overawed.

Mr. Mehmet looked around the room. Everyone seemed deeply involved in one conversation or another, so he decided it was a good time to slip out. He had already noted a side door that seemed little used at the end of a hallway lined with storage rooms, and made sure no servant saw him leave.

Mehmet walked quickly around to the side of house, where there was only a little moonlight. He peered until he saw a spark of light in a knot of trees bordering the lawn, then headed toward it.

"Kerem, you smoke too much. It'll be the death of you," he said in Turkish, laughing quietly.

"You want one?" He lit a fresh one and handed it to Mehmet. "And what have you for me?" asked Kerem.

Mehmet reached into his pocket for an envelope, which he handed to Kerem, who in turn handed Mehmet another envelope.

"It's questions and information from—"

"No names, not even here," said Mehmet, and Kerem nodded.

"From our 'friend in London,'" he said, using English for that one phrase. "I assume this is your report, which I will give him on my return. But what do you really have for me? I've been standing out here for nearly an hour."

"I can't help it. These English parties—it's not easy to slip away. But here—" He produced a silver flask and handed it to Kerem. "It's brandy." Kerem took a deep drink.

"The Prophet would not approve of drinking so much, so quickly," said Mehmet.

"The Prophet never experienced an English autumn," said Kerem. "I have a very practical view of religion. Just as well I became a soldier, not an imam." They both laughed again. "But when are you coming back to London?"

"I'll be here a while longer," said Mehmet. "There is more work I can do, more people to meet."

"Much longer and the pasha will start wondering. He suspects you and dislikes you anyway. Meeting Englishmen for fun or for advancing the family business is acceptable, but there will be questions if you don't return soon."

"If I go back to London, the pasha can find a way to kill me there."

"If he believes that you, Sir Calleford, and our 'friend in London' are in league, he'll kill you wherever you are. Come, Mehmet, I'm not just your friend—I'm your cousin. There is something else, isn't there? If you can't trust me, you can't trust anyone."

Mehmet peered at Kerem. There was concern there—what they were doing could get them killed.

"You worry too much. The pasha trips over his own two feet and the sultan is all the way in Istanbul."

Kerem turned and spat at the mention of the sultan.

"I know," said Mehmet. "Anyway, I've been gone too long. Take the brandy and I'll keep you notified of any change of plans. Where are you staying tonight?"

"A simple inn near Morchester." He grinned. "I told the waitress there I knew the secrets of the sultan's harem. She was entranced. Perhaps tonight . . ."

Mehmet chuckled. "You're incorrigible. You know nothing of the sultan's harem."

"And neither does the English girl. Thank you for the brandy, and be careful." He disappeared into the dark. Mehmet finished his cigarette and headed back to the house. He quietly opened the forgotten side door again, stepped in, and bolted it behind him before heading along the hallway back to the drawing room. Mehmet didn't expect to see any of his fellow dinner guests and was particularly surprised by whom he saw outside of Sir Calleford's study. But on second thought, perhaps it wasn't such a surprise. What was that useful English word? He thought there might a . . . liaison. He stepped behind some decorative Greek statuary until he was alone, then leisurely returned to the drawing room.

<hr />

Back in the drawing room, an American, Mr. Hardiman, was talking with Mrs. Blake. In her elegant dress and perfectly styled hair, she was not his idea of a farm wife—at least not the farm wives from back home in western New York. But a casual query about local agriculture proved she knew a great deal about the estate's farms. He bet she knew every dime (*no, shilling*, he reminded himself) that went in and out of the lands, and wished etiquette didn't prevent him from asking for a full account.

As she spoke, amused at her guest's curiosity, she noted the heavy chain that led to his large gold pocket watch, which he consulted from time to time. Like everything else Mr. Hardiman seemed to own, it was vulgar—and very, very expensive.

His daughter was not discussing farming. Miss Hardiman was engaged in a lively talk with Mrs. Blake's son, Christopher. A tall, striking girl, she was laughing—a little too loudly—at a funny story Christopher was telling. He had a cheerful, handsome face made for smiling, and clearly enjoyed making the young woman laugh. Once or twice, she gently rested a gloved hand on his arm.

"I do envy you, growing up in this magnificent house," she said, looking around.

"I actually grew up on a neighboring estate," he said, "but I was always a favorite of my uncle's, Sir Calleford, and I spent much of my time here."

"So your uncle owns it?" she asked, looking at him closely.

"No one really owns a house like the Eyrie," said Christopher. "The family is merely its caretaker."

Miss Hardiman wrinkled her nose and said, "But I don't understand . . . I thought . . ."

"My ancestors have lived here for more than three hundred years." He waved a hand carelessly and grinned. "But I'm speaking in riddles. Has anyone really shown you this house? I'll give you a detailed tour tomorrow."

Miss Hardiman clapped her hands together and said that would be delightful.

"Meanwhile, may I escort you outside to see the moon? It's particularly fine tonight."

⁕

Across the room, the lord of the manor, Sir Calleford, was speaking in French with M. and Mme. Aubert. The two men were having an animated talk about history, voices rising, but in amusement rather than anger. Sir Calleford said Gibbon's classic history *The Decline and Fall of the Roman Empire* held the answer to their disagreement, and M. Aubert laughed and said he doubted it. Sir Calleford was threatening to fetch it from his study.

Mme. Aubert became bored and headed over to the two widows, Mrs. Bellinger and Mrs. Sweet. They were usually with each other at gatherings like this. They were single women past their first youth, with little money and no property, so few ever bothered to ask their opinion or try to impress them. But although her English was weak, Mme. Aubert thought stumbling through a discussion of gardens was better than listening to intricacies of Roman history.

Although they were lumped together as "the widows," they were really not at all alike. Mrs. Bellinger looked like she had been carved out of beautiful marble, with a pair of cool eyes that seemed to look down on everyone. No actress could possibly fake such an aristocratic attitude. Mrs. Sweet, on the other hand, lived up to her name, with cheeks that dimpled when she smiled. Her dress was good, but a fine eye would catch the minor repairs that had been made over time. They both managed to admit Mme. Aubert to their talk—Mrs. Sweet with cheer, Mrs. Bellinger with condescension. The Englishwomen talked about how nice it was outside, and Mme. Aubert agreed, although she had a typical French prejudice against drafts.

Mrs. Blake had to step out of the room periodically to have a few words with the servants, including a reminder to the head housemaid to make sure rooms would be readied for Gwen and her friends, who would be arriving later that night. She'd have to talk to Gwen—it was time the girl settled down, found a suitable husband, and prepared for the day when she would be mistress of Kestrel's Eyrie. Mrs. Blake had no illusions about Gwen's ability to run a household like the Eyrie, but she would stay and guide her. Hadn't she made the manor what it was, done what Sir Calleford's late wife had not been capable of? She took great pride in her work. But it was time to begin reminding Gwen of her future role in life. *Men never think of these things*, she thought ruefully.

She'd sit down privately with Gwen, where they wouldn't be disturbed. She'd have to get her alone, of course. Get her away from that rather odd friend of hers, Thomasina. Of course, Gwen was a little odd, too. And Lady Frances Ffolkes as well—between her suffrage work and rumored police involvement, she was making quite a reputation for herself. But Mrs. Blake was confident; she had handled worse than this.

Later, no one could agree on the timetable, who left the drawing room, and when, and for how long. But at some point Mrs. Sweet said she would be heading home and wanted to say good-bye to her host. The last thing anyone remembered was Sir Calleford laughing with M. Aubert, saying he'd prove he was right, and dashing off to his study.

But no one would ever see Sir Calleford alive again.

CHAPTER 2

Frances strode into the lobby of Miss Plimsoll's Residence Hotel for Ladies, still feeling light in her step from her "bohemian holiday." She picked up her letters from the piecrust table where mail was kept for residents and greeted the manageress, Mrs. Beasley.

"Welcome home, Lady Frances. I trust you had a good trip?"

"Very much so, thank you." She headed up the grand staircase to her suite. Mrs. Beasley had said "welcome home," and indeed it felt like home. As much as she liked visiting Charles and Mary in the house where she had grown up, this felt like her place now.

Everyone knew about Miss Plimsoll's. She was the last member of an old family, living in a huge house but finding her money was all gone. She had turned her house into an exclusive residence only for single, well-born women who for one reason or another had no other place to live. Mrs. Beasley guarded the virtue of the residents from a desk by the staircase. At Miss Plimsoll's, Frances found the same freedom and casual way of life as she had in college in America.

Mallow was sewing in their little sitting room but stood up and smiled when her mistress entered.

"Welcome back, my lady. Did you have a good visit with your friends?"

"Yes, thank you, Mallow. I have a note here from Lady Seaforth saying you did as good a job as Garritty. Considering Garritty has been working as a lady's maid for far longer than you, that's a high compliment."

Mallow reddened a little. "Thank you, my lady. I am glad I was able to be of service."

"My brother tried to pump you, no doubt," she said with a smile.

"His lordship asked me several questions about you, my lady, which I was of course unable to answer," she responded coolly.

"Bless you, Mallow. You're a gem."

Her maid had started unpacking Frances's bag meanwhile, and looked with such disdain on the men's clothes she had worn that Frances almost wilted.

"You have gotten these somewhat muddy, my lady. I will have them laundered. Unless you are done with them and wish to donate them to the poor box."

"Oh, thank you, Mallow. These clothes are warm and very comfortable. We'll be taking them to Kestrel's Eyrie tonight. A quick sponging should do it; they're just for outdoor wear anyway, so they don't need to be perfect."

"Very good, my lady." Her tone said it wasn't very good at all. Frances decided to tweak her.

"If you would like, Mallow, I will buy you similar clothes."

"Thank you, my lady, but that won't be necessary." She said it with great stiffness, and Frances felt bad for teasing her.

"I think we'll have a good time at the Eyrie, Mallow. It's an enormous house—a nice change from our little suite here."

Now that caught Mallow's interest. "It must have a very large staff, my lady."

"Oh yes, Mallow. And as you're lady's maid to the daughter of a marquess, you'll have precedence in the servants' hall." Mallow preened at that. "We'll be traveling by train with Miss Kestrel and Miss Calvin." Mallow knew both of them well from their frequent visits to Miss Plimsoll's.

"Very good, my lady. I shall be particularly attentive to Miss Kestrel during our trip, since it has been my experience she tends to drop and forget various personal items."

Frances smiled ruefully. "Yes, Miss Kestrel can be somewhat scatterbrained."

"I was not criticizing your friend, my lady. My late mother, God rest her soul, used to say the vicar at our church was always losing his spectacles because he was too busy thinking of how to help others, and I expect it's the same with Miss Kestrel." Indeed, Gwen was known to empty her purse of an entire week's allowance into the hands of beggars, or be late for lunch because she stopped to help an overwhelmed nanny on the street soothe the fussing children in her care.

"Mallow, it's clear you're not only a fine maid, but a talented diplomat as well."

"Thank you, my lady. We are mostly packed for this evening. I understand that we will all leave together from Miss Kestrel's residence?"

"Yes. We'll dine on the train, arrive late tonight, and be able to start work bright and early tomorrow."

"Very good, my lady," said Mallow. She gathered a few final personal items and frowned as she did what she could with the "walking clothes" before folding and packing them as well.

"I hope you're not too tired, my lady. You were just traveling this morning and we're leaving again tonight."

"But it was a most relaxing trip, Mallow. I feel very invigorated." She gave her maid a sly smile. "Mr. Wheaton was also a guest."

"I'm pleased to hear it, my lady," said Mallow, scarcely looking up from her tasks. "I trust he is well."

"Quite well. It's just that . . . I know you are concerned, and I want you to know he treats me very well." Mallow gave Frances the barest hint of a smile.

"I would be deeply disturbed and surprised if he did not, my lady."

"What do you think of him, Mallow?"

"I'm sure it's not my place to comment on your ladyship's friends . . . or suitors," said Mallow.

"But I'm asking your opinion, Mallow, as I would for a hat or dress."

Mallow saw the mischief in Lady Frances's eyes. "I could say then, my lady, that I think that Mr. Wheaton is almost good enough for you."

Frances laughed. "You really are a diplomat!"

"Thank you, my lady. Now, I packed your green dress. It's suitable formal for dinners at a great house, and sets off your hair nicely."

Mallow summoned two hotel maids to help her bring the bags to the lobby, then turned the bags over to a pair of porters to take them directly to the station, making sure they had the correct train.

"Be careful with them. They belong to Lady Frances Ffolkes, the sister of the Marquess of Seaforth. I will be very displeased if these bags are lost or damaged. Very displeased." The porters were over thirty and Mallow not quite twenty, but her tone and the seriousness of her face wiped away any thoughts they had of merely humoring her. They just touched their caps, said, "Yes, miss," and moved along.

"And I'll be checking with the conductor," she called after them. Then she went back upstairs to get Lady Frances dressed for travel.

Within the hour they were on their way to Gwen Kestrel's London residence. Some years before, Sir Calleford, caring little for London society, had put Gwen in the charge of an aunt of his late wife's to sponsor her debut during the "Season"—the spring and early summer in London, where the cream of English society came together for one house party after another. A key goal was arranging marriages for the young people. In that respect, the Season had not been a success for Gwen. But she found London much more to her liking than her father's country mansion and stayed on with her great-aunt, making only occasional visits home.

On arrival, a maid showed Frances and Mallow into Gwen's bedroom, where she was dithering over her packing. Although wealthy, it never occurred to her to engage a lady's maid, and Tommie was trying, gently, to organize Gwen. Too gently, because little progress was being made.

Frances smiled fondly at the seemingly mismatched pair. Gwen wasn't much taller than Frances, with a pretty but rather vacant face surrounded by golden curls. Tommie, on the other hand, was taller than average, and although a more confident woman would've used that to her advantage, Tommie tended to stoop so as not to stand out. She came from a family of much more modest means than either Gwen or Frances. Her widowed mother was a martyr to her health, and with their few servants run ragged to meet the difficult woman's demands, no one in the household took time to care for Tommie. She was not anyone's idea of pretty, but as Frances observed when she looked at Gwen, there was a Madonna-like beauty in her face.

"So glad you're here, Franny," said Tommie. "I'm ready, but Gwen is a little behind."

"Mallow, I think Miss Kestrel could use your help."

Yes, she could, thought Mallow. *If Miss Kestrel were left to her own devices, they'd never leave.*

Mallow picked appropriate dresses out of Gwen's closet, as Gwen looked on wide-eyed.

"Now, let's get you out of your current dress, miss, and into something more suitable."

"But I like this dress so much," said Gwen.

"And I will pack it for you. It's too elaborate for train travel. You will have trouble making yourself comfortable and the wrinkles will be almost impossible to get out." Ignoring further protests, she began undressing Gwen.

"I already have a hat picked out," said Gwen tentatively, looking at a magnificent confection well-accented with feathers.

"I will pack it most carefully, miss. But it, too, is unsuitable for train travel. It is too ornate."

"Yes, Mallow," said Gwen, meekly.

"It doesn't pay to argue with Mallow," said Frances. "She knows these things."

Mallow had Gwen ready to go in a few minutes, then turned to Tommie. "Now, if you will have a seat, Miss Calvin, I'll just touch up your hair."

"That's quite all right, Mallow—"

But Mallow was already practically pushing Tommie into a chair. The maid's nimble fingers quickly turned Tommie's soft brown hair into a neat and fashionable arrangement. Then Mallow replaced Tommie's hat at an attractive angle.

Mallow turned back to her mistress. "We are ready to go now, my lady."

Gwen's great-aunt kept a coach, which took them to the train. Mallow saw the ladies settled on board, then Frances sent her to the dining car to get herself something to eat.

"Was there a particular reason your father wanted to see you now?" Frances asked Gwen.

"It wasn't Father so much as Aunt Phoebe. Father writes me every week without fail, but never mentions my visiting, except maybe for Christmas. But Aunt Phoebe wrote to say at my age I should take a little more interest in the family estate." She seemed confused by this, and Tommie laid a gentle hand on hers.

"Your Aunt Phoebe—she's your father's sister?" asked Frances.

"No, Phoebe isn't really an aunt at all, or even a true relation, except by marriage. She was married to Father's first cousin, Captain Jim Blake. He was great friends with my father, and after he died and mother died, Aunt Phoebe came to run things for him. Her estate was much smaller, and Christopher takes care of things there."

"Who's he?"

"Oh, Christopher. He's Aunt Phoebe's and Captain Jim's son. He's delightful; everyone loves him. When we were children, he was my best friend, although a few years older. The estates aren't far and he visited often. He was awfully kind; he let me play his games. But he also loved the Eyrie. Father always said that no one loved the Eyrie more than Christopher did. I always found it too . . . much. I liked Christopher's house better, actually. It was . . ." she searched for a word.

"Warmer?" suggested Frances.

"Yes, Franny. You always know the right word." She yawned. "Why do trains make me sleepy?"

"I suspect it's the rocking motion," said Tommie. "We'll be getting in rather late. Take a nap if you like."

"I think I will."

Tommie helped Gwen get comfortable, and by the time Mallow returned, she was peacefully sleeping.

"I'll keep an eye on her, my lady," said Mallow, who produced her knitting and went to work.

Tommie and Frances made their way to the dining car.

"I'm not very hungry . . . perhaps just some soup," said Tommie.

"You are having something substantial," said Frances. "You never eat right." Her mother's cook was too busy trying to get the fussy old lady to eat to prepare something for the self-effacing Tommie.

She smiled softly. "You're right. I'll have the chicken cutlets and maybe even some dessert."

"And wine," said Frances. "You look a little nervous." Tommie may have been anxious about her first visit to such a great house.

"It's not the visit—it's . . . Oh Franny, something so awful happened to me." Her deep eyes looked so sad, Frances thought she might cry. "I don't even know if I can talk about it."

But Frances pressed Tommie, and she related the story of the man in the cathedral.

"But that's . . . horrible. There can be no excuse for that . . . it's appalling," Frances said at last, watching her friend blink back tears at the memory. "Come, let's put our heads together and figure this out. Tell me about this man."

With patient questioning, Frances teased the details from Tommie. It was something she had learned in college: careful exploration yielded results. The man had the clothes and manner of a gentleman and certainly looked English. Was it a London accent? At that, Tommie hesitated. She was a careful, detail-oriented woman, and even in her fear and horror she noticed small things.

"I think so . . . but there was something odd about it, when I think now. Too exact, if it doesn't sound strange."

"Perhaps like someone trying to create a London accent. Maybe to hide where he was from?" Frances frowned. That would bear thinking about. "Tommie, have you ever met Sir Calleford?"

She grew wide-eyed at that. "You mean maybe Sir Calleford sent a man to threaten me? I can't believe that. We met a few times when he came up to London. He was always perfectly polite, if a bit distant."

"He never seemed upset at your friendship or that you brought Gwen into the suffragist group?"

Tommie shook her head. "That was the saddest thing. He didn't seem to care what she did, as long as she didn't embarrass the family." In fact, Gwen was perfectly happy with the clerical work she did for the suffrage group, and never showed any wish to do any speaking or other public work. "I don't want to criticize our host, but I don't think he had much interest in his daughter at all."

That wasn't a surprise. Wealthy and prominent men like Sir Calleford rarely involved themselves much with daughters, beyond seeing that they were properly married. And Frances had to admit even if he objected to Tommie's influence on his daughter, he would've brought his daughter home to the Eyrie, not sent an agent to threaten Tommie.

"You won't say anything to Gwen, will you?" asked Tommie.

"Of course not." She gave her friend a slightly embarrassed look. "Gwen looked so unhappy about her summons home that I was the one who suggested she ask her father if you and I could come for a working visit. He said yes, of course."

"That was very forward of you," said Tommie with a trace of censure. And then she grinned. "But I'm glad you did. I never would've done it, and she's so much happier with us joining her."

They talked over suffrage matters, then Tommie asked the waiter for some rolls and jam for Gwen. "It's all she'll want. No doubt she'll have something more substantial when we arrive."

In fact, Gwen had woken up and was perfectly happy with what Tommie brought her. Meanwhile, Mallow had managed to get her a cup of tea.

"Gwen, will there be other guests at the Eyrie this week?" Frances asked.

"Oh yes," she said. "We have ever so much room there. Father says only Pennington, our butler, knows how many bedrooms. Father wrote me and said the Auberts were staying. They're French. He's an old friend of Father's, and they've visited a lot. And some Americans Father met, a father and daughter. I don't know many Americans, but he said they were nice. And there's a big dinner party tonight, with the usual locals. Mrs. Bellinger and Mrs. Sweet, widows who rent cottages. And the doctor and his wife, who always come. And of course Christopher."

That was interesting, thought Frances. Sir Calleford was a well-regarded diplomat; her brother knew him well and thought a great deal of his skills. French and Americans staying over—that spoke of international discourse and negotiations. These men were no doubt representatives from Paris and Washington.

"Oh, and one more guest. I can't remember his name. It was funny and foreign." Gwen pursed her lips in concentration.

"Do you think it was Russian?" asked Frances, trying to be patient. "German, perhaps?"

"He had an odd-sounding name. Oh, I remember now, he's Turkish. Father said he's a friend from London."

Turkish. An envoy from the Ottoman Empire? The situation in the East was volatile. Frances wondered what they were walking into. It also explained why Gwen's aunt had apparently encouraged them to come so late in the evening. Gwen disliked large, formal dinner parties. *And it would be disturbing*, thought Frances ruefully, *to place noted suffragists among such august diplomats.* Frances knew she was making a name for herself as a speaker and writer in London. Sir Calleford might welcome an outspoken progressive woman to his house, but would think twice about seating her at a dinner with international implications.

It wasn't much longer until they arrived in Morchester, which had once been a sleepy village but had become large and prosperous with the coming of the trains half a century before. Handsome new redbrick buildings were replacing the old wooden ones. Mallow, however, was unimpressed. Born and raised in London, she found every other town in England second-best. *Who knew what services were available in a small place like this*, she wondered, *especially at this late hour?*

"Are we to be met by a motorcar or carriage from the house, my lady?" she asked.

"I imagine things are run very strictly at a great estate like the Eyrie, Mallow, so I'm sure we'll be met. But perhaps you can find some porters?"

Mallow was excellent with porters, and a few minutes later returned with two, leading them like a colonel with his troops. Fortunately, coming up behind them was a chauffeur.

"Mrs. Blake sent me to meet you." He bowed briefly to Gwen. "Welcome home, Miss Kestrel. I will have your luggage brought up by wagon shortly, but you ladies may join me now in the motorcar."

Frances loved motorcars and was thrilled when her brother traded in the family coach for one of these new technological marvels. Mallow, however, as much as she liked train travel, distrusted motorcars. Gentlemen and ladies should be traveling by coach with a team of strong grey horses.

Frances gave the Kestrel car an admiring look. She had heard about this—the remarkable new car from Rolls-Royce.

"This is the Silver Ghost, isn't it?" asked Frances.

"Ah . . . Yes, my lady," said the astonished chauffeur. He had driven many ladies, but none had any interest in motorcars.

"My understanding is that it has a six-cylinder, 7036 cc engine. Is that correct? I've been told that it's almost silent, hence the name 'ghost.'"

Frances relished the look on the chauffeur's face, and Mallow took pleasure in watching her ladyship amaze him. Lady Frances was special.

The chauffeur roused himself from his stupor, helped the women into the car, and started it up. Frances was pleased to discover it was indeed a quiet engine, as they drove out of town to the Kestrel estates.

The car's headlights lit up an elaborate iron gate that had been forged more than a century ago and opened onto a long tree-lined drive, the entranceway to Kestrel's Eyrie. At the first sight of the house, brightly lit, Frances and Tommie forgot their patrician upbringing, and Mallow forgot her servant's training, and cried out. The house seemed to rise from the road in all its Tudor splendor—welcoming, but still ancient and strong in a way the later Georgian manors could never match.

"It is something, isn't it?" said Gwen. "Everyone is stunned the first time they see the Eyrie." But her tone was more sad than proud.

Mallow continued to be dumbstruck by the house, but Frances cast a practiced eye on the grounds. Even by nothing more than the lights from the car and manor house, she could tell the lawn was well-tended, and properly pruned trees dotted the parkland. Signs that someone was overseeing the estate with a sharp eye.

The motorcar had barely stopped when two footmen emerged from the front door to greet them. Following at a more sedate pace was a tall woman dressed for a formal party. She looked to be in her fifties, and Frances saw a little gray among the auburn of her hair. A welcoming smile softened her strong cheekbones and chin.

Gwen was out of the car first, and greeted her aunt with a hug. "So good to see you again, dear. It's been too long. And your friends are welcome, too."

"Aunt Phoebe, these are my very great friends from my suffrage club. This is Miss Thomasina Calvin. She and I work together on so many projects and she's my dearest companion. And this is Lady Frances Ffolkes, who is absolutely the cleverest girl you ever met. This is Mrs. Phoebe Blake, my aunt."

"I know you have other guests. We hope we're not imposing," said Frances.

"Nonsense. I'm glad you could be here to offer companionship for Gwen. And as you can see, there is no lack of room in this house."

Mrs. Blake led them through the spacious Elizabethan hall, with its exposed beams and high windows designed to provide light to the vast space. Frances guessed that even on a clear day, the corners of the expansive room remained lost in shadow.

Then up the stairs and onto a long corridor. "All three of you will be here. You in this room, Lady Frances, and my maid will be along to show your maid her room in the servants' quarters. Gwen, your usual room is available, and you, Miss Calvin, will have an adjoining room. Now, I have things to see to, but if you want, you may gather later in the solar. I'll have some refreshments sent there."

"A solar? You really have a solar here?" asked Frances. It was a gathering room in homes built centuries before. The term had long gone out of fashion.

"It seems silly, I know," said Mrs. Blake. "But an old house has old terms. We have a large drawing room, and the hall, which we rarely use, but we still like the old solar for family events."

"It could take days to get used to a house like this," said Frances.

"It takes years, I assure you. A lifetime," said Mrs. Blake. "Again, welcome. Now Gwen, Miss Calvin, I'll see you to your rooms." She floated out.

Frances found that her room was a large space for a guest room, with a view of the back lawn and the farmlands beyond. Again, Frances noted it had been immaculately cleaned and well-appointed. Footmen followed shortly with their luggage.

Mallow was a practiced hand at unpacking, and soon had Frances's clothes put away and her ladyship refreshed.

"Mallow. I had a talk with Miss Calvin on the train. It seems that someone has been threatening her and Miss Kestrel, although Miss Calvin is the only one who knows."

"I am upset to hear that, my lady," she said, her voice thick with indignation. "If I may say, there are no nicer ladies in London."

"I agree. I am going to try to find out who, and why. Miss Calvin was told not to come here this week, so it may be some-one in the house. So just keep your ears open—if anything odd is happening here, or there is any gossip, let me know."

"Of course, my lady. And may I say I hope the local vicar is an effective preacher, so whoever did this will see the error of their ways this Sunday and repent."

"I hope so too," said Frances, although she had far less faith in religious conversion than her maid.

Mallow had just finished unpacking when there was a knock on the door.

"I am Jenkins, my lady, Mrs. Blake's maid. I will show your maid to her room." She cast an eye on Mallow, who stood straight and met her look right back. Jenkins was about the same age as her mistress and as tall—and not just tall. *She was a large woman, built more like a cook than a maid*, thought Frances.

"This is my maid, Mallow."

Mallow tried to look serious, even haughty. Mallow was young for a lady's maid, promoted when Frances went out on her own. She was sensitive about being taken seriously by older, more experienced maids.

"Of course, you will be known as 'Miss Ffolkes' in the servants' hall. We follow traditional ways here, and visiting servants are known by the names of their mistresses and masters, for simplicity."

"We follow the same customs in Seaforth Manor, country seat of the Marquess of Seaforth," said Mallow with such clarity that Frances suspected she had rehearsed it. The meaning was clear: Jenkins may be lady's maid to the mistress of Kestrel's Eyrie, but Mallow was lady's maid in a noble household.

Jenkins's mouth gave a twitch, which Frances suspected was as close as she came to a smile. "Then there will be no confusion. We dine each evening promptly at eight o' clock." Mallow told her mistress she'd be back later to help her get ready for bed, then followed Jenkins. When they were gone, Frances grinned and shook her head. Her mother always said that even the greatest duchess in the land was not as snobbish as a superior servant.

Frances wasn't tired, so she started making some notes for some suffrage speeches, but it wasn't long before there was a knock on the door.

"Come in!"

It was a housemaid.

"I beg your pardon, my lady. I just wanted to make sure all your luggage arrived."

"Yes, thank you. But since you're here . . ." She looked at the little table in the room. "I have some work to do and this table is very small. Is there an estate office or somewhere where I could spread out?"

The maid expertly hid any surprise that a lady would have "work" to do requiring office space.

"There is an estate office, my lady. Gentlemen from the accounting firm are reviewing the books there this evening, but there is plenty of room. I can take you there, if you like."

Frances gathered up her papers and followed the maid to a spare and practical room in a far corner of the mansion. She knew from her own family's experience that late-night work was common for accountants going over quarterly accounts. The two accountants, clearly the senior partner and a junior, greeted her briefly as the maid refilled the tea pot.

Frances set herself up on a broad table and happily got to work.

"Oh, and please tell my maid Mallow where I am, in case she comes looking for me," she said.

"Very good, my lady," said the maid. The room lapsed into silence as the two accountants and the lady scribbled away with their pens.

Meanwhile Mallow was acquainting herself with the house. She had been to great houses before, but never one this large. Miss Jenkins had told her that visiting servants could join the house staff in the servants' hall. Cook had laid out some evening snacks, as the staff would be up late due to the party.

"Thank you, Miss Jenkins," said Mallow, putting just a little hauteur in her voice. "I will join the staff as soon as I have unpacked my own case."

It took a couple of false turns, but she eventually found her way down to the ground floor and headed toward the servants' hall entrance. There was indeed a nice spread laid out, and Mallow was introduced to a few of the other servants, one of whom told her, with some surprise and curiosity, that Lady Frances was working in the estate office. She clearly hoped Mallow would enlighten her as to why a titled lady needed access to an office.

"Her ladyship runs several important charitable groups and must work at all hours to meet her responsibilities," said Mallow grandly. She stayed for a while, then decided to head back to her room until Lady Frances was ready for bed. Along her way, she passed a footman knocking on a door and frowning.

"Excuse me," said Mallow. "But one doesn't knock on doors, except for bedroom doors."

"Oh, ah . . ." He seemed at a loss.

"I'm lady's maid to Lady Frances Ffolkes, who is a guest here. And you're not supposed to knock on the doors of living areas."

"Oh, yes. Quite. But you see, the master, that is, Sir Calleford, is quite particular. This is his special study, and Mrs. Blake asked me to get him . . ." His voice trailed off. He was clearly unable to decide how to handle this. "Perhaps I should get the butler, Mr. Pennington?"

"Oh, for heaven's sake," said Mallow. "Do you want to show your butler you can't handle a simple task like this? Do you want to be a footman for the rest of your life?" She stepped up to the door and rapped sharply. "Sir Calleford? The mistress would like to speak with you." Mallow put her ear to the door, but heard nothing. So she tried the doorknob and pushed open the door.

"Oh dear God," she said. The footman, right behind her, gasped and started to say something, but couldn't speak. Mallow ventured a few steps into the room, but it was clear nothing could be done. She turned, half dragged the footman with her, and closed the door behind him.

"You stay here. Allow no one in and say nothing. Is that clear?" With the house full of guests, there was no reason for the butler or any other servant to be in that corner of the house in the next few minutes. It would only take a few moments to get her ladyship. She would know what to do.

"Where is the estate office?"

The footman stammered directions, and Mallow took off to find her ladyship with two men working with ledgers. Frances looked up in surprise at Mallow's concerned face. The maid leaned down to whisper.

"My lady, there is something you should see, right now."

Not wanting to attract attention in case they were seen, they walked as fast as they could without breaking into a run.

The footman was still guarding the door, and brought himself up straight when the two women approached.

"My lady, I don't know if you—"

"Just keep standing there," said Frances. She opened the door and entered, followed by Mallow, who closed the door behind them.

Sir Calleford was slumped in his chair. Sticking out of his chest was an elegant, curved dagger, and blood had flowed over three large rubies set in the handle as if to join the jewels in continuous red.

There was no point in checking, Frances realized. The man was dead. She looked at the wound and then glanced around the room. It was clear where the dagger had come from. The wall opposite the desk was decorated with swords and daggers of all kinds. She saw a huge Scottish claymore, a navy cutlass, an Italian dueling sword, an American Bowie knife, and an exotic-looking weapon with a wavy blade. The dagger's scabbard was still on the wall. *The artistry was Turkish*, Frances concluded.

What an odd collection, she thought, *especially for a diplomat*. But gentlemen often liked to collect things. *De gustibus non est disputandum*; there was no accounting for taste.

The rest of the room was masculine, as these offices were. Lots of polished wood, brass, and leather.

"There is nothing else for us to see here, Mallow. Let's go." Outside, the footman was sweating out of fear.

"Go get Mrs. Blake. Tell her that her presence is requested," Frances told the footman, and he left with great relief.

"I hope Mrs. Blake can summon the vicar tonight," said Mallow. Frances smiled briefly. It was so like Mallow to worry about someone's soul. But Frances was saving her concern for the living. Gwen was her father's only child, and most likely had just become the mistress of the Eyrie—and one of the wealthiest women in England.

CHAPTER 3

Everyone stumbled through the evening. Dr. Olcutt, who was there socially, formally pronounced Sir Calleford dead. Then came the chief constable of the county, along with a local inspector named Bedlow, several other constables, and the vicar.

Gwen couldn't seem to take it in, crying until she was sick as Tommie soothed her and fed her tea with honey.

Frances eventually sent Mallow to find some sweet sherry, which she pressed on Gwen.

"I don't drink," whimpered Gwen.

"Now is a good time to start," said Frances, and practically poured it down the girl's throat. Eventually, Dr. Olcutt gave her a mild sedative and she slept.

"I'll sit by her in case she wakes," said Tommie, pulling up a chair.

"She should be out for a while," said the doctor.

"I don't mind," said Tommie. "When she does wake, I'll be here."

Tommie insisted on watching her through the night, but Gwen slept continuously, if restlessly. In the morning, maids came with breakfast trays for the three women. Frances noticed they wore black armbands—someone was very quick and efficient. *Was it Mrs. Blake, or someone else, who had such presence of mind as to make sure the undertakers provided them for the whole staff within hours after the master's death?*

Gwen woke up, still a little dazed, but over her hysterics.

"You won't leave, will you?" she said, hugging Tommie.

"Of course not. Not me, not Franny. We're here for you."

Mallow then showed up and helped the ladies dress, then constables came to take preliminary statements from everyone. But as the women arrived late, the questions were brief. Frances longed to ask the constables what they had discovered so far—even to speak with the inspector—but she knew they wouldn't say anything to her. There would be time for that later.

While Tommie tried to coax Gwen into eating, Frances pulled Mallow aside.

"How are the servants taking this?" she asked.

"Very upset, of course, my lady, but . . ." Frances waited while Mallow found the words. "But most of them didn't really know him, did they?"

Frances nodded. A wealthy and important master like Sir Calleford probably only spoke to his valet and butler. He would be a remote figure to most of the staff. The footmen who served him his dinner would know how he liked his meat and whether he took an extra helping of peas, but not much else.

"I see the household seems to be running well this morning. The butler must be very good, and judging from the organization of the maids this morning, so must the housekeeper."

"But that's a strange thing, my lady. There is no housekeeper. Mrs. Blake takes on the responsibility herself. Very odd, if I may say, my lady."

Odd? It was unheard of. Houses half the size of the Eyrie had a housekeeper. And seeing how well-appointed the house was, it clearly wasn't penny-pinching on Sir Calleford's part.

"Did anyone offer an opinion as to why there is no housekeeper?"

"No, my lady. I only know that there hasn't been one since Mrs. Blake came here after Sir Calleford's wife passed on. She's taken on the housekeeper's job herself and runs the house with

Mr. Pennington, the butler. She addressed the staff this morning, my lady, right after breakfast. Told everyone that the house was to run as normal. Meals in guests' rooms through lunch tomorrow, but then there would be dinner as usual. She was rather . . . fierce about it, my lady."

"Fierce?"

Mallow frowned. She clearly didn't like criticizing the lady of a great house, where she was a servant and her mistress was a guest. "She said that she expected every servant to carry on as usual, my lady. And she said that any servant who couldn't . . . well, was welcome to give notice and depart."

"That does sound a little cold, Mallow. But let us make allowances for the strain of the master's death. And not just death, but murder."

"Yes, my lady."

Tommie was getting Gwen to take a little beef broth, which pleased both of them, but Frances was chafing at the inactivity.

"Gwen, where is your telephone kept? I think I should let Mrs. Elkhorn know about the tragedy." Winifred Elkhorn was president and founder of the League for Women's Political Equality—their suffrage club.

"Oh, yes . . ." she said, vaguely. "There's a closet next to Father's study . . ."

"You just rest, my dear," said Frances, and headed out. Maids and footmen were about their tasks in the household, with only the armbands as a reminder anything unusual had happened. She found the telephone closet and got the exchange to connect her with Mrs. Elkhorn in London. She hoped her friend and mentor was in.

"Frances? Good hearing from you. I trust you, Gwen, and Tommie are working well in the Eyrie?"

"Actually, Mrs. Elkhorn, no . . ." And she proceeded to summarize Sir Calleford's murder.

"My deepest sympathies to Gwen. It must be some sort of lunatic."

"Yes, but there's more. Shortly before this happened, Tommie was threatened while in London and told not to come here by a stranger—a man who said horrible and revolting things about her friendship with Gwen. I can't find a connection, but I don't want to believe it's a coincidence."

"My goodness. You have landed in it, Frances."

"I want to see what this is all about. Gwen and Tommie may be in danger. So we may be a little late with those speeches and pamphlets."

Mrs. Elkhorn gave a quick laugh. "Frances, you've never let me down. It's more important that women are there to support each other—the pamphlets can wait. Gwen will be besieged by men: police, her fathers' advisors, solicitors. The whole point of the League is women working together to help each other."

"I'll take good care of Gwen," promised Frances.

"Let Tommie take care of Gwen," said Mrs. Elkhorn. "She's very nurturing to her. That is not your strong point, Frances. You have other skills."

It was insulting. But honest and true. "Of course, Mrs. Elkhorn. 'We each have a role to play,'" she said, quoting one of her mentor's favorite quotes back to her.

"Very good, my dear. Keep me posted, if you can, and I'll see you when you return. If anyone can succeed, you can."

Frances felt flushed with pride after the call. She valued no one's opinion more than Mrs. Elkhorn's.

Next, she called her closest friend Mary, who was also her brother's wife. Cumberland, the butler, answered the call.

"A pleasure to hear from you, my lady. I will connect you to Lady Seaforth, who is in the drawing room." A moment later, Mary was on the line.

"Mary? I'm at Kestrel's Eyrie. I came up with Gwen Kestrel and Tommie Calvin to work in quiet on some suffrage projects . . . but you must've already heard what happened."

"Yes, a special messenger came from Whitehall. Charles is closeted in his study with foreign office staffers. You know of course he was a distinguished diplomat. How is Gwen faring?"

"Not well. As you know she's a rather sensitive soul and this hit her hard. Tommie and I are doing what we can."

"Of course." She paused. "Are you going to . . . insert yourself into this? I can't imagine it's anything but a lunatic who slipped into the house somehow. It's an enormous residence, probably with half a dozen doors."

"I have been known to help the police," said Frances.

Mary laughed. "And they'll be lucky to have you, even if they do resist the advice of a civilian—and a mere woman at that! But do be careful. Meanwhile, I can give you a clue. It was a secret, but now that it's over, I'm sure Charles won't mind. Sir Calleford was hosting a special meeting, or a series of meetings. A high-ranking French diplomat was there, and a Turkish diplomat as well. The Foreign Office has been very concerned with the instability in the Ottoman Empire, and concerned about what France would do. Oh, and more . . ." she reduced her voice to a whisper. "Charles has been receiving and sending an unusual number of special coded cables to the Eyrie, with confidential messengers arriving at all hours. Cumberland has been driven to distraction. Of course Charles can't discuss the details, but something special, something unusual, was going on. Anyway, last night was the concluding dinner."

"Another interesting angle," said Frances. This clarified the purpose of the dinner, which Gwen had told her about, but also made it clear that there was something secret going on.

"Aha, you said 'another.' The Lady Sherlock is already on the case. Best of luck, my sweet, and make sure Mallow is by your side to guard you. But one more thing—" And even with the crackly phone connection, Frances heard a sharp change in Mary's tone. She always backed up Frances's suffrage work and police involvement with support and amusement, but now turned serious. "When you are settled back in London, you must come over for a long chat—lunch, or tea, just the two of us. I miss you."

"No more than I miss you. We will get together—I promise. Give my love to Charles."

One more call. A deferential clerk answered: "Caleb Wheaton, Solicitors."

"Mr. Henry Wheaton, please. Lady Frances Ffolkes calling." And a moment later Hal was on the phone.

"I can guess why you're calling. We heard early this morning, but no details. How are you Franny?"

"I'm well. It was Mallow who found the body and I was next on the scene."

"The two people most likely to keep a cool head over a killing."

"Thank you, kind sir. But it's already more of a mare's nest than you can imagine . . ." She quickly summarized what she knew of the murder—and the threat to Tommie. When she was done, Hal wasted no time or energy on being appalled.

"If you're looking for agreement from a legal expert that this is no coincidence, you have it. These are connected—as I'm sure you've already concluded."

It was reassuring to have Hal agree with her on that. "Finding the connection is going to be hard. It's not obvious."

"But I have faith in you, my love. Meanwhile, a piece of advice on how these things play out. There is going to have to be an arrest. It is impossible, inconceivable, that a man of such importance and wealth is murdered and someone doesn't hang for it. And perhaps, whoever did this is aware of that. And someone—not the right one, but the most obvious—will be made to pay. Think on that."

"Indeed . . ." His advice sent her mind going in several different directions. But no. She had to be organized and logical. "You are a wise man, Mr. Wheaton. You really do earn your exorbitant fees." He laughed.

"You know, Franny, if you need my help, one call and I'll be on the next train to Morchester."

"And what if I don't need your help . . . just want you to come anyway?" Her tone was half teasing, half serious.

"Again, the next train."

"I do love you," she said.

"I love you too," said Hal. And they rang off.

CHAPTER 4

Franny gave herself a few moments to replay the conversation before rousing herself. Having done what she could, she looked in on Gwen, who was napping again, and Tommie, who was watching over her. She went back to her room to make some notes and then read her book for a bit. It was about a family called Forsyte, written by John Galsworthy, an incisive look into personal relationships and class issues. It made her think of Hal . . .

She read for about half an hour—but the murder kept inserting itself into her mind. A Turkish blade . . . a Turkish diplomat. Was this a message? But why threaten Tommie? Frances paced in her room. There was no helping it. She had to find Mrs. Blake, the mysterious mistress of Kestrel's Eyrie.

Normally, in a situation like this, the lady of the house would be found in her own rooms, but if Mrs. Blake was running the household, she could be anywhere. Frances thought the butler's pantry would be a good place to start—the de facto staff headquarters. But she didn't have to go so far. She found Mrs. Blake in the hallway, just staring at the door of Sir Calleford's study, the scene of the murder. She turned at the sound of Frances's footsteps, and Frances got a good look at her for the first time, as she had seen her only briefly the night before. She was a handsome woman, who when young had certainly been beautiful. But the strain revealed itself around her eyes.

"Lady Frances. People have told me that their first visit to the Eyrie is something they remember for the rest of their lives. I am so sorry yours has been marred by tragedy."

It was a strange speech, but Mrs. Blake was in a strange position. She was the mistress of the house, but not the widow. The wife of a cousin—technically speaking, she didn't even need to wear mourning.

"I hope Gwen is bearing up? Her late mother was my greatest friend, and she wasn't very strong—emotionally or physically. I know Gwen takes after her."

"She had a good night, and Tommie is looking after her."

"How fortunate for her to have such good friends. I've instructed the servants to get her anything she wants, and that applies to you and Miss Calvin as well. The formal meals will resume at dinner tomorrow. Now, as you can imagine, I have a great many details to see to. If you'll excuse me . . ."

"Actually, Mrs. Blake, I was hoping to have a few moments of your time."

Mrs. Blake raised an eyebrow, and Frances wondered if she'd refuse her outright or fob her off on the butler.

"I see. Come with me then." And she led Frances to what apparently was a morning room. In most houses, such a room was used as an informal gathering place, but here it looked like an office and retreat for Mrs. Blake. Frances guessed she used it for intimate conversations, and indeed, she closed the door when they entered. They made themselves comfortable.

"It was my maid, of course, who found Sir Calleford dead. I couldn't help but wonder if the dagger had any significance. I'm not an expert in weapons or antiques, but even I could see what an exquisite piece of workmanship it was."

"What an extraordinary question. If you didn't come from such a distinguished family, I'd suspect you of gross curiosity." A thin smile. A challenging smile.

"Not at all. But my people have always been involved in foreign affairs. I know the weapon was Turkish. And you have a Turkish guest."

"I see," she said. Frances suspected she could read Mrs. Blake's mind: *What can you do about these modern London girls?* "You couldn't help but notice that Sir Calleford collected bladed weapons. I don't know why; he never discussed his reasons. But he enjoyed talking about the collection itself. That piece—the ruby dagger, he called it—was his particular prize. He picked it up some years ago on a trip to Istanbul. According to the story, two centuries ago the three rubies were a gift to a powerful Turkish family from a royal emissary in Burma, where you'll find the finest of these gemstones. The Turkish nobleman had them set in the hilt of a dagger, made to his specifications."

"I imagine it was cursed?" asked Frances. "One hears that all great jewels come with a curse."

Mrs. Blake smiled briefly. "You've read Wilkie Collins's celebrated mystery novel, *The Moonstone,* I see. Yes, the dagger comes with quite a backstory. The original nobleman who owned it died without sons. A son-in-law and a nephew fought over it, and the nephew actually stabbed the son-in-law to death with it. The daughter eventually gave it to her son, who in an absent moment cut himself with it and died of blood poisoning. The cousin who then took possession enjoyed keeping it on his person, and was attacked by a pair of thieves. He successfully defended himself but died of his wounds days later. Meanwhile, the family had done something to offend the sultan and went into decline. Suspecting it was worth a great deal, the last owner quietly put it on the market through discreet agents for dealers, who have lists of serious collectors, and Sir Calleford bought it."

Mrs. Blake shrugged. "Who knows if all that is true? All I know for sure is that he spent a small fortune for it. I can't imagine it has anything to do with our Turkish guest, Mr. Mehmet. He is—was—a recent acquaintance of Sir Calleford's, but I know little about him. But let me ask you a question, Lady Frances. As you said, that rather remarkable maid found Sir Calleford. Why did she go directly to you?"

Now Frances raised an eyebrow. "Mallow is remarkable, but I didn't know you realized that."

"It's obvious. Only a remarkable maid would've kept such a cool head. Most would've fainted or started screaming. And my guess is that she's barely twenty, awfully young to be a lady's maid, especially to a titled lady. Even more remarkable. And yet, as calm as she was, she fetched her mistress, and not me as lady of the house."

Frances shrugged. "Not knowing you, she probably felt I was in a better position to give her immediate instructions."

"Perhaps you're right," said Mrs. Blake, but her tone said she didn't believe that for a minute.

"I understand you were in the middle of a dinner party. Why was Sir Calleford in his study?"

"More research for the Foreign Office?" She smiled again, but Frances didn't respond. "Oh, very well. Dinner was over, and the gentlemen had rejoined the ladies. We were talking in knots, and Sir Calleford said something about a passage he had come across in Gibbon. He kept *Decline and Fall of the Roman Empire* in his study. We kept talking among ourselves in the drawing room. People wandered outside for a bit of fresh air; it was cool, but not unpleasantly cold if you had a wrap or jacket. When he didn't come back, I sent a footman to find him—and that's when your maid stepped in."

For a few moments, the mask of the grand lady of Kestrel's Eyrie fell away, and Frances saw deep sadness. She had been married to Sir Calleford's cousin; she had no doubt known the master of the Eyrie for many years.

"I'm wondering if you could now answer me some questions. I said I was glad you and Miss Calvin came, but I am still trying to figure out how our Gwen ended up in a women's suffrage group. I wouldn't have thought it of her. Understand I am not criticizing, but I was surprised."

It was only fair. She had satisfied Frances' curiosity, and expected the favor returned.

"You don't think Gwen would have the convictions?" asked Frances.

Mrs. Blake smiled coolly. "Frankly, no. That is not the type of thing I ever thought Gwen would be interested in. I admit I don't know her very well; she has spent most of her adult years in London, so I rarely see her. But I should say that even though you and I just met, your name is not unknown to me, Lady Frances. You are a true believer. I imagine Miss Calvin is as well. But I wonder if Gwen is even clear on what Parliament does."

"Different types of women join us for different reasons. But our founder and president, Mrs. Elkhorn, believes that every woman has something to contribute. Every woman is accepted and valued and every woman in our group is treated with kindness and respect. For someone like Gwen, who felt deeply uncomfortable with the arch and artificial conversations of a debutante ball, a group like ours has been a little oasis for her. She has found a place in life."

Frances knew as she finished that she had spoken too fully and too sharply. It was one of her sins; once she got on her hobby horse, she rode it till the end.

But Mrs. Blake didn't seem affronted, merely amused. "How interesting. Then I am very glad for the League for Women's Political Equality and its ability to provide a life for my niece."

Frances decided to press the point. "I'm pleased you agree. I know Gwen was worried that her father would object to her activities with the group."

Mrs. Blake echoed what Frances already knew: "Sir Calleford was a busy man with many intellectual pursuits. Men like that often take little interest in their daughters. As long as she was reasonably discreet and didn't embarrass the family publicly, he was happy to leave her to her own devices. As the daughter of the Marquess of Seaforth, a minister of the crown, I'm sure you have personal experience with that."

Mrs. Blake was absolutely right. Her father had not been unkind, but he had many interests and responsibilities, including seeing that his son would be prepared to take over the family someday. Frances was merely supposed to marry well.

Of course, reflected Frances, she had not been reasonably discreet and had indeed embarrassed the family. Her father had had to pay a lot more attention to his daughter than he had anticipated. He only agreed to send her to college in America because her mother had pointed out that if Frances was to misbehave, better in America where no one knew them than in London in front of all their friends and relatives.

Mrs. Blake brought Frances back to the present. "I know you are Gwen's friend, but Tommie—they seem to have a particularly close friendship. I haven't met her before, but Sir Calleford told me Tommie is mentioned frequently in her letters. And yet I know nothing about her. Can you tell me how Gwen and Tommie met?" asked Mrs. Blake.

"They took their first Season together," said Frances. "But I'm sorry to say that both for your niece and for Tommie, the Season was a disaster. Gwen is sweet, as you know, but not especially quick, and she had been unable to keep up with the other debutantes, with their flirting and inside jokes. And Tommie had just plain felt left out, with her introverted personality and intellectual interests. In a London town house, they found each other in the library. They happily spoke to each other about their interests, and a friendship was born."

"Gwen never told me that," said Mrs. Blake. She gave a wry smile. "But I have heard tales of your debut—the following year. Their Season may have been disappointing. Yours was notorious."

Frances didn't blush. It was true her behavior had been over the top and she didn't apologize for it. Instead of limiting her conversation to society fashions, Frances had insisted on discussing politics and avant-garde literature. Finally, completely bored at one party her mother had insisted she attend, she convinced a few other debutantes to follow her on an adventure. She bribed a coachman to take them on what turned out to be a high-speed champagne-fueled race through the park that only ended when a constable pulled them over for disturbing the king's peace. Frances's father had threatened to send her to a Spanish convent school after that episode.

"I have no regrets," said Frances.

"No, I don't suppose you would," said Mrs. Blake, more in admiration than censure. "The Seaforths are well-known, and even up here we've heard that in some circles you're referred to as Mad Lady Frances."

"I expect to have that name on my tombstone someday," said Frances. She was rather proud of the moniker.

"I really must go now, but make yourself free of the house. If you want, have a look at our gardens, which we're expanding and renovating. Perhaps Gwen can give you a tour, if she's up to it. It might do her good to have something to occupy her. I know it does for me. Meanwhile, I also have let everyone know that the police have requested that our overnight guests remain for the time being." She made a face. "Won't it be fun passing that news on?"

Frances thanked Mrs. Blake again, and decided it would be a good idea to look over the grounds. She came across the constables examining the ground-floor windows, no doubt trying to see if someone had sneaked into the house. They were taking directions from a well-fed-looking man who almost strutted as he walked. *The local police inspector*, Frances gathered, making sure the gentry saw how actively he was seeking out the culprit.

Frances again cast her eyes over the house as she walked around it. True, it was enormous, and an intruder would have to find just one loose window or a forgotten basement door with a broken lock. But once inside, what then? The household was crawling with servants and a stranger would instantly stand out. How would he know where to go, especially during a lively dinner party? It didn't seem to make any sense. What were the odds

they'd find someone alone in the study? Sir Calleford would have
to stay perfectly still while this mythical robber pulled a dagger
from the wall and went at him.

Back inside and on her way back to her room, she ran into
the butler.

"I beg your pardon, my lady, but I know you are with
Miss Gwendolyn's party from London, and I was wondering
how she is bearing up."

He called her "Miss Gwendolyn." He was clearly old enough
to have been in the house since well before Gwen had been born
and had known Gwen her whole life.

"She is doing as well as can be expected and had a good
night. Thank you for your concern, which I'll convey to her. It's
of course a very difficult time for her."

"I am sure, my lady." He paused. "It's a very difficult time
for all of us." Pennington probably mourned a good employer,
someone he was close to. He might also be wondering what
would happen to the house and staff. He looked near retirement,
and likely Sir Calleford had left him a legacy, but still . . .

"I am sorry for you, too, Pennington. I imagine it was a
privilege serving a great man like Sir Calleford."

She saw surprise and then understanding in his eyes. "Yes,
my lady. For forty years I've served here. And if I may say, he
wasn't just a great man; he was a good one. You won't find anyone to say otherwise."

And that, thought Frances, was a fine epitaph.

"I am sure the police have already asked, but were there any
arguments during the evening? Any unpleasantness during or
after dinner?"

But the sentiment in his face disappeared immediately. "Nothing at all, my lady."

Even though Frances was a guest and friend of Gwen's, and a
daughter of a noble family, he wasn't going to share anything. It
was one of the great strengths of a good staff—but it made any
investigation very difficult. And if he wouldn't share anything

with the sister of the Marquess of Seaforth, he was even less likely to cooperate with the police.

She headed back upstairs to see how Gwen and Tommie were doing.

⊷⊶

The next morning started with breakfast trays again, and Frances decided that Gwen, who had again slept through the night, had to get up and get going.

"Jenkins, Aunt Phoebe's maid, said she'd help me get dressed, but she's a little . . ."

"Yes, a little overwhelming. Mallow, could you see Miss Kestrel into her dress?" A black dress had been found for her, and Mallow did some last-minute alterations to fit her into it.

"I'd like to see your solar here," Frances said. "Is it a pleasant room?"

"Oh yes," said Gwen. "It's my favorite room. Not too big, with a lovely view of the grounds."

"Good. We'll settle there for now, and maybe get some tea. Your father was always a busy man, Gwen, and wouldn't want you idle. We can at least talk about some of the suffrage issues." Frances doubted suffrage politics was what Sir Calleford had in mind, but anything to keep her thoughts occupied.

The solar was indeed a pleasant, old-fashioned room. The furniture was good, as befitted a fine house, but less elegant than what was found elsewhere in the Eyrie. This was a room for the family, not generally for guests. And the view was indeed excellent, showing acres of lawn and farmland.

"When Christopher and I were little, we played here," said Gwen. "He'd pretend to be a king, and this was his court. That big, old chair there was his throne. And when he wasn't here, I'd bring my dolls in and we'd have tea . . ." She prattled on, and Tommie seemed pleased for the change of attitude. They talked more about Gwen's childhood while sipping tea.

The conversation ended with the arrival of the vicar, a young, scholarly looking man with somewhat unruly hair. *He probably absently combs his fingers through it when he's anxious*, thought Frances, and he proved her right by doing it then and there.

"Miss Kestrel? I am pleased to see you again, although I am sorry for the circumstances, of course. Your Aunt Phoebe told me I'd find you here. She and I have settled most of the issues regarding the funeral, but I was hoping we could go over some hymns—a chance for you to add your personal insights, so to speak." He smiled and pushed his spectacles back up his nose.

Gwen did her duty and introduced her friends to the Rev. Jellicoe, who praised the young women for supporting their friend. Frances suggested Gwen and the vicar make themselves comfortable at the small table by the far window, and that gave Frances a chance to bring Tommie to the other end of the room to talk quietly.

"Gwen seems to be coping," said Frances. "But how are you? I haven't forgotten how you were threatened yet you came here anyway."

"I am not like you, Franny. I'm petrified at the thought of making speeches in the park or making calls on government officials. But I should hope that I can find enough courage to stand by my closest friend in her hour of need." She half smiled, and Frances reached out and squeezed her hand. The two women looked out the window, across the expanse of lawn. She saw a party of workmen cross the grounds on their way to the village road and could just hear their talk.

"I wonder what those workmen are doing. Something with the funeral?"

"I imagine the gardens. Gwen told me a while ago that her father was having some major improvements made. That's the one thing Gwen said she really missed in London, having a very nice garden."

Frances nodded. Tommie would remember something like that about Gwen. She remembered what Mrs. Elkhorn said:

Tommie was there to take care of Gwen. Frances had other duties. She wondered if Mallow was picking up anything in the servants' hall and started considering when it would be best to tackle the local police inspector.

───────◆◈◆───────

Despite the tragedy, Mallow was enjoying being in the servants' hall of a great house. It was so much larger and more formal than Miss Plimsoll's. *What if her ladyship married a duke or earl, and moved to a manor house like this? But no . . . not Lady Frances.*

When the servants' breakfast was over, she saw one of the footmen hanging back to speak with the butler, Mr. Pennington. She walked from the table slowly so she could hear what they were saying.

"I checked as you asked, Mr. Pennington, and the constables are still walking around the grounds."

"Tramping on the flowers and leaving holes in the lawn, no doubt," he said.

"And the visitors from London have arrived. I set them up in the blue parlor, as you instructed earlier."

Pennington sighed. "Very good. You saw they were served tea, as Mrs. Blake asked?"

"Yes, sir. With the second-best china, as you said." The footman flashed a cheeky smile.

"I daresay they'd have preferred beer, Mr. Pennington."

Mr. Pennington was not amused. "I daresay you're right. But they're not going to get it."

That was curious. Lady Frances would be interested. Mallow quickly headed up to the solar and found her ladyship with her friends. She pulled her ladyship away into a quiet corner.

"I heard something that may be important, my lady," Mallow said before recounting what she had overheard.

"Visitors from London," Frances said at last. "But not important ones. The butler seems unhappy with them. They're only getting the second-best china and it's assumed they'd want beer rather than tea." Only servants drank beer. And only on their own time. "I think our visitors are London police. Guests, but not quite gentlemen. Scotland Yard detectives, for sure. The blue parlor?"

"Yes, my lady."

Frances told Tommie where she was going and left with Mallow.

Not being from these parts, Frances knew she'd have little influence with the local constabulary, unlike in London. They might not like her in London, but they certainly knew her, knew her persistence, knew her willingness to use connections to push her way into the offices of the most senior Scotland Yard officials. She knew chief inspectors and superintendents—even the commissioner.

The blue parlor was on the ground floor, a small and cozy room suitable for half a dozen people to have a quiet talk during a party. The door was open, which probably meant the police were not yet meeting with anyone. Frances stuck her head in— and her heart leapt. This was better than she had dared hope. The two men in the room had their backs to her as they reviewed the chamber's elegant appointments.

One was enormous, both tall and broad, in a loud check suit. The other was slightly built, in a quiet but rumpled suit that she remembered from previous meetings.

"Inspector Eastley?"

The man turned sharply. Then he closed his eyes and sighed dramatically. "Lady Frances. What are you doing here?"

"I'm a guest here—I arrived two nights ago. It seems we'll be working together again, inspector. Isn't that exciting?"

CHAPTER 5

"I had hoped after our last meeting, you were done inserting yourself into crime and involving yourself with the police," Inspector Eastley said. "I hate to think you've taken to following me. You weren't here at the dinner party, were you?"

The officer standing next to him, Constable Smith, consulted a sheaf of papers, and in his heavy cockney accent said, "She's not on the list, sir."

"I wasn't at the dinner party myself. Miss Kestrel, another friend, Miss Thomasina Calvin, and I came late that night."

Inspector Eastley turned to his constable. "Smith? Isn't Lady Frances somewhere among the interview notes that the local inspector, Bedlow, gave to you?"

Smith shuffled through the pages. "Here we go, sir. We had only worked our way through the actual party guests. Lady Frances is listed back here, along with anyone on the estate who was not actually at the dinner, sir."

"Inspector Bedlow's organization leaves something to be desired," said Eastley. "Anyway, the question remains, Lady Frances. What are you doing here? How do you know Miss Kestrel?"

"Miss Kestrel, Miss Calvin, and I all know each other from the suffragist group."

"That figures," said Inspector Eastley.

"I fail to see how that 'figures,' inspector. But never mind. I am just here to support my friend." His features softened somewhat, so she made her move. "Of course, if there is any information you can share, I know it would put Miss Kestrel's mind at ease."

"Absolutely not, Lady Frances. You should know better than to even ask."

But Frances already knew something. Eastley and Smith were members of an elite Scotland Yard unit called Special Branch. They had responsibility for high-profile cases where the security of the realm might be involved. As Sir Calleford was a diplomat and several visitors were from overseas, it made sense they were present.

"Now, inspector, you did admit that I was of help to you last time."

"I was desperate and you were lucky." He held up his hand to forestall any further discussion. "We're very busy, so if there's nothing else—yes, constable?"

One of the local uniformed constables had entered the room, a young man who removed his helmet and stood at attention. His tunic was neat. Frances bet he had a wife—no, he was too young, probably a mother—who cared about his appearance.

"Begging your pardon, inspector. We just found out that several of the witnesses don't speak English."

"What? Morchester station should've passed that on to me before I left London. Another mistake. Who doesn't speak English?"

"There are a Monsieur and Madame Aubert, sir, from Paris, France. They also have two servants. Madame speaks a few words of English, I ascertained, sir, but not enough for an interview. The servants speak no English at all. Monsieur speaks perfect English, but of course we can't have one witness translating for another. I am based in the village, sir, and I know our doctor speaks a little French. He said was willing to try, but it's been some years."

"Thank you for your diligence," said the inspector with a sigh. "But we'll have to call London, and that means a day is lost. I hope the French guests were planning to stay for the funeral. I can't hold them."

"Excuse me inspector—"

"What is it, Lady Frances? You see I'm busy. Why are you still here?"

"No need to be rude, especially as I'm about to help you. I speak perfect French." She just had to hope Inspector Eastley wasn't going to be stubborn. But he was too intelligent to turn away such a good solution. "I was tutored as a girl, studied in college, and have been to France multiple times."

She could see him thinking it over, trying to find a reason to reject her.

"There is a problem. You're technically a suspect."

Frances rolled her eyes. "Really, inspector? That's ludicrous."

"Sir," said Constable Smith. "According to the interview notes, Miss Kestrel and Miss Calvin were just with each other for most of the evening. But Lady Frances was in the estate office with a pair of chartered accountants during the relevant period. They were absolutely sure Lady Frances never left."

"We just have their word for it, I suppose?"

"They are from a well-known and reputable firm, sir. Inspector Bedlow said he saw no reason to question their statements."

Eastley gave him a sour look, then turned back to Frances. "You're really fluent?"

"I can almost pass for French."

"And you don't know the Auberts? I have to make sure there are no conflicts of interest."

She assured him she knew none of the guests; the inspector sighed again. "Very well. I'm not happy about it, but I see no other solution. Smith, make a note that Lady Frances Ffolkes is being engaged as an official police interpreter. And you, constable . . ."

"Dill, sir, Arthur Dill."

"Dill, we'll start with Madame Aubert's maid."

"Leonie, sir. I'll send her up."

Frances was thrilled. Not only would she possibly learn something, but this would be a new experience, and new experiences tended to be both educational and entertaining. Of course, it would be a challenge, too. It was one thing to know a foreign language, and quite another to translate rapidly from one to the other.

Inspector Eastley sat her down and gave her some strict instructions. She was only a translator. She was not to add questions or comments, or decide what was or was not relevant. And everything she heard was a secret; nothing left the room.

"My family has been in public service for generations," she said, feeling a little patronized. "And I'm sure you will find me satisfactory."

Leonie was darkly pretty, and even the rather shapeless black dress she wore, standard for a lady's maid, didn't completely obscure a lithe figure, much like a dancer's. She didn't seem nervous or excited. She took a chair when invited, and Eastley began asking questions while Smith took notes. If she thought it odd that a lady of quality was acting as translator, she said nothing.

Frances was able to jump right in, and found the simple questions and answers easy to handle: Her name was Leonie, and she had been with Madame for four years. Madame had told her to answer all the questions of the English inspector of police. This was her third trip to Kestrel's Eyrie. She knew nothing about Sir Calleford, had only seen him in passing. She had heard him speak French to Madame—pleasantries, nothing more.

No, she had not heard anyone arguing at any time. Everyone seemed to be having a good visit. Madame never said anything about Sir Calleford, one way or another. Frances heard Leonie shut down at that. If Inspector Eastley thought he could get Leonie to pass along any confidences she held with her mistress, he was very much mistaken.

Leonie knew nothing about the murder until she heard it from her ladyship. Had she been in her room, all evening? Here, there was just a moment's hesitation, and Eastley seized on that.

"Ask her where she was, and what she saw. Tell her if she wasn't supposed to leave her room but did so anyway, we will not give her secret away to her mistress."

Frances emphasized that the English inspector would be discreet, but Leonie wasn't impressed or rattled. "It was stuffy in my room. I was outside for a few minutes for some fresh air. But I got cold and came back. I don't know how long I was outside. I didn't look at the clock."

"Inspector, I think I know what she was up to—" started Frances.

"Lady Frances, you have been most helpful in the past, and I'll be the first to admit that. But these are just simple statements right now, so let's stick to the task at hand, shall we?"

"Duly noted, inspector," she said, stiffly.

He had a few more questions, which yielded no useful information. Leonie had neither seen nor heard anything unusual. The inspector dismissed her and told her to send up Jean, Monsieur's valet.

Frances used the break to dab her brow with her handkerchief.

"Difficult work, my lady?" asked the inspector, with a brief smile.

"Intellectually challenging," she countered. When she got back to London, perhaps she could add her name to an official list of translators at Scotland Yard. She was always looking for ways to insinuate women into the police force, and this could be one route.

Jean was considerably older than Leonie and had a world-weary, almost sardonic tone about him. He seemed curious at seeing Lady Frances, but said nothing.

He had been with Monsieur for nearly twenty years and had visited the Eyrie more times than he could remember. It was his understanding that his master and Sir Calleford were friends of long standing, but when Eastley pushed for details, he shut down just like Leonie had. No gossip here. He never discussed Sir Calleford with his master. During the evening, he said he played a friendly game of cards in the servants' hall with three of the footmen—Benjamin, Adam, and James—he knew just enough English for that.

Jean was dismissed, and told to send the request that Mme. Aubert come, if it was convenient.

"So far, so good, Lady Frances. Thank you. It will be a little trickier now. Madame is the wife of a diplomat, and we don't want to offend." Frances wanted to add that she was used to talking to diplomats and their wives, in English and French, but decided there was no point in getting the inspector's back up, especially when things were going so well.

"I will be very careful with my phrasing," she assured him.

Mme. Aubert was an elegantly dressed woman in her late fifties, with well-coifed silver hair. When she was seated, Inspector Eastley thanked her for her cooperation, and Frances translated, as Mme. Aubert briefly smiled.

"She says she is happy to be of assistance—and also expressed surprise that the police employ ladies of quality to translate. I told her I was a friend of the family's and volunteered to help. I assume that was satisfactory?"

"Yes," he said dryly.

"Have you been to the Eyrie before?" asked Frances, on behalf of the inspector.

"Yes, several times, and my husband has been here by himself over many years. My husband and Sir Calleford were great friends, and had known each other through diplomatic channels for many years. No, there were no arguments during the evening or at any time. Intellectual disagreements of course, but nothing serious."

"What happened during the course of the evening?"

"We had all gathered in the drawing room after dinner. During our stay, it had just been ourselves and a Turkish gentleman, Mr. Mehmet. I didn't really speak with him, as he spoke English but not French. On the last night, many other guests were invited. Everyone was chatting, stepping outside for a breath of air—it would be impossible for anyone to keep track of who went where."

Frances had already heard the Gibbon story from Mrs. Blake, and now she got to hear it again from Mme. Aubert: "Sir Calleford and my husband were in a playful discussion about something political—I become bored and moved on. And suddenly, I heard Sir Calleford laugh and say he'd prove his point and get his Gibbon."

"Was it Sir Calleford's idea to get the Gibbon? Or your husband's?"

Madame shrugged. "I couldn't say. I wasn't paying close attention. It was something that happened frequently. The two old friends enjoyed intellectual combat."

"Her word was 'combat'?" asked Inspector Eastley.

"That's the best translation," said Frances. And he nodded.

The inspector next asked what she thought of Sir Calleford. And that gave her pause. When she did speak, she chose her words carefully, and Frances gave a moment's pause herself to find the best English words.

"You hesitate, Lady Frances," said the inspector with a smile. "Is your vocabulary not up to the task?"

"My vocabulary is excellent," snapped Frances.

"My apologies for teasing you. You are actually much more fluid than our usual man in London." He glanced at Constable Smith, who was writing furiously. "Smith has no problem keeping up with him, but you're much faster."

"Thank you," said a mollified Frances. "Anyway, Madame is an intelligent and thoughtful woman. She was choosing her words with great care so I want to make sure I choose the English words with equal care. She said she found Sir Calleford intellectual and always exceedingly polite—courtly, in fact. But he was reserved and did not discuss feelings or thoughts on his family. Well, what could you expect from the English?"

"Lady Frances—that last bit. Was that Madame or were you editorializing?"

"That was Madame—I did not add anything, as you instructed," said Frances, a little affronted that she was accused of disobeying orders. But she had to add: "Nevertheless, I do agree. But her tone was not one of criticism."

Frances was dying to ask Mme. Aubert if Sir Calleford had said anything about his daughter—or if she had formed any opinion of Gwen herself. But there would be a chance for that later; she'd get her alone at some point before they returned to France.

"There is one more thing, Monsieur le Inspector," said Mme. Aubert. "One doesn't like to tell tales, but as you probably already heard, people were stepping outside from time to time for fresh air. Indeed, I stepped out once myself." She smiled. "Between following my husband's and Sir Calleford's intellectual discussion in French and forcing myself to speak my limited English with the other guests, I had developed a headache and wanted some quiet outside alone. It was a fine evening. I saw one of the other guests—Mrs. Bellinger—just along the walk." She paused. "I don't think she saw me. She was in a discussion with someone. I wouldn't say it was an argument. But it was—animé."

Frances translated it as "animated."

"I didn't want to pry, you understand, but I wanted to make sure she was all right. So I stayed in the shadows until I saw whom she was talking to." She paused again, clearly struggling with her desire not be seen as an eavesdropper. "It was the Turkish visitor, Mr. Mehmet. But they were speaking in English, so I couldn't understand them."

Inspector Eastley leaned back and looked thoughtful. Frances was poised for more questions, but he just said, "Thank you for being so frank. I will be discreet with what you have told me."

Mme. Aubert responded by saying that she and her husband mourned the loss of their friend and hoped the famed English police would spare no effort in finding the murderer. She thanked the inspector and Frances again, and on her way out, she said that if there was a Catholic church nearby, she would say prayers for his soul.

Eastley remained lost in thought for a moment, and Constable Smith quietly wrote in his notebook, the pen moving neatly in his huge hand. Frances had a dozen questions—but reminded herself to be patient. She would be able to ask them later.

"Lady Frances, thank you very much," said Eastley. "You saved us a great deal of time and bother. I will remind you, however, that your part in this investigation is over." Without waiting for a response, he turned to Constable Smith. "I have to place a call to London. Then we'll proceed with the next witnesses."

"Yes, sir," said Smith, and without a look back, Inspector Eastley left.

"I have something for you, m'lady," said Smith. He handed her a piece of paper. "This is a voucher. Submit it to Metropolitan Police Headquarters to be paid for your services."

"Constable—" said an astonished Frances. "I did this to help, not for money."

If Constable Smith saw anything odd in paying the wealthy daughter of a powerful aristocratic family, he kept it to himself.

"I have to give it to you, m'lady. It's the rules," he said, and Frances took the paper authorizing His Majesty's Exchequer to pay Frances Ffolkes for providing translation services to the Metropolitan Police Service. Imagine that—getting paid! She had no intention of submitting it, but as soon as she got back to London she'd have it framed.

"Thank you, constable. And good day." She stepped into the hallway. First things first. That French maid was lying, but Frances had no illusions about being able to get her to admit it. She was far too self-possessed for that, and as Frances was not her mistress, there was no leverage. But footmen were another story.

Jean, the valet, said he was playing cards with three footmen. A house of this size would need at least four. At least one was not at the card game. And Frances knew how to find out without raising anyone's suspicions.

With a few false starts, she found the dining room, and as she suspected, maids were already setting the table in preparation for dinner.

"Excuse me, but I was wondering if you could help me?"

"Of course, my lady," said one of the maids, young and wide-eyed. Good—she looked naïve and wouldn't think too much about Frances's questions.

"The footmen were very helpful with our luggage today. I wanted to make sure I gave them all the proper thanks." Tipping servants in a country house, especially when they had been helpful, was common.

"Of course, my lady. There are four, Mark, Adam, David . . . and Owen." She blushed at that last name. "He's still new, my lady." Another maid snickered, but quickly covered up. Well, that made it all clear.

"If you're looking for them, they might be in the drawing room. Mrs. Blake likes the furniture set up special for after dinner." Frances thanked them, but didn't say it was unlikely anyone would feel like gathering after dinner tonight.

As Mrs. Blake had said, it was larger than the solar. Few houses boasted a drawing room like this, which served as the main social room for all gatherings smaller than a full-fledged ball. Indeed, you could even set up a small orchestra right in this room.

Two footmen were working on the furniture.

"Excuse me, is one of you Owen?"

"Yes, my lady." His accent, like his name, showed him to be Welsh. His handsome features showed why the maid blushed at his name. He stepped over to Frances.

"I understand that all of you, and you in particular, were both helpful and careful with my luggage, and I want you to know that I will remember that when I depart."

"Thank you, my lady."

"Also, since you're here, I have a quick question. I know you have been keeping company with Leonie, Madame Aubert's personal maid, and while I have no interest in your personal life, I would like to know if you saw anything during your evening tryst." She smiled.

Frances rather admired him for not buckling immediately.

"I, ah, my lady . . . I am not quite sure I understand what you mean." Unlike Leonie, he was a very bad liar.

"Now, Owen, I have no intention of reporting anything to Mrs. Blake, Miss Kestrel, or to Mme. Aubert. Or the police, for that matter. But I do have a need to find out what you saw that evening. It may have to do with your master's death, and as a friend of Miss Kestrel's, I am asking a few questions. This is a family matter, Owen." She was counting on his loyalty to the Kestrels for cooperation, and his respect for authority to not inquire why a lady was asking these questions.

Owen nervously slid his finger around his collar. "Well, if you put it like that, my lady, I will admit that I did take an evening walk with Leonie."

I bet it was a lot more than a walk, thought Frances.

"However, we didn't see anyone that night. We, ah, paused, by the gardener's shed near the formal gardens, my lady, but we had the place to ourselves."

"Are you absolutely sure?"

"Yes, my lady." She studied him—he wasn't lying outright, but there was something he was nervous about. She wasn't going to give up. Frances just kept looking up at him, and eventually he spoke again. "But the night previous, my lady—the night before the dinner party that ended in the master's death—that evening, Leonie and I did see two people in the gardens." He took a deep breath. "It was the master, my lady."

"I take it this was unusual?"

"Unheard of, my lady. The master was very regular in his habits. He'd have a last cigar and brandy in his study and then straight to bed. He never went out after dark. His schedule was so regular you could set your watch by him, my lady."

"And who was he with?"

"Mrs. Sweet, my lady. She's a widow who rents a cottage on the estate and was also a guest at the dinner party the following night. She's been here for dinner before, with all what we called the local worthies, my lady—squires, the vicar, solicitor, doctor, and so forth. But they've never been out walking."

"Did you hear them say anything?" At that, Owen became uncomfortable. This time, she was asking a servant about eavesdropping—and repeating a master's conversation was a major sin below stairs. But of course, the master was dead.

"Just one thing, my lady. I was distracted." As he realized what he said, his cheeks flamed. Leonie's sultry face and supple body—of course Owen was distracted. "I beg your pardon, my lady. But I heard Sir Calleford say one thing to Mrs. Sweet. He said, 'It won't always be like this.' Or something very close to that. But if she said anything, I didn't hear it."

Frances nodded. "Thank you, Owen. You've been very helpful—you may go back to your duties."

"Very good, my lady."

"One piece of advice—do be careful. You've begun what could be an excellent career in service in a great house—you don't want to complicate it. And thank you again for being careful with my luggage."

Frances turned and left. Owen might've stood there the rest of the afternoon gaping after Lady Frances, but the other footman said, "Hey! I could use a little help here." And so he shook his head and went back to work.

CHAPTER 6

Mallow had received instructions from her mistress to keep an ear out for gossip. Servants always knew what was going on, especially in a place like the Eyrie with a large staff. Of course, one had to give gossip in order to get it, and a proper lady's maid did not gossip about her mistress. But Lady Frances had approved areas of discussion that were fair game for Mallow to relate to other servants.

Nothing worked with Jenkins, Mrs. Blake's maid. As they were equals, they might've chatted, but Jenkins proved quiet and moody—almost sullen. She had showed Mallow her room and reminded her of when she needed to dress Lady Frances, and that was it.

Downstairs, however, over tea in the servants' hall, the large staff was more welcoming, and more than a little curious about Lady Frances, a member of a powerful aristocratic family. Mr. Pennington oversaw the proceedings with a strict eye, but allowed a certain latitude to talk to a visiting servant.

The servants were subdued, but not in mourning. Again, most of them hadn't really known the master, and for the young maids in particular, who didn't even serve at dinner, the event was more thrilling than tragic. After all, life in the country with a semiretired master was probably boring day-by-day.

"It must be exciting, working in a great house in London," ventured a housemaid named Nellie, whose ingrained cheerful nature was not appreciably dampened by the recent tragedy. "All the lords and ladies coming by."

"I came from the household of the marquess, but now her ladyship and I live in a private hotel for ladies."

That amazed everyone—even the butler seemed startled. Young ladies did not live on their own.

"Lady Frances likes her freedom," said Mallow loftily. "She was used to it after attending university in America."

"Oh, go on," said a footman. "Ladies don't go to college."

Mallow glared at him. "There are colleges for ladies in America, and Lady Frances went to one. She's very unusual." And everyone became wide-eyed when she told them about her political work getting the vote for women—they clearly didn't know Miss Kestrel was also involved in the group. "Lady Frances has also been to police headquarters at Scotland Yard. I've even been there with her." That astonished everyone.

After answering questions, Mallow ventured one of her own. "I suppose Miss Kestrel will come back here from London to live, and Mrs. Blake will return to live with her son?"

Before anyone could respond, the butler said, "It would be unseemly to speculate at this point." And that ended the conversation.

However, Mallow was able to pick it up later, after tea, when she sat at a small table with Nellie to catch up with their sewing. Nellie made sure Mr. Pennington was not around, then said, "To be honest, we are concerned that Miss Kestrel will not want to return. She's lived in London for years now, and she doesn't . . ." She lowered her voice to a whisper. "I'm not sure she's well-suited to running a house of this size, even if she hired a proper housekeeper."

"Maybe she'll get married," suggested Mallow. "And you'll have a new master."

"Maybe. There's been talk that she might marry her cousin, Mr. Blake—then the two estates would be joined. He visits a lot. A very fine man." She paused. "I suppose Lady Frances will get married someday, and you'll move to a fine house."

"Yes, but right now her ladyship is too busy to get married."

Well, that was something. Nellie knew women who were too old to get married. Or too poor. But too busy?

Nellie pursed her lips and looked thoughtful. "A friend of the master's visited once. A young man, from a good family. We thought he might've come to possibly court Miss Kestrel and even marry her. But his valet said his master wouldn't because of some old poet Miss Kestrel liked . . . let me think . . . a funny name . . . I don't see why he wouldn't marry her because she liked the poet . . . Oh, it was such a funny name . . . Oh, now I remember . . . Saffy? No, it was Saffo. That was it for sure."

They chatted a while more, before Mr. Pennington called Nellie away for other duties. However, Mallow was not alone long. Another woman came to join her, but the new arrival did not look like a proper servant. Her hair wasn't as neat as it could be and Mallow thought her clothes were a little casual for a maid. She was holding a fine evening dress.

"Excuse me," she said. "We haven't been introduced, but I was watching you sew and I've never seen such perfect stitches. Could you help me?"

"Oh . . . yes, of course," said Mallow. She took pride in her sewing and was flattered. "Bring a chair around into the light."

"Thank you so much. I'm Amy, Amy Hopp, although here I'm supposed to be Miss Hardiman, because it's my mistress's name. Dumbest thing I ever heard, but if that's what they do, I guess I gotta go along. Anyway, my mistress is a guest here, with her father, and back home we don't dress like this so much."

Mallow was a bit overwhelmed by a servant who so freely offered such sharply worded opinions, but again, she knew her ladyship was relying on her.

"I would be Miss Ffolkes, after my mistress, but—" and she gave a welcoming smile. "My name is June Mallow."

"Glad to meet you, Junie." She stuck out her hand and gave Mallow a firm shake. She was a strongly built girl, not especially tall but with broad shoulders and lots of straw-colored hair.

Her mistress had a tear along the seam of her evening dress. For Mallow, it was an easy job, but Hopp was impressed. "I never would've done it like that."

"You have to, if you want the stitches to remain invisible. See? As good as new. You could never tell." Mallow handed her the dress back.

"Well, wait'll I tell Miss Hardiman what I learned."

Mallow leaned over the little table and whispered. "Don't do that. Take credit yourself. I don't care, and don't let your mistress think that there was something you didn't know."

Hopp grinned. "Say, aren't you the clever one! Like I said, back home we don't dress so fancy."

"And that would be—America?" asked Mallow. The accent was a giveaway.

"That's right. Took a ship here, and wasn't that something. We've been mostly in London, kinda fun, more lively than back home. You're from London?"

"Yes. My mistress is Lady Frances Ffolkes. She's the daughter of a marquess. They're a very important family, lords and ladies, bishops and members of parliament. Lady Frances knows everyone, famous writers and artists and actors. Once, the king himself came to dinner at her brother's house. Lady Frances started talking with him about politics and almost caused a scandal."

Hopp's eyes got bigger and bigger. "You sure have more fun than we have, I can tell you."

Mallow saw nothing but admiration in the maid's eyes, which thrilled her.

"Do you have moving pictures in your town in America?" asked Mallow.

Hopp shook her head sadly. "No. There's one in Buffalo, but it's too far from our house. And we've been too busy in London."

"Well, when we get back to London, on your evening off, you'll come with me and my friends from other good houses, and we'll go see a moving picture. Then we'll have a glass of cider in a respectable establishment."

"Well aren't you the best!" cried Hopp.

Now to move in. "So tell me, Miss Hopp, why did you come to England? Is Mr. Hardiman also in government?"

"In government? I don't really know. I do know he's very rich. I think he just wanted to travel a bit, and well . . . I shouldn't really say." She lowered her eyes.

"Oh, but you can tell me . . . Amy."

The girl looked around. "Oh, very well. It's just us. The real reason . . . Miss Hardiman is looking for a husband. That's why we were staying in London. Going to parties to meet a lord who'd marry Miss Hardiman."

Mallow nodded. "Your secret is safe with me."

Hopp looked down at the repaired dress. "I ought to go back upstairs with this. Thank you again, Junie."

Mallow looked up at this cheerful, sloppy American. "When we are alone together, you can be Amy and I can be . . . Junie. But among others, I will be Miss Ffolkes and you will be Miss Hardiman."

"It sounds like a silly rule, like I said. First name, last name, it's all the same to me."

"They are not silly rules. As a lady's maid I have earned the right to be called 'Miss Mallow' at home. To be called 'Miss Ffolkes' when we travel to great houses—it is something I'm proud of. Women must achieve and must proudly insist on recognition of their achievements, no matter what their station in life. Lady Frances says so."

Amy looked a little stunned at this. Mallow was young, but her words lent a gravitas to her face.

"Are there a lot of English ladies like your Lady Frances?"

"No. Of that I am sure." When Mallow was just a housemaid in the household of Lady Frances's parents, she had more than once overheard old Lady Seaforth sigh and say "There is no one like our Franny," and old Lord Seaforth mutter, "Thank heaven."

Mallow finished her sewing and then headed upstairs to help Frances get dressed for dinner. It would naturally be a subdued affair, Mr. Pennington had said, but he expected it to be done right. Mallow was going to make sure her ladyship was a credit to the House of Seaforth.

"Getting on with the other servants?" asked Frances.

"Yes, my lady, although Miss Jenkins was a bit standoffish, I must say. They say downstairs she's a good lady's maid, very devoted to Mrs. Blake. She knew Mrs. Blake even before her marriage—in fact, she's from these parts. But still, she keeps herself to herself."

"Any talk about Sir Calleford?"

"Not much, my lady. No one said he was ever unkind, rather reserved. But they had some things to say about Mrs. Blake. Runs a very tight ship, she does."

"Cruel or unfair?"

"Not exactly, my lady. But heaven help the maid who forgets to dust a vase or a footman with unshined shoes. You get a dressing down. And a speech. She lectures the servants on the history of the house, and how you're letting the family down if you're less than perfect."

Not just strict, but odd, thought Frances.

"But she can be nice, too. She told Sir Calleford's valet he could stay on until he found a new position, and has already written him an excellent reference."

Kind and wise, thought Frances. It was important to keep up the servants' morale. A house like this would fall to pieces without proper staffing, and a murder was terrible enough without servants worrying about getting dismissed.

And then Mallow proudly launched into her real discoveries, her conversations with Nellie and Amy. Frances listened carefully without interrupting.

"Well done, Mallow! That's a lot of excellent information. So there was some thought or hope that Gwen would marry Mr. Blake, her second cousin." *Was it just rumor, or had there ever been a real plan?* "And speaking of young women getting married, we have Miss Hardiman looking to become a countess or even duchess. Where were they staying in London?"

"At Claridge's, my lady." *Of course. The most elegant and prominent hotel in London. The perfect place to start meeting the "right people."* Miss Hardiman would not be the first young American woman to trade a huge dowry for a match with an aristocratic but impoverished English family. This was no doubt engineered by Mr. Hardiman. An alliance with one of the great English families would be good for his career as well—especially if it was his goal to ingratiate himself with London's diplomatic elite. Were there disagreements with Sir Calleford? Something to embarrass Miss Hardiman?

"If I may say, my lady," said Mallow with a little hesitation. "Miss Hopp, although pleasant and respectable, would not pass muster in England. She would not be more than a simple housemaid or scullery maid in Lady Seaforth's house."

"I'm sure you're right, Mallow. My guess is that the Hardimans are what are called *nouveau riche*. That means the new rich—people, usually Americans, who had very little money but then suddenly became rich. Now they want to mix with other rich people, those who may have been rich for generations." Frances's family had been aristocrats since Kestrel's Eyrie was new.

Mallow nodded. There were "new rich" people in London, people who had money but no ties to the aristocracy or even the landed gentry—the well-off landholders who had owned large tracks of farmland for generations. The servants knew who these new rich were. Lady Frances numbered some of them among her friends in charitable circles in particular and in the suffragist group. She didn't care where the money came from, as long as it was honestly made, but her late mother wouldn't have them at her dinner parties.

And the new rich often didn't make the wisest decisions in hiring servants.

"And one more thing, my lady. I don't really understand, but it may be important." She told how someone said that Miss Kestrel liked some poet too much, and seemed to think this was very funny. "Nellie remembered it, as it was an odd name, my lady, and I wrote it down as best I could, although we don't know if I got the spelling right." She produced a piece of paper from her sleeve and showed it to Frances.

"Saffo." *A close approximation for* "Sappho." *Oh my.*

"Sappho was a Greek poetess who lived a long time ago. From what little we know about her, she lived a very . . . unconventional life." That was one way to put it.

"Oh. Like you, my lady," said Mallow.

"Not exactly. You see, Sappho didn't like the company of men. She had . . ." Frances struggled to find the words to explain it to Mallow. The poor girl would be shocked. "She had romantic feelings for other women, rather than men."

"I see, my lady." She cast a critical eye on Frances's evening dress, to make sure it was smooth. Mallow was reacting coolly to the whole thing, and Frances realized she had misjudged her maid. There was no telling what Mallow had seen growing up in one of London's poorest neighborhoods. Behavior was much the same everywhere, Frances had observed, but some things were easier to hide in the large houses of the rich than in tightly packed tenements.

"So I'm afraid that visiting gentleman was suggesting Miss Kestrel was like Sappho," concluded Frances.

"If I may say, it's very wicked, my lady."

Frances turned. "What is wicked, Mallow? The behavior or the telling of tales?"

"Oh, my lady, the telling of tales! What people do is none of my concern. Now if you could hand me one more hairpin, my lady, we'll be all ready."

Frances smiled at her remarkable maid. "Thank you. Again, you did very well today."

And Mallow flushed with pride while Frances reflected: *So at least one other person wondered about Gwen. Who was spreading these tales?*

"So, do you like being in a great house in the country, with a big servants' hall?" asked Frances. "Should I marry a great lord and settle in a grand estate like this?"

"It's a very nice house, I'm sure, my lady, but since you ask, I think I would miss London."

"You would miss the cinema, certainly," teased Frances. "I don't think the little village here shows moving pictures yet."

Mallow's eyes lit up. "Oh, my lady, I would miss them. Miss Hopp sounded so disappointed she lived in a town with no moving pictures yet. I went with Mabel last week, and the stories, and what they can put on the screen—you can't imagine, my lady. The music hall stage is wonderful too, my lady, but the moving pictures are something special." She lost herself for a moment. "It's a very grand house, my lady, but I would miss city life."

"I would too, Mallow."

CHAPTER 7

Frances allowed herself plenty of time to walk from her bedroom to the dining room for the first formal meal since Sir Calleford's death. She was early, but found a man was already waiting in the hallway outside, studying some miniature oil paintings. As she got closer, the man heard her and looked up. Frances judged him to be in his thirties, and he was handsome in an exotic way. His clothes were English, but somehow seemed incongruous with his looks.

He bowed.

"A pleasure to meet you," he said, in lightly accented English. "Do I have the honor of meeting Lady Frances Ffolkes? My name is Mr. Mehmet."

"You're correct. I heard there was a representative from the sultan. That must be you?"

"I am from Istanbul, but have been residing in London," he said, not quite answering her question.

"And how did you know who I was?"

"It could be because I heard you had arrived, and I know the other guests. But in fact, you look very much like your brother. I compliment you on having such a distinguished relation. His work has brought honor to your king and your house."

"Thank you for your kind words. I take it then that you have had meetings with my brother in his role as a Foreign Office undersecretary?"

"I have many interests, and move in diplomatic and business circles, so I number many prominent Englishmen, like your brother, among my acquaintances," he said. That wasn't odd. Anyone important in the diplomatic community in London would've met Charles at one point. "Indeed, although I rent a house in London, I am fortunate enough to have friends with country houses like this. May I take it you are here as a friend to Miss Kestrel, to support her in this difficult time?"

"Yes, two of us, Miss Thomasina Calvin and I, came down here with her for a visit, but will be staying indefinitely." She paused. "I know Miss Kestrel finds it upsetting to see so many police officers around, a reminder of how her father died. They seem very busy investigating the death, but so far have not made any arrests. As you have been here some days, perhaps you were able to assist the police in their investigations? Have you seen or heard anything that throws suspicions on anyone here?"

Mr. Mehmet smiled again. "You are direct and curious, also like your brother. Do you have an official position with the police?"

"You're teasing me, Mr. Mehmet. The authorities haven't seen fit yet to employ female officers in London any more than they do in Istanbul. I act on behalf of my friend, Miss Kestrel. Given that this was a political meeting and that Sir Calleford had a long Foreign Office career, I was wondering if you thought the killing was politically motivated."

"A political meeting? You were misinformed. It was merely a meeting of friends, old and new. The discussion did center on foreign affairs—that is Sir Calleford's great interest. But he does not have an official position in the Foreign Office, I understand."

"Really?" said Frances. "That is interesting. Because I was thinking that a murder with a dagger—he was killed with a dagger, if you hadn't heard—is a very personal sort of murder."

That seemed to get Mr. Mehmet's attention. The slightly amused look on his face disappeared. "I had not heard. But yes, it does sound like a personal murder."

"And you may be interested to know the murder weapon was Turkish."

"Not the ruby dagger? Sir Calleford showed it to me. He was very proud of it. Aside from his tragic death, the crime is compounded by the . . . desecration of a work of art. I suppose because of Sir Calleford's importance, and the dramatic manner of the murder, even more English police from London head-quarters will swarm all over the house."

He now looked positively gloomy. Frances decided to push further. "I imagine you're right. And it's not a very, how should I say, English method of murder. I was told that the dagger once belonged to a noble Turkish family. Yours, by any chance, Mr. Mehmet?"

Mr. Mehmet just stared for a moment—then laughed. "No, my lady. Not at all. You overreached, but that was an excellent theory. You have far more imagination than the local inspec-tor, Mr. Bedlow, who questioned me earlier today. He seems convinced it's an outside gang—kept asking if I had seen any strangers. I wouldn't have thought a band of violent robbers would operate in such a peaceful county, but I can't imagine any other solution. I have confidence the police will discover them soon enough. But others are coming—perhaps we should change the subject."

Joining them were a handsome young man dressed in a fashionable suit, a large older man in clothes that didn't fit per-fectly, and a tall young woman whose dress, Frances quickly noticed, was the wrong cut for her figure and wrong color for her complexion.

The gentlemen bowed and the woman looked at her with a mix of curiosity and welcome.

"You must be Lady Frances," said the young man. "I am sorry we haven't met earlier today, but with the tragedy . . . I'm Christopher Blake, Miss Kestrel's cousin, and Mrs. Blake's son. May I present some guests—Mr. Ezra Hardiman, and Miss Effie Hardiman, his daughter, from America. This is Lady Frances

Ffolkes, a close friend of my cousin Gwen. And I see, Lady Frances, you have already met Mr. Mehmet, a guest from London."

Mr. Hardiman gave her a strong welcome, with a formal speech. "I am very pleased to make your acquaintance, Lady Frances, although I wish it were in better circumstances. Normally, we would leave to give the family some privacy, but your police have asked the guests to stay while they make their investigations."

Frances said that was perfectly understandable.

Miss Hardiman reminded Frances of some of the American girls she had known in college: robust and healthy-looking, with a friendly voice just a little bit too loud.

"A pleasure, Lady Frances. I understand you come from London? Father and I were staying in Claridge's. London quite took my breath away. But oh, I do apologize, Mr. Blake; no offense was intended to this house. I have never seen anything like this— words fail me. Nothing like this near Buffalo."

"Buffalo?" asked Lady Frances. "I was educated in New York, but never managed to make it to Buffalo."

"Really? May I ask where?" asked Mr. Hardiman.

"Vassar College, a school for women, in Poughkeepsie."

"I've heard of it. And it's a fine town, Poughkeepsie, right on the Hudson. Important for river shipping and rail. I hope you get a chance to see Buffalo someday, Lady Frances. We'd be happy to play host—we live just outside it. A wonderful city, isn't it, Effie?"

"Yes, Father," she said, but with very little enthusiasm.

The Auberts then showed up as well, looking calm and politely greeting everyone. Pennington stepped out of the dining room to ring the gong, as was typically done in large houses to summon everyone to dinner. Even as he did so, the rest of the party arrived: Mrs. Blake, Gwen, and Tommie. They all had been dressed and groomed nicely for dinner, and Frances was pleased to see Gwen looked rested and composed.

"Good evening, Mother. I've made introductions," said Christopher.

"Very good," she said with a wan smile. "Shall we go in?"

Dinner was quiet. No one felt they could really talk about Sir Calleford, given the tragic way he died. Mrs. Blake mentioned the work on the gardens, and that led to a brief discussion of flowers. Frances let her eyes dart around the room. Effie Hardiman seemed eager to discuss the gardens, and commented extensively on the house and grounds. Mr. Hardiman said little, but seemed to enjoy his food. Gwen also joined the discussion of gardens, but Tommie was quiet. Mr. Mehmet also spoke little but watched carefully. M. Aubert was smoothly polite, and Mme. Aubert exchanged pleasantries with Frances, as the other French speaker at the table.

Christopher supported his mother in her conversational gambits, and was also solicitous of his cousin Gwen, reminding her it was a good idea to eat, and noting no one would think less of her if she wanted to retire early.

Frances studied him. *Here was a man not made for mourning,* thought Frances. *He was made for laughing, not because he was disrespectful, but because it was his nature to be cheerful,* Frances concluded. Indeed, he was very handsome, and he couldn't help the charm coming through, even now. Frances saw it. Miss Hardiman had many questions about the house and grounds, and Christopher responded pleasantly to all of them.

The dinner broke up early, as expected. Mrs. Blake led Gwen away for a few moments of conversation, probably about the funeral plans.

"How is she faring?" Frances asked Tommie.

"Surprisingly well. I don't know if it has fully hit her yet. Our bedrooms are next to each other, so I'm near her if she needs company in the night."

Frances said goodnight to everyone, and was about to head to bed herself, when she felt a hand on her arm.

It was Mr. Mehmet.

"I do not wish to be offensive," he said, "but I have heard that in London society you are now referred to as 'Mad Lady Frances.'"

"Your information is correct," said Frances. She kept her tone even. "I earned it by being unconventional."

"Does that mean you don't believe everything you hear?" he asked.

"Absolutely, Mr. Mehmet. And I ask many, many questions before I decide what I believe."

"Many questions?"

"How else will I find out who killed Sir Calleford?" *And*, she thought, *who is threatening Tommie.*

"Would you mind some advice, Lady Frances?"

"I hope I'm not closed-minded."

"Think of your own life. Which I'm sure is blameless." Frances laughed. "But aren't there . . . aspects of your life you would rather not be widely known? People may resent your questions, not because they are guilty of a crime, but because . . ." and he just waved his hand.

"Very good advice, Mr. Mehmet. There is much talk of the wisdom of the East, and I see it is well deserved."

Now Mr. Mehmet laughed.

"Nevertheless, sir, I may have questions for you in the future. Good night, Mr. Mehmet." And she headed up to her room, happy that she had had the last word.

CHAPTER 8

Frances didn't expect to accomplish much the next day. Life would be held in suspension until after the funeral. But she could still observe and give instructions to Mallow. The police would be speaking to everyone, no doubt—even those who had arrived after the murder, and Frances would see that she and her maid were prepared.

Almost everyone made it down for breakfast, and Mrs. Blake was presiding over the table. "Miss Calvin said Gwen hardly slept—I think the horror of it all finally reached her. Miss Calvin was up with her much of the night, I found out, when I called on Gwen this morning. I ordered Gwen a tray in her room and I offered Miss Calvin a tray as well, but she firmly declined." Of course. Tommie wouldn't give in to that kind of coddling just because she hadn't slept. "And Mr. Mehmet rose early and took an early walk, as is his custom." Apparently, the Auberts were sleeping in.

Tommie was at one end of the table talking to Miss Hardiman, while at the other end, Mr. Blake and Mr. Hardiman were in deep conversation. Mr. Blake had apparently stayed the night, perhaps to help his mother and cousin, even though his own house wasn't far away. After greeting Frances, Mrs. Blake rejoined her son and Mr. Hardiman.

Frances helped herself to breakfast from the platters on the sideboard and then sat with Effie Hardiman and Tommie.

"Franny," Tommie began, "Miss Hardiman was anxious that she and her father not be seen in a poor light having to continue to accept hospitality here because of the police request. They'd be willing to relocate to a hotel in Morchester."

"Not at all," said Frances. "Nothing in Morchester will be very comfortable—there will be nothing like Claridge's here. I am sure Mrs. Blake is not at all put out having you continue to stay here."

"I am very glad to hear you say this, Lady Frances." Miss Hardiman placed a hand on Frances's arm. Americans touched a lot. "I hear you come from a very important noble family, and your brother is a marquess, which is very high up, they say, so this means a lot to me."

Frances couldn't help but smile.

"I am glad I could reassure you. But do tell me, Miss Hardiman, what brings you to England?"

"It was Dad's idea. Why? I don't know. Maybe he was restless. My brothers do most of the business work now. I didn't question it. I was just glad to get out of Buffalo."

"Did he say anything about meetings here? People he wanted to see? My brother and I know a lot of people, and we can help."

"Well that is very kind of you. I'll let Dad know. But so far, he's just taking it as it comes, no real plans."

"But how did he know Sir Calleford?"

"I'm afraid I don't really know, although I'm glad to see this house. It's unbelievable. I don't think even the White House in Washington matches it. He just told me he knew someone who knew someone, and we'd be checking out of Claridge's to visit the country for a bit."

So someone wanted Mr. Hardiman here. Was Sir Calleford acting indirectly? At any rate, these were people to cultivate, if she wanted to find out more about what was happening at the Eyrie.

"When we all go back to London, Miss Hardiman, I will call on you at your hotel. We will take tea with my sister-in-law, the Marchioness of Seaforth, and other ladies. Also, if you would like, I will introduce you to the dressmaker who serves both me and the marchioness. You might like some English dresses while you're here."

Frances thought Miss Hardiman would hug her with delight. "This is the nicest thing that has happened to me that I can remember. Thank you very much." *Tea with noblewomen! And wait until the girls back home saw dresses made by the seamstress to a marchioness!*

"Oh, and one more thing . . ." Miss Hardiman was all ears now. "Miss Calvin, Miss Kestrel, and I belong to a club." She glanced at Tommie and saw her raise an eyebrow. "The goal of the club is to gain the vote for women in England. I understand there are similar groups in the United States. If you'd like to stop by, we welcome visitors."

Miss Hardiman slammed her hand on the table, drawing attention to herself. She realized it and lowered her voice. "That beats everything. Dad would have ten kinds of fits if I did that, wants me to be a good girl, meet the right sorts. But . . . well anyway, I'd be happy to come, and I can keep a secret. Now if you'll just excuse me for one minute, I'm going to get more of these fishes. What are they called again?"

"Kippers," said Frances. "You can't have breakfast in England without them."

"Kippers. Right. Thank you!" And she was up.

"My goodness," said Frances, when Miss Hardiman had gotten up. It was not often that someone left Frances feeling overwhelmed.

"Yes, 'my goodness' says it all," said Tommie. "It never would've occurred to me to invite her to a suffragist meeting, but that's a marvelous idea. Mrs. Elkhorn will be tickled. Let's keep her around. With a voice like that, she'll become our principal speaker." They stifled their laughter. "But I don't doubt she has a good heart."

And that was Tommie, always looking for—and finding— the good in everyone.

"But tell me, how is Gwen?"

"Tossing and turning all night. It's everything, really. The murder of her father, and it's beginning to hit her that this place is now hers. At least—she said her father told her it would be hers, but he no doubt assumed she'd be married by that time." Tommie shook her head, then leaned in close. "And I can't help thinking about the horrible man and his disgusting threats."

Frances nodded. She understood Tommie's feelings. "I understand. The odd thing is that there has been no hint of Sir Calleford's thoughts—if he had some particular thoughts about Gwen that were hidden from us, and from her. Perhaps when the solicitors talk to Gwen about the will—if he added something about Gwen having to move home to inherit, something like that."

Tommie's eyes grew wide, and she asked if Frances really thought that was likely. Her voice trembled a little.

"No, I don't. It sounds awful, but I don't think Sir Calleford cared enough for his daughter to disown her just for her affiliations. It's someone else who hates her. That's as far as I've gotten. But don't worry."

Miss Hardiman made her way back with plenty of kippers, and with Mrs. Blake.

"Lady Frances, I've just found out we will be playing host to another member of your family. Your brother Charles has just sent a telegram that he'll be coming. The Foreign Office had said a trusted clerk would come to take possession of some important papers belonging to Sir Calleford, but it seems Lord Seaforth will be coming personally."

Frances was briefly rendered speechless. It was because of her—she knew it. Mrs. Blake seemed somewhat amused at hosting two members of the Ffolkes family. Tommie raised an eyebrow again. And Miss Hardiman could barely contain her excitement at meeting a real, live marquess.

After breakfast, Frances found Mallow in her room organizing her clothes. She told her that his lordship would be joining them.

"The late Sir Calleford was involved in diplomacy, Mallow, as is Lord Seaforth. However, I'm afraid he's really coming because of me. You know how upset he was the last time I became involved in things he didn't feel were proper."

"Yes, my lady." That wouldn't be something Mallow would forget anytime soon.

"It's a big house, with extensive grounds. I could hide. But that would be cowardly, and ultimately futile." She sighed. "You know, this wouldn't be happening if I didn't have to sneak around. If I were a minister in the Foreign Office myself, I could make legitimate inquiries."

"I think you would be an excellent minister in the Foreign Office, my lady," said Mallow loyally, despite having only a vague notion of what the Foreign Office did.

"Thank you, Mallow."

"And perhaps his lordship won't be quite as angry as you fear, my lady. You've only come here to support your friend."

"But will his lordship believe that?"

"Probably not, my lady," said Mallow, shaking her head. "But you've always talked him around."

"Dear Mallow, your faith in me is always a tonic." And thus emboldened, she left to see how Gwen was doing. But then she glanced out the window and saw the Rolls-Royce pull up with Charles and his valet.

Very well. She'd face up to him. In the hallway, she stopped a footman to tell him that if Lord Seaforth, who just arrived, asked for her, she would be in the solar. When she arrived there, she found Gwen and Tommie, along with Miss Hardiman.

"Oh, Lady Frances, do join us," called out Miss Hardiman. "We are trying to assure Miss Kestrel that she has our full support in these difficult times." Tommie and Gwen both looked a little alarmed by the American.

Frances sat down with them. Gwen was looking wan, but Tommie seemed in control. She flashed a quick, wry smile at Frances.

"It's the two things," said Gwen. "I barely seemed to be able to take in that my father had died, when it became clear that I was mistress of the Eyrie. I never thought, you see . . ." She looked confused, as much as anything.

"I am sure the solicitors will take care of the details. And your Aunt Phoebe will stay on as long as you need her." *That was something to think about—would Mrs. Blake want to return to live with her bachelor son on their estate?*

"I—I don't think I could ever manage this place," said Gwen. "It sounds silly. I never really thought of this as a home. It was more like living in a sort of museum than in a proper home."

And that was probably the most insightful thing Frances had ever heard Gwen say. She was mulling it over when Miss Hardiman jumped in.

"I think being mistress of this house would be the greatest thing in the world," she said.

No one had time to respond to that, because of the arrival of a well-dressed man with a masculine version of Frances's features that gave him a boyish look.

"Charles, do come in. We heard you were arriving. Miss Kestrel, Miss Calvin, Miss Hardiman—my brother Charles, Marquess of Seaforth. Charles—my old friends Gwendolyn Kestrel and Thomasina Calvin, and my new friend, Effie Hardiman, from America."

Charles gave Frances a brief, hard look, but nothing would stop him from being polite. "Miss Calvin, Miss Hardiman, a great pleasure to meet you." Tommie greeted Charles with a brief smile, and Miss Hardiman almost swooned. "Lord Seaforth, your sister has told us all about you," she said.

"Only good things, I hope, Miss Hardiman," he responded, and she found that very amusing. He turned to Gwen. "Miss Kestrel, my deepest sympathies on your loss. He was a fine man. I speak for His Majesty's government when I say your father's death was a loss for all of England."

"Thank you for your kind words," said Gwen. "Your sister has been a great support."

"Indeed," he said. "I am so glad to hear it." Was there sarcasm there, or was it Frances's imagination? "Franny, would it be possible to pull you away from your friends for just a few minutes for a brief discussion? The weather is warm for this time of year, and we could walk through the gardens."

Oh, I'm in for it, thought Frances. *Very well.* She girded herself for battle and said goodbye to her friends.

Charles didn't seem inclined to talk as they walked down the stairs.

"Mary is well?" asked Frances.

"She was fine when I left her earlier today. But this is an official visit, not a social one, which is why she didn't come." He had that strict, slightly pompous look he had inherited from their father.

The workmen were busy at one end of the garden, but even half of it provided enough room to walk and talk. When they were alone, he began.

"I was going to send my chief clerk to take care of Sir Calleford's papers, but after Mary told me you were here, I thought I'd come myself and then serve as the Foreign Office's official representative at the funeral. You told Mary that you were staying here to support Miss Kestrel."

"Miss Kestrel, and our mutual friend Miss Calvin, are all members of the League for Women's Political Equality," she responded, putting as much superiority into her tone as possible. "We support each other in times of crisis."

That made Charles stop. "You're telling me that Gwen Kestrel is a suffragist? I don't believe it. I've known Calleford for years—he never said anything to me. I can't believe he'd tolerate it, and from what little I know of his daughter, she doesn't strike me as someone who'd defy him."

"Well, she is. Call Mrs. Elkhorn if you don't believe me. It's no secret. And frankly, I don't think Sir Calleford cared one way or another about what Gwen was up to. Typical attitude about girls. If she had been a son—" She was on a roll but Charles was quick.

"Franny, I don't have time for this. Very well, so a suffrage meeting coincided with a murder. It figures."

That was what Inspector Eastley had said. "Someday you will explain how crime and the suffrage movement are related."

Charles chuckled, and they resumed walking. "And of course," she said airily, "I, like you, have my official duties here."

"Official? What government department has secured your services?"

"The Home Office. I am an official translator for the Metropolitan Police Service."

"You're what?" He seemed genuinely astounded.

"Inspector Eastley of Special Branch had some French nationals to interview and I volunteered my services as a French translator."

"For whom?" he asked, uncharacteristically sharply. He was often frustrated with Frances, but rarely snapped at her like this.

"Oh! Mme. Aubert, her maid, and her husband's valet. M. Aubert's English is excellent, I was told, and so he didn't need a translator."

"And what did they tell you?" he asked. He looked positively stormy, but Frances just glared right back.

"The inspector swore me to secrecy. He answers to the Home Office. You work in the Foreign Office. You haven't been cleared." Neither said anything for a moment—and then Charles burst out laughing.

"Franny, you are completely in the right and I am absolutely in the wrong." He bent down and kissed her on the cheek. "I so wish Father was alive to see you like this. He'd be proud of you."

"Thank you, that means a lot to me," she said softly. And then she decided it was time to get back to the subject at hand. "You see I can keep a secret. What is going on here?"

Charles sighed. "Oh, very well. I can give you the outline. There's a bit of a mess brewing on the Continent—France,

Germany, Russia, the Ottoman Empire, everyone jockeying for position. Sir Calleford was as shrewd a diplomat as we have. M. Aubert was the best France has as well. They were genuine friends, and this week were expected to talk and reach some important conclusions. Mr. Mehmet, who is staying here, represents certain Ottoman interests."

"'Certain interests.' That doesn't mean the sultan, then?"

"A shrewd observation and conclusion, Franny."

"Thank you. But why weren't you there yourself—but I know. This was quiet and unofficial. That's why a senior government official like you couldn't come."

"Very good, Franny. What a shame you're not in the Foreign Office yourself."

Frances wanted to start again with her usual line about admitting women to the ranks of government, but now was not the time to get sidetracked.

"Sir Calleford never sought out an official position in government, never stood for parliament. He was an intellectual with many interests, and it suited him, and us, for him to be a sort of unofficial diplomat. And a very good one."

"I see, thank you. But what about—"

"That's all, Franny," he said.

But she wasn't put off. "But back to Mr. Mehmet. Whose interests does he represent?"

"He's a man with connections to various businesses and to the sultan's government. As well as his own interests. Stay away from him."

"But—"

"Franny. He is a dangerous man. Stay away from him." He looked hard—and then once again broke into his charming smile. "This isn't about your being a woman. It's about some very secret and delicate negotiations."

"Can I conclude then that Mr. Mehmet is not an *official* representative of the Ottoman Empire? Or does he combine work with the sultan with other interests, as you say?"

"Come, Franny. You know that the Ottoman Empire is very shaky. Let us say Mr. Mehmet is an unofficial representative, just as Sir Calleford was for Britain and M. Aubert was for France."

"So that means—"

He cut her off. "You already know much more than you should. Help your friend through the funeral tomorrow, then come home with me."

"Thank you. But Miss Kestrel still requires my support. I will be staying on a while longer."

Charles knew there was no point in arguing with her, but as they headed back to the house, he said anyway, "Do as you please. Right now, I have to meet with Inspector Eastley—and no you can't sit in. It's government business."

"Oh, very well. But can you tell me about another guest? Who is Ezra Hardiman? He and his daughter are visiting from America. What is he—a senator? An ambassador?"

"Hardiman? Never heard of him."

"You must've. I know he's wealthy and I assumed he was also invited here as a representative of the American government."

"Franny, I may decline to tell you something, but I won't lie to you. I have no idea who Ezra Hardiman is. It's very possible that he speaks officially, or even unofficially, for Washington. I keep up with Europe, but America is not my department. Sir Calleford may have found it useful to have American insights at this time. As I said, Sir Calleford was unofficial. He worked his own way and had his own contacts."

"So, could I call the Americas desk at the Foreign Office?"

"Yes, you could. And they would tell you precisely nothing." Frances looked exasperated, and Charles continued. "But we've strayed from the subject—which is your interference with the police investigation of a murder."

"That's not why I'm here—" she said primly.

"Franny, I just told you I'm busy and I don't have time for all this."

"You sound just like our father. But never mind; you trusted me, and I will trust you. Tommie Calvin came to me—before Sir Calleford died. She was threatened with ugly accusations—something that could destroy her reputation, hers and Gwen's both—although Gwen knows nothing about it, and can never know. I'm not going to see my friends' lives destroyed."

"Oh, very well. It sounds like a crank, but if anyone can help, you can. And I'm not being patronizing about that—I mean it. But promise me you'll stay away from the police. Give me that much."

"I will. If I can."

"What do you mean, 'if you can'? Of course you can. Franny, this isn't London—"

As they exited the gardens, Frances saw they weren't alone. Tommie had joined them; she had clearly been running from the house.

"Oh! I'm sorry. I didn't realize I was interrupting. I'll just . . ."

"You're not interrupting. My brother has very important work and was leaving anyway."

Charles sighed. "Miss Calvin, good day. Franny, I'm staying for the funeral tomorrow. We'll talk more." And he left.

"Franny, I'm sorry, but I wanted to show you this." She looked stricken—and when Frances saw she was holding a piece of paper, she knew what was in it.

"A note—it was slipped under my door sometime after I left for breakfast."

It was cheap notepaper, and the penmanship was poor.

"DEAR MISS CALVIN,
YOU WER WARNED NOT TO COME HERE. YOU HAVE AN UNATURAL FRIENDSHIP WITH MISS KESTREL AND YOU ARE NOT WANTED HERE. WE NO YOU ARE A KILLER. YOU SHULD LEAVE NOW."

It was written in awkward block letters, not in script, and there was no signature.

"There are several spelling mistakes," said Frances "This was written by someone ignorant—or someone who wants to appear ignorant. Now the man who threatened you seemed a gentleman. That's odd. And it's someone in this house—although I suppose a servant could've been bribed—I'll have to think about that." She looked up at her friend. "Are you frightened?"

"I am angry," said Tommie. She was almost shaking. Anger was not an emotion one associated with Tommie.

"One thing we know for sure. Whoever is threatening you is a coward. The man in the cathedral was just an agent and this note is anonymous. A bully and coward."

"I'm not leaving," said Tommie.

"Of course not. We're staying in this together."

They slowly began walking back to the house. "I can cope with this," said Tommie. "But can you imagine what this would do to Gwen? She's missed it twice now."

Frances frowned. "That's interesting. It would terrify her, destroy her. If someone wanted to ruin your friendship, Gwen would be the best person to attack. And yet, they attack you. Someone wants Gwen left whole."

"I see what you're saying, but why?"

"I don't know," said Frances. "Not yet, anyway."

Chapter 9

Mr. Pennington, the butler, announced to the staff that the police would be speaking privately with each servant. He sounded very aggrieved about this—he could not see the necessity. It was impossible that a servant had seen anything and not spoken, and inconceivable that one had been involved. "Naturally, it is Mrs. Blake's and Miss Kestrel's wish that you cooperate fully. Of course, that does not mean you share any gossip."

He paused and looked around. "Those of you who work for guests of the family—I'm sure the same instructions apply to you as well."

Lady Frances had already told Mallow they might be questioned, so Mallow was not surprised when a young, uniformed constable called for her. He was given permission to use the butler's pantry for privacy.

Despite being prepared, Mallow was deeply affronted from the beginning—never mind that her ladyship knew senior officers in Scotland Yard, and now was so proud of having actually worked for the police as a translator. In the neighborhood where Mallow was born and raised, people didn't want to be involved with the police. At least in London her ladyship met with high-ranking London constables, not a common village bobby. This one was tall and strong-looking—Mallow would've taken him for a farm worker if it weren't for his uniform.

She sat straight up in her chair. The constable produced a pad of paper and pencil, licked the tip, and began. He surprised her by being well-spoken.

"I am Constable Arthur Dill, of the Greater Morchester Regional Constabulary. I understand you're June Mallow, maid to Lady Frances Ffolkes, of Miss Plimsoll's Hotel, City of Westminster, London. You arrived yesterday. Is that all correct, Miss Mallow?"

"Yes. Your particulars are all correct."

The constable looked up, startled. She was a young maid but spoke like a duchess.

"Yes, well. I will ask you a few questions, then." They were very simple questions: When exactly had they arrived? Had they been here before? Mallow answered them briefly.

Then came another question. "Why did you come? Does her ladyship know the family?"

"You would have to ask her ladyship," she said. "It's not my place to comment on her ladyship's social circle."

Constable Dill smiled. "Oh come, Miss Mallow. It's hardly a secret. I can find that out elsewhere, but my guvnor will be very pleased with me if I can get it from you."

Mallow thought. He was right—it was hardly a secret, and Lady Frances had told her to see if she could uncover any hints from the police questions. She should be cooperative.

"Very well, Constable Dill. Miss Kestrel, Miss Calvin, and Lady Frances are all friends from London. They belong to a . . . club for ladies. We all traveled down together."

"One of the housemaids told me Miss Calvin was up half the night taking care of Miss Kestrel. It sounds, then, like Miss Calvin and Miss Kestrel are especially close friends." It was half a statement, half a question. Mallow looked closely at him. He didn't seem to have that arrogant look so many other constables had. He appeared to be . . . sympathetic.

Mallow mulled over his question. Her ladyship had said there were some wicked stories about Miss Kestrel and Miss Calvin.

Maybe this kind constable knew something. Her ladyship would be very pleased if she could uncover something.

"My lady has said that Miss Kestrel and Miss Calvin are particularly close, like sisters."

"'Like sisters,'" said Constable Dill, quoting her. "Really?"

"Are you doubting me?" asked Mallow, coloring. The constable was embarrassed.

"Oh, no, not at all, Miss Mallow. It's just that someone else said the two ladies were like sisters, and Inspector Bedlow laughed and said, 'Oh sure. That's not what I heard.'" The constable shook his head at the oddness of his superior. Mallow filed the information away for later.

"Just one more question, Miss Mallow, for our records. I assume your address at Miss Plimsoll's is temporary, that you live with your mistress with a father or brother normally."

"We do not," said Mallow stiffly. "It is our permanent residence. It's only for ladies from the best families and their personal servants."

He raised an eyebrow. "That's very unusual, isn't it?"

"Lady Frances is very unusual. She went to university, in America."

"Did she indeed? It sounds like you have a very interesting position. How did you get it?"

"Is it necessary for your investigations to know that?" asked Mallow. The constable smiled. *A little cheekily*, she thought.

"No, not really. But my mother was in service you see, in a great house, until she married my father, a local farmer. So I have an interest in, and admiration for, young women like yourself who are in service."

Well that sounded reasonable. And respectful. "I was housemaid to her ladyship's parents, the late marquess and marchioness. When she went on her own, Lady Frances promoted me as her lady's maid." She preened.

The constable closed his notebook. "It was thought I'd follow in my father's footsteps. But I took the police exam and passed.

And I took the exam to become a sergeant and passed that too. When there's an opening I'll get my sergeant's stripes." He stood and smiled again. Mallow thought it was a very pleasant smile. "I think we have something in common, Miss Mallow, rising through the ranks as we have."

Mallow hadn't considered that, but the constable had a point. She hadn't really thought of constables as, well, as people, growing their careers just as maids and footmen in great houses did.

"I suppose you're right," she said softly.

Constable Dill stood. "Thank you for your cooperation, Miss Mallow."

"You're most welcome." She paused. "And I wish you luck on your promotion."

———◆⋅×⋅◆———

Upstairs, things were not going nearly as smoothly for Lady Frances and Inspector Bedlow, the local man from Morchester she had seen outside earlier.

The inspector had expected to get just the basics from Lady Frances for the record. Nothing much else there—she hadn't even come down to the Eyrie until the night of the murder. She was the sister of that Whitehall lord who had come down from London, but no surprise in that. All the nobility were connected, even related to each other.

But Lady Frances was determined to give her opinion, he found. Bedlow blamed that secretive Special Branch man, Inspector Eastley; he had used her as a translator and that had given her airs. Eastley had even seen fit to snap at him for not noting that there were foreign nationals in the house. It never did to argue with the Scotland Yard boys, but he had wanted to tell him off. Ah well, he'd be gone tomorrow.

After giving her name and address and confirming how she knew the family, Lady Frances said, "Now, inspector, I was wondering if you had considered—"

"Thank you, Lady Frances. We're considering several lines of inquiry."

Frances colored. She hated to be interrupted like that, but realized she should've expected it from the police.

"I was only saying that there are some issues that I have been made aware of that might have bearing on the case."

"That's quite all right, my lady. I assure you we have everything in hand." He smiled indulgently. Worse than being interrupted, Frances hated being patronized.

"Maybe Inspector Eastley will be interested."

"Inspector Eastley will be going home tomorrow." He put a little steel into his voice. "I am in charge of this case."

"I thought the chief constable called in the Yard."

"You were misinformed, my lady. The Yard has not been called in. Scotland Yard came down just to take charge of Sir Calleford's papers. But thank you for your interest. Good day." He snapped shut his notebook and left.

This was very irritating. Inspector Eastley was also difficult, but he was intelligent and at least he listened to her—some of the time, anyway. And of course, her brother was also adding to her frustration by being prickly—although she had to admit, he had given her some clues.

But then Mallow came up, smiling.

"You look like the cat who got at the cream," said Frances. "Let's sit—and do tell me."

"Well, my lady, a rather kind constable questioned me—"

"A kind constable? How wondrous!"

"Well-spoken and polite, my lady, and I answered him proper." She related their conversation and Frances listened intently, showing great interest when Mallow repeated the information about Inspector Bedlow laughing at the thought of Miss Calvin and Miss Kestrel being something other than close friends.

Frances frowned. This was another hint that others suspected there was something odd about Gwen and Tommie. First Gwen's brief suitor and now the inspector. Where was this coming from?

There had been no nasty rumors in London; Frances would've heard. She shook her head, then smiled again.

"Very good, Mallow—well played. This was important. Just continue to keep your ears open and we'll get to the bottom of this."

"Yes, my lady," she said, looking very proud of herself.

"I suppose we'll have another odd and awkward dinner tonight, but we'll be turning in early. Tomorrow is the funeral. I think it's going to be a very long day."

CHAPTER 10

In the morning, Tommie and Frances worked with one of the maids to get Gwen dressed. The poor girl seemed still in shock. Aside from losing her father, she was stuck playing the role of chief mourner. Gwen had never put herself forward and was horrified at having to take the lead in the elaborate performance that was a funeral for a great and wealthy man. With no reaction, she allowed herself to be dressed, and when she was done, she turned her eyes on Tommie.

"You'll be with me, Tommie? You and Franny—all day?"

"Of course," said Tommie. "Your family, too."

"You're my family," she said.

The village church was not large, and it was stuffed to overflowing. More would be coming to the reception; the great hall at Kestrel's Eyrie would be used for the first time in anyone's memory.

It wasn't usual for nonfamily members to be seated up front, but for Gwen's sake, they made room for her friends. Frances found herself seated next to Gwen's cousin, Christopher Blake, who leaned over and whispered. "We owe you and your friend thanks for all your help." She smiled and nodded.

Gwen leaned against Tommie, and Frances looked around the church. Her eyes, as usual, were restless. She saw it was a typical old church with a cool and clean design, except for some fussy Victorian memorials marking the death of worthy citizens of past generations. She saw her brother Charles, but he was deep in conversation with other gentlemen. She became aware of a ripple in the back and craned her neck; two servants were helping in a large, elderly woman.

Frances's first thought was that Queen Victoria, dead these six years, had miraculously returned. The woman was clearly ancient and dressed in clothes that had gone out of style decades ago.

"I can't believe it," said Christopher. "It's Betsy Tanner. I don't think she's been out of her house in more than a decade."

"Oh, it's dear Betsy," said Gwen, smiling and crying at once. "She made it. Christopher, see that she's properly seated?"

But it was not necessary. With great deference, other men gave up their seats for her.

Christopher explained it to Frances. "She was a servant here for years, then married a groom and had half a dozen children, who had half a dozen each. Practically the whole staff is related to her one way or another. Pennington is her nephew or cousin or something. She is respected as part of the 'old school' and even gentry in these parts defer to her because of her great age and knowledge about 'how things are done.'" He smiled. "How's your history, Lady Frances? Local lore has it she was born on June 18, 1815."

"Let's see—oh, that was the Battle of Waterloo. That was her birthday? That would make her well into her nineties."

"Yes. Her nickname is Battle-Born Betsy," said Christopher. "It was said that a messenger from the Continent interrupted her baptism in this very church with news of the victory. But that makes no sense; we're not between any port and London—"

"Betsy is very proud of that story," said Gwen with unusual sharpness. "She'd be hurt if you doubted it."

"Sorry, cousin. I forgot how close you two are. No offense intended. She honors us with her presence." He gave her hand a reassuring squeeze.

An old servant. This was someone Frances wanted to talk to. Old servants knew everything.

The funeral service began, and it was no different from the funerals of other important men. A few words from colleagues, including Charles. Frances felt family pride at how smoothly he spoke, the elegant turns of phrase. It was no wonder he was the Foreign Office's fair-haired boy.

The funeral, and the following graveside service, seemed to go on forever, but Gwen made it through without a fuss, although she occasionally leaned on Tommie. Finally, it was back to the hall, where a large buffet feast had been laid out for the crowd of mourners. Frances and Tommie saw Gwen into a comfortable chair in the corner. She said she wasn't hungry, but Frances said she had to eat and dispatched a maid for some cold ham, potatoes, and sweet sherry.

Frances let her eyes dart around. There were two more attendees at the dinner party whom she hadn't met—Mrs. Sweet and Mrs. Bellinger, who rented cottages on the estate. Mrs. Sweet had been seen in a nighttime conversation with Sir Calleford, and Mrs. Bellinger with Mr. Mehmet. She expected they would appear at the hall and, like everyone else, offer their condolences to Gwen.

Meanwhile, she saw Mr. Mehmet across the room, helping himself to some sliced chicken. And then she saw Charles approach him. The two men shook hands and engaged in serious conversation in a far corner—not angry, but serious.

Then Inspector Eastley joined them. Charles made introductions and the three spoke. She would've given anything to know what they were saying, but knew there was no chance any of them would share it with her.

But she was kept busy supporting Gwen as streams of people stopped by to say what a wonderful man her father had been. Gwen just sank further and further into her chair, responding automatically to the well-wishers, most of whom were strangers to her. Mrs. Blake spent most of her time circulating and supervising the servants but stopped by several times to see how her niece was doing and quietly thank Tommie and Frances for their help.

Eventually, Frances's patience was rewarded as two women approached. They were in their thirties, dressed in country clothes: appropriate and respectable, with none of the style one found in London.

One stood a little in front of the other. Her hair was swept back to reveal a high forehead. She had a cool eye and set mouth.

This is a proud one, thought Frances, as Gwen made introductions. Gwen was doing that rather well when she actually knew one of the mourners, falling back on training all girls from good families received when they were very young.

"Frances, Tommie—this is Mrs. Celia Bellinger. Mrs. Bellinger—Lady Frances Ffolkes and Miss Thomasina Calvin, my dearest friends."

"You are fortunate to have such good friends to support you in this difficult time," she said, and Frances detected a note of irony.

"I understand you were at the dinner party?" asked Frances. The question was unnecessary and even impertinent, but she was curious about Mrs. Bellinger's attitude.

She gave a small smile. "Yes, I have also been fortunate in my friendships here." And again, that ironic tone. That would bear follow-up.

Mrs. Bellinger slipped away, and Mrs. Sweet stepped forward. She was a different type. Her face was warm and open, and there was a comforting look about her. Another round of introductions and then she bent down and kissed Gwen on her cheek.

"Your father was a delightful man, and he spoke often to me of you. He was proud of the woman you had become."

Frances was sure that was a lie—that Sir Calleford had never discussed his daughter with anyone. That was becoming clear. But it was a good lie, and Gwen accepted it gratefully after hearing so many meaningless lines about what a great man her father had been. She gave Mrs. Sweet a hug and teared up.

"Did he really?" she asked. "Did he really talk about me?"

And Frances saw Tommie was crying too, to see Gwen so pitifully grateful for a hint that her father cared for her.

<hr/>

Eventually, the crowd thinned out and the servants began clearing.

"Do you think I could lie down now?" said Gwen. "Aunt Phoebe said the solicitor needs to see us later, but an hour or two would be awfully nice."

"Of course," said Tommie.

Frances suggested Tommie see Gwen upstairs—she had some people to speak with and set off briskly out of the hall.

Indeed, she was in time to catch Charles standing by his motorcar, again talking to Inspector Eastley. Except for her brother's valet standing a few paces away, they were alone.

"Gentlemen," she said. "I am so glad to catch both of you together."

"Inspector, I know that you have been . . . involved with my dear sister in the past. Has she been pestering you again?" Charles asked with a wry smile.

"Not at all, my lord. She has been of great use. And may I say, she has an organized and disciplined mind. If she were a man, my lord, I'd be happy to welcome her into Special Branch—and I don't say that in jest, but in all seriousness."

"Thank you, inspector. Maybe you'll be a good influence on my brother. I know you would find me an excellent addition to your department. But to the subject at hand, I answered some questions from Inspector Bedlow, and he indicated that you would not be continuing your investigation here. Is that true?"

The inspector glanced quickly at Charles, then spoke. "Yes it is, Lady Frances. Scotland Yard only comes in at the request of the local chief constable. That hasn't happened—not yet anyway. And even then, it would not be my unit." Special Branch involved itself in matters concerning the safety of the realm, not a mere murder.

"My understanding was that you came to take charge of certain papers. But I doubt someone of your rank was needed to do that. And you were questioning witnesses, as I well know. May I ask why you really did come?" she asked.

"You may not," said the inspector.

"I don't mind," said Charles. "Franny, Special Branch is here at my request because of Sir Calleford's work, which is highly classified. Only highly ranked personnel could handle them. The questions for the witnesses were routine for Whitehall records. That's all you need to know."

"Indeed," said Frances with a skeptical look. *Why were they making such a secret fuss about everything? There was something more to this.*

Charles sighed. "Franny, help Gwen get settled and then come home. You've been running around a lot, and Mary misses you. Now, I'm due back in London, and I believe Inspector Eastley is as well."

But Frances was not giving up yet. "Will you at least tell me, perhaps in a general way, what you were discussing with Mr. Mehmet? He was a guest here, and it would help Gwen if she understood the relationship."

Inspector Eastley just grinned and shook his head, but Charles became stormy.

"Franny, that's one of your more transparent attempts to insert yourself into a situation where you don't belong. I told you before—stay away from Mr. Mehmet."

"Besides, my lady, I was talking with Inspector Bedlow, and it seems very clear this was simply some outside intruder, likely trying to commit robbery. He knows the local lay of the land, so to speak, and will no doubt track down the murderer. It's nothing very complicated, just a lot of leg work, that's all."

Frances looked doubtful again.

"Both of you have a good trip back to London. Tell Mary we'll speak soon." And with that, she turned sharply and headed back to the house. She didn't believe that robbery story for a minute, and there was indeed something important about Mr. Mehmet.

Back inside, Frances was going to see how Gwen was faring, but ran into Mme. Aubert, who greeted her warmly. It made sense: she spoke almost no English and her husband was probably busy speaking with others in the diplomatic community who remained.

"Lady Frances, we are leaving on a train later today for London, and will then be heading back to France in a few days. I wanted to see you again and tell you how I enjoyed meeting you, even in such terrible circumstances. When you next visit Paris, please come stay with us."

"Thank you—I'd like to see Paris again. For now, do you have a few moments to talk?"

"The pleasure is mine."

They found a seat outside.

"Gwen Kestrel is a good friend of mine, and is feeling rather desolate after her father's death. Like many busy and important men, he was not very close to his daughter. I was hoping to uncover whether he spoke to you about her—something I can pass on to her."

Mme. Aubert thought about this for a while—so long, Frances thought she might not answer at all.

"I have three brothers. My father was also in government and had extensive business interests as well. I hardly knew him. When I came of age, men were paraded past me, and when one I formed a bond with asked my father for permission to marry me, I did. Fathers and daughters, Lady Frances. I did what I was supposed to do, and that was the extent of my father's interest." She spoke lightly, without bitterness. "I didn't meet Sir Calleford until after his wife had died. His daughter was in the hands of a nanny and then a governess. I wouldn't have even known about her if my husband hadn't told me of her existence."

Frances nodded. "And in later years, he never spoke of Gwen?"

"No. I only met her briefly, once or twice."

"What about Mrs. Blake? Was she interested in her niece?"

"I don't think so. She didn't talk about her much either. She was very . . . solicitous of her son, Christopher. I think Miss Kestrel spent so much time in London, she wasn't well known up here. I am glad she has good friends in London—she wasn't close to her family, I imagine."

"But was there any indication that he wanted Gwen to leave London and return to the Eyrie?" *Had he found out about the rumors and wanted to separate Gwen and Tommie?*

Mme. Aubert shrugged. "I saw no sign of that, and had my husband known, he would've told me. Sir Calleford mentioned in passing that Gwen was happy in London, and that was fine with him. I think he would've found her . . . oh, what is that English expression . . . 'under his feet.' I wondered if he thought she'd have a better chance of finding a suitable husband in London, under the supervision of her London relations."

They sat in silence for a while, lost in thought. Then Mme. Aubert smiled, and said, "But you, Lady Frances. You are in no rush to get married?"

"I am unconventional. That's how my father put the best face on it."

"Your brother spoke earlier today with my husband. I got a sense he is worried about you."

Frances laughed. "He is like my father."

"Men. Busy and important men," said Mme. Aubert. "They just want us to be safe—and married. You choose not to marry, not because you have no suitors, but because you value your independence too much."

Frances tried to control her reaction, to keep Mme. Aubert from seeing just how close to the truth she was.

"But, Lady Frances, despite the annoyance you no doubt feel about your brother fussing over you, at least you have the satisfaction of knowing that although your brother's French is as good as yours, your accent is better."

And Frances laughed again. "Thank you, Madame. And may I ask, do you have children?"

"Three sons. They are wonderful boys." She smiled wryly. "And my husband is very interested in them. And now, I should find my husband. Again, Lady Frances, it has been a pleasure."

———————

With Mme. Aubert's comments flowing through her mind, Frances sought out Gwen to see how she was doing. She came across Tommie quietly leaving Gwen's bedroom and putting her finger to her lips.

"I just got her down. She was making an awful fuss, but eventually fell off—let's find somewhere to talk."

They headed toward the solar, which was empty, and she continued after they sat down. "The funeral took a lot out of her. And now she's saying she doesn't want to see the solicitor for the reading of the will, that she can't face it."

"Then we will face it with her," said Frances.

"But that's quite against the rules. Only those who are named in the will can be present for the reading."

"Oh, but as the saying goes, 'There's more than one way to skin a cat.'" Frances struck a histrionic pose. "Dear Mr. Solicitor, my great friend Gwendolyn, with no father, brother, or husband to support her, begs your indulgence and hopes you will stretch the rule to let her two good friends sit with her at this solemn legal reading."

Tommie laughed. "You're terrible," she said. "And yet, I'm sure it will work."

And so it did. When Gwen awoke, Frances was there to instantly soothe her and promise that she and Tommie would accompany her in her meeting.

"Really?" she asked.

"Absolutely. Just follow my lead." And arm in arm, the three women headed to the drawing room, where servants were arranging the chairs. The solicitor was already there, arranging papers on a table. Frances delivered her lines perfectly, and was aware that Tommie was struggling not to laugh again.

Not that the solicitor, who introduced himself as Neville Small, seemed to notice. He was old and old-fashioned, in a well-made but out-of-date suit. He was no proof against ladies appealing to his sense of strength and chivalry.

"Well, my ladies, it's not quite proper—" he smiled indulgently. "But in this case, I think it will be quite all right if your friends accompany you. But please, no talking," he said, speaking to them as if they were children. In London, political men and men of business knew the value of sophisticated women, even if they weren't open about admitting it. But in the country, it was different. No one would be less likely to work with young women than a rural solicitor. Indeed, Frances wanted to strike him. But this was not the time or place to make a stand for women's rights.

They took three seats up front, and gradually others who had been summoned showed up: Mrs. Blake and her son Christopher—who asked Gwen how she was doing—and some senior and long-term servants. Everyone quietly took their seats.

Mr. Small cleared his throat.

"Thank you all for coming. Sir Calleford left a fairly simple will, so this shouldn't take very long." He started by announcing some legacies for the servants, which Frances thought were very generous. The butler and cook, among others, could retire on their legacies and seemed suitably grateful.

"If there are no questions," said Mr. Small, "the staff may leave, so I can continue just with the family." And a moment later, the room was almost empty.

"Very well," said Mr. Small. "The rest is also very simple." He read directly from the will: "To my cousin-by-marriage and dear friend, Phoebe Blake, I leave one thousand pounds in gratitude for years of selfless help, as well as the Gainsborough portrait of my ancestor, Lady Caroline Marchand, which she has always admired." The financial gift was also generous, Frances knew, and a Gainsborough was extremely valuable.

At that, the cool Mrs. Blake broke down and cried into her hands. Christopher gently soothed his mother, while Mr. Small diplomatically paused.

"To my nephew, Christopher Blake, in grateful recognition of his excellent job in running the farmlands, I also leave one thousand pounds, plus the remaining bottles of my best port, which he has always enjoyed with me."

Christopher smiled and just shook his head. "Good show, uncle. I'll drink to your memory every time I have some."

"The rest of the estate is left to you, Miss Kestrel. That is, this house, all the lands, and the invested monies." He explained patiently. "It is in trust. It's yours, but I am a trustee. That means I will supervise everything on your behalf, until you get married. I manage the estate and pay you an allowance for your personal needs, as your father did. You have nothing to worry about," he added with a paternal smile.

Gwen just nodded. Frances doubted she understood what was going on. But one thing Frances had had her fill of was Mr. Small's patronizing tone. And knowing that she shouldn't, Frances spoke anyway.

"I think Miss Kestrel would benefit from knowing the size of the estate and its financial position," said Frances.

Mr. Small glared at her. Indeed, everyone took notice: Gwen's eyes grew wide, and Tommie gave a small smile. Mrs. Blake raised an eyebrow and Christopher Blake openly grinned.

"Thank you, Lady Frances, for explaining how my job should be done." His voice was full of sarcasm, which she ignored. He picked up his pen, and there was silence in the room except for the scratching.

"This, Miss Kestrel, is the current valuation of the house and grounds, and your father's investments, minus the recent legacies.

The next line is the income, and the final line the expenses. It should be clear the estate is in a sound financial position." Gwen took the paper and murmured a thanks.

However, Frances wasn't finished. "And I know Miss Kestrel would appreciate knowing when she can review the books."

This time, there were gasps all around.

"Excuse me?" asked Mr. Small. "You are here as a favor. You shouldn't even be speaking."

"It's just as well I am here, Mr. Small. I know something of the law, and I know Miss Kestrel's rights." *Rights that would be easily granted if Gwen had a brother or husband.*

She felt her heart beating. Everyone's eyes were on her, and Mr. Small looked at her with pure contempt.

"You know something of law and finance, do you?"

"I am treasurer of the Ladies Christian Relief Guild in London, the largest ladies' charitable agency in England. I work closely with both solicitors and chartered accountants, and my books balance to the penny. I would be happy to assist Miss Kestrel in reviewing the estate accounts under your care."

Mr. Small wants to yell at me, she realized. The only thing stopping from him losing his temper was the thought of how foolish he'd look.

"Lady Frances, I can only assume that the recent tragedy has unhinged you, or you would not be behaving like this." He gathered his papers with more violence than was warranted. "If there are further questions, I can always be reached in my office. Miss Kestrel, again, my deepest condolences." And with that, he walked quickly out of the room.

CHAPTER 11

Frances looked around again. Gwen and Tommie were simply astonished. Mr. Blake was still grinning. And Mrs. Blake was unreadable. In truth, Frances wasn't embarrassed. She was proud of what she had done, making a stand for women's rights. Why shouldn't Gwen have the same access to her estate's books as a male heir would?

Still, it wouldn't hurt to observe some proprieties.

"I apologize for any upset I caused in your house," she said to Mrs. Blake.

A thin smile. "Not at all, Lady Frances. As you said, you just asked for Gwen's rights." She then turned to Gwen. "My dear, I will be happy to work with Mr. Small on your behalf in the future so you won't have to. I worked with him alongside your father. If you will excuse me now, I will see how Cook's preparations for dinner are proceeding." She stood up and left as well.

Christopher stood and bowed to Frances. "For putting that pompous bore in his place, you've earned my deepest respect. I said I'd drink to my uncle's memory with his best port. I will drink to your health as well."

"I am glad you approve, Mr. Blake," she said.

"I do. Dear Cousin Gwen, you have chosen your friends well. I do not joke when I say that if this is how suffragists behave, you have my full support. And now, I just want to look in on the

Hardimans. A bit out of their element I'm afraid. I'll see you at dinner." And chuckling, he left the women alone.

"Well," said Tommie. "Is it any wonder Mrs. Elkhorn and the rest of the suffrage group admire you so much?"

Frances turned a little pink and waved away the compliment. She turned to Gwen, who was still looking a little shocked.

"I'm sorry if I embarrassed you, dear Gwen. The last thing you need is more disturbance today." Gwen responded by hugging her.

"I didn't understand what Mr. Small said or what you said either, but I am fortunate to have such fine friends. And that Aunt Phoebe said she would help. Would you like to see what Mr. Small gave me?" Frances took a look. If Mr. Small's figures were accurate, the estate was indeed in a good position. It cost a fortune to run the house and grounds, but the investments were extensive.

"You have staunch allies, I promise," said Frances. "Now, we have to decide what to do next." She didn't want to speak in front of Gwen, but she knew why those account books needed opening—and glancing at Tommie, she knew that her friend also knew why. Sir Calleford had been murdered, and money could be part of it.

"You mean, meet with Mr. Small again?" asked Gwen. "Or have Aunt Phoebe do it?"

"Oh no. He's not going to be of any help at all. And we don't want to put your aunt in the awkward position of questioning a man who has served the family for years. We have to make what is called in military circles a 'strategic retreat.' And then we call up reinforcements. May I use your telephone, Gwen? I need to reach London."

"Of course. There's no need even to ask."

"Excellent. The only way to battle a solicitor is with a better one. And I know the best. For now, I think it would be a kindness to thank some of the locals who came today. Can I do that for you, as you're so overwhelmed? On behalf of the family?

I particularly would like to visit Betsy Tanner, as she made so much effort."

"That would be lovely Franny, thank you. Use the car, if you want. Also, Mrs. Tanner has a bit of a sweet tooth and loves the ginger snaps the village baker makes. If you could bring her a box on my behalf?" And Frances said she would.

So Tommie took Gwen back to her room, and Frances placed a call.

She felt full of energy, and there was still plenty of time left in the day. Frances knew tomorrow would be busy, and there were people to speak with today while everything was fresh in their minds.

The first call would be to Betsy Tanner, the old servant. It was only half a mile to the village, but her feet were already hurting. She thought about the boots she had worn at the cottage with Hal. Solid footwear for men who worked. *Why should only men have comfortable boots? Of course, women were meant to merely sit around and be decorative.*

But what would everyone think about her if she put them on now? What would Mallow say? She smiled to herself as she thought of the last time she wore the boots, and decided to seek out the Kestrel chauffeur for his services as she was making calls on behalf of the family.

⋆━✦━⋆

Betsy Tanner was spending her retirement years in a small cottage in what amounted to a tiny hamlet of grounds keeper and gamekeeper cottages. A sense of quiet hung over the place; most of the occupants had something to do, especially with the work for the master's funeral, plus the ongoing work on the gardens.

The chauffeur had pointed her to the correct door, and Frances knocked. A girl of about twelve opened it.

"Hello, my name is Lady Frances Ffolkes. I'm here to see Mrs. Tanner."

"Oh! I'll see if she is in," said the girl, using the phrasing suitable for the very best London houses. This girl had been trained well, even at her young age.

Frances waited in the entranceway, then was ushered into a small sitting room. Mrs. Tanner was ensconced in an old but comfortable chair. She had changed out of her good dress and was wearing something simple now. There was indeed a definite resemblance to the old queen, an imperiousness, but she had a welcoming expression nonetheless.

"Good afternoon, Mrs. Tanner. I'm Lady Frances Ffolkes, a friend of Miss Kestrel's, who asked me to extend her thanks to those who attended Sir Calleford's funeral. She was very touched you took the effort to come."

"Well, isn't that nice, my lady," she said in a voice heavy with the local accent.

"And Miss Kestrel asked me to bring you ginger snaps," said Frances, holding up the box. Mrs. Tanner laughed.

"She never forgets, does she!" she said. "But please, my lady, take a seat. And excuse me for not getting up—it's something of an effort at my age." Frances dismissed her concerns. Mrs. Tanner then called for Dolly, and the girl returned. Mrs. Tanner asked her to put the biscuits on a plate and to bring in some tea, which the girl did quickly and efficiently.

"That girl has been well-trained," said Frances.

"She is my great-granddaughter. And she should be good—I trained her," she said proudly. "Someday I expect she'll get a position at the great house. But first, her mother thinks it would be best if she had more schooling." Mrs. Tanner clearly thought that was a waste of time.

"It's not like the old days, I'm afraid," said Frances. "There aren't as many positions as there were in service. There are other opportunities for girls like Dolly, but they require some education." Education for the poor, especially for girls, was a subject near and dear to Frances's heart.

Mrs. Tanner pursed her lips. *It didn't matter what your station in life was,* Frances concluded. *People didn't like change. Especially the elderly.*

"I daresay you're right, my lady. It's not like it was." She took a ginger snap. "It was kind of Miss Gwendolyn to remember these, and kind of you to fetch them, my lady. I've known her since she was born, and since leaving for London she writes me every month from the city, the goings-on, what's happening in society. And she brings me a cake at Christmas."

How Mrs. Tanner must appreciate that. No longer in a servants' hall, robbed of the gossip that servants loved, she no doubt looked forward eagerly to hearing the latest London scandals. That would be something to plumb—but first, Frances wanted some insights into Gwen from someone outside her family who knew her.

"I've only known Gwen for a few years. Can you tell me what she was like as a girl, since you've known her for so long?"

"Oh, that would be a pleasure, my lady. I can tell you she was always the sweetest girl, kind to everyone, even when people weren't kind to her. She loved dogs and horses. And she always did what she was told, as best she could, my lady."

Frances watched Mrs. Tanner's eyes lose their focus as she returned to the past.

"When you said people weren't kind to her—why would anyone be cruel to Gwen?"

Mrs. Tanner looked thoughtful. "Ffolkes," she finally said. *Was her mind wandering?* "Lady Frances Ffolkes—I have that right, don't I, my lady? Your father is Marquess of Seaforth. In government, he is."

"Yes. He passed on some years ago. My brother holds the title now." She watched the old lady closely. She had been wrong; her mind wasn't wandering. She was at something, but wanted to find out something about Frances first.

"Of course. So your grandmother—no, great-grandmother— was Lady Helena Norwich, who married Viscount Bellmawr."

Frances was astonished that Mrs. Tanner knew her family so well. But then, Mrs. Tanner probably had little to do these days other than revisit the past.

"Very good, Mrs. Tanner! Age has not diminished your memory." The old servant looked very proud of herself. "I remember her in particular, my lady. She was here for the celebrations at the end of the Crimean War, some fifty years ago. A fine and gracious lady she was, I am happy to tell you."

"So family lore has it," said Frances. Mrs. Tanner nodded.

"If I may be so bold, my lady, may I ask why you're here? Why you're really here? It's kind for you to call on Miss Gwen's behalf, my lady, but there's something else, isn't there?"

Frances looked into the old woman's eyes. There was a shrewdness there. Mrs. Tanner now looked at Frances as she would at a junior housemaid who had done a careless job dusting the drawing room knickknacks.

"What makes you ask that, Mrs. Tanner?"

"You're one of the old families, Lady Frances. The Seaforths have been leaders for generations. I know I can talk to you, my lady." *Ah, there it was. Another snobbish servant.* Frances was trustworthy because of her name. But there was more. "I wonder what a lady from a great family wants from an out-to-pasture servant such as myself?"

"You're not out-to-pasture. You may not work, but you have knowledge. You have memories. And so you're of more use to me than a score of maids and footmen." Frances saw she'd have to trust Mrs. Tanner. And hope that Mrs. Tanner would trust her. "I am Gwen's friend, and so is Miss Calvin, who also came up with her from London. I don't know who else is her friend. Her father was killed. And someone has been spreading wicked stories about Gwen. I'm trying to find out who. And why."

"Stories about Miss Gwen? It was ever so. I was just a housemaid in the house in 1837. I won't forget that year, my lady, being the year Queen Victoria ascended to the throne. General Sir Robert Paddington owned an estate nearby, a frequent guest he was. Stories started flying. I hope I don't embarrass you, my lady, but your name isn't unknown here, and I don't think much upsets you. But Sir Robert's name was whispered—stories of late evening parties . . . with young men." She shook her head. "When it became too much, he shot himself. It was the talk of the county for months."

Frances leaned forward. "I don't want Gwen to become the subject of gossip. I think you know that. I love Gwen like a sister. Stories or no stories, we will stand by her, Miss Calvin and I both. Her protection is my only concern. And I think you are the one—the only one—who can give me the stories that will help."

Mrs. Tanner just looked for a while, thinking. When she had reached a decision, she continued. "As I said, Miss Gwendolyn was kind, but I'm afraid she was the butt of jokes. I'm too old to bandy words, my lady, so I'll just say that as sweet as she was, she was never the smartest girl. It was easy for other children to fool her and tease her. Her only champion was her cousin, Mr. Christopher. Almost like brother and sister, they were. He was at his own house, but when he was around, no one dared show any disrespect to Miss Gwendolyn in his presence. A fine boy he was and fine man he became."

"Do you think he'd make a good husband for her?" asked Frances. She watched Mrs. Tanner closely for a reaction—but she just laughed.

"Bless you, my lady. We all thought that a good idea and hoped for it, but that's not to be. I think, as I said, they were raised almost like brother and sister. Nevertheless, I think Mrs. Blake had hopes, bringing the two branches of the family together, and the two estates. But still, I think she'd make some man a good wife, and hope she does soon."

"Do you, Mrs. Tanner?" Frances spoke emphatically, and the old woman seemed a little confused.

"Well, yes, my lady. Not to a political family such as yours, but a solid country squire. They'll hire a proper housekeeper.

I think Mrs. Blake will want to return home now. And Miss Gwendolyn will entertain in country style. I could see that, my lady. What else is there for a young lady like Miss Gwen except for marriage?"

"Of course. She may lack the companionship she had in London though. Perhaps her dear friend, Miss Calvin, would join her as a sort of companion?" *I threw out the bait*, thought Frances. *Will Mrs. Tanner bite?*

"That might work very nicely, my lady. Miss Gwendolyn has written about her good friendship, and Miss Calvin, though I never met her, sounds like a young lady of sober sense. A good idea, my lady." She fixed her eye on Frances. "But you spoke of rumors, my lady. There are always rumors. We are as God made us and you'll get no judgment from me. What Miss Gwen does or feels is her own business. Not my place to comment on it. Still, one way or another, she'll need a husband to run the great house, never mind feelings to the contrary."

So she had heard something, but she would clearly say no more, not even to Gwen's friend. But Frances knew there was also a chance to find out more about Sir Calleford.

"I am sorry that when she does marry, she won't have her father to walk her down the aisle. Although I never met Sir Calleford, I've only heard good about him."

Her face lit up. "Oh yes, my lady. He was a fine man. He and his cousin, Captain Jim. Not to be disrespectful, but that's what everyone called him, my lady. Cousins they were, but as close as brothers, as different as they were."

Frances got excited at this. Here was someone who had known Sir Calleford as a young man. Perhaps she had some insights, something in the family history that would explain his sudden death or the accusations about Gwen and Tommie.

Mrs. Tanner sipped more tea and had another biscuit. Frances took note of how much she was enjoying herself. No doubt everyone here was tired of her stories and reminiscences, so a fresh audience was deeply welcome.

"It was always the two of them, Captain Jim Blake and Call-eford Kestrel, always back and forth between the great house and Captain Jim's estate, Blake Court—now run by his son, Mr. Blake. Now Mr. Kestrel, as he was before he was knighted, was a quiet, studious man. Always polite and friendly like. But Captain Jim was very outgoing, always laughing and cheer-ful, ready for anything. A bit of mischief as a boy, but he was never unkind."

He sounds just like his son, Christopher, Frances thought.

"As they grew up, they frequently made a party with two young ladies from neighboring manors, Miss Phoebe and Miss Bronwen, the four of them playing tennis and lawn games and having picnic lunches. We knew there would be marriages, and you may laugh to hear me say it, my lady, but as close as they were, there was much discussion about who would marry who." She nodded at the memories, remembering garden parties of another age.

"But they sorted themselves out. Miss Phoebe, a sensible and well-organized young lady, married Captain Jim and helped him settle down. And Miss Bronwen married Mr. Kestrel. She was gentle and romantic, and very beautiful. If I may be so bold, my lady, she found herself a little overwhelmed running the great house, but no one ever faulted the warmth of her hospitality. I know you never met her, but if you know Miss Gwendolyn, then you know her mother."

"Did the friendships continue after their marriages?"

"Oh yes, my lady. They dined together every week. Sir Call-eford and Captain Jim hunted and the ladies did good works together. Then one by one they were called to God. First, Cap-tain Jim, who took a chill after a long ride one winter. And then Sir Calleford's wife, the former Miss Bronwen, who was never very strong and never quite recovered from Miss Gwen's birth. That's when Miss Phoebe—that is, Mrs. Blake—came to keep house for Sir Calleford, her cousin-in-law, and it seemed to work very well." She sighed. "And now this tragedy. Lord save us, my lady, cut down like that. May God forgive whoever struck him down at the great house."

And Frances offered an "amen." She had learned quite a bit from Mrs. Tanner, but now something bothered her.

"Mrs. Tanner. You have several times referred to Sir Calleford's manor as the great house. Everyone here has called it Kestrel's Eyrie."

"I suppose they do," said Mrs. Tanner, letting a sour note creep into her tone. It looked like she would say nothing more, but then she sighed again, and continued. "That's not the real name. It was a joke of Mr. Jethro Kestrel, Sir Calleford's grandfather. This house—and I worked there back then—was Marchand Towers, and the lords of Marchand had lived here since Queen Elizabeth's day."

Mrs. Blake told the story with much embellishment, but in the end, it was an old tale and a common one: a noble family running out of blood and money, until there was no one left but a young woman and her widowed mother living in the rambling, drafty house. Jethro Kestrel had been nothing more than some squire's son, who made a fortune "doing something in the East," said Mrs. Tanner. "He married this last daughter of Marchand, and after renaming the house for himself, restored it to its former glory. The Honorable Miss Marchand, now Mrs. Kestrel, got to stay in her home, and Mr. Kestrel got to graft himself onto an aristocratic tree. Those of us who remember the old days—and there are very few—have trouble calling it Kestrel's Eyrie, my lady. Some of us remember the Marchands."

"Are you saying it was wrong for Sir Calleford's grandfather to marry above himself?" Frances asked. There was a little humor in her question, but Mrs. Tanner just shook her head. She may like gossip, but she had served three generations of Kestrels, whatever she may think of them. "It's not for me to say, my lady."

Frances didn't respond. She had learned that if you let a silence hang, you might get more. She was right.

"I will say, my lady, that marriage is very important. The proper choice of your companion for the journey of life can make your life."

Mrs. Tanner would clearly say no more, and she was looking tired. But Frances was determined to gather more information and come back with more detailed questions, now that she had Mrs. Tanner's trust. For now, Frances just stood and said, "Mrs. Tanner, you have been too kind, first coming to pay your final respects to Sir Calleford and now giving me the benefit of your insights."

Mrs. Tanner thanked her for the biscuits and asked Frances to give her regards to Gwendolyn before Frances departed.

That was a lot, Frances thought, standing in the little yard outside of the cottage. There was some knowledge Gwen was who she was, but nothing to reduce Mrs. Tanner's affection—or change her expectation that one way or another, Gwen needed to marry. She thought about Sir Calleford and Gwen's mother. It was hard to imagine this man she had heard so much about, the polished and erudite diplomat, as the ardent suitor of the sweet and beautiful Miss Bronwen.

The chauffeur had said the widows' cottages were not far, so she had sent him home and used the walk to think. She reflected on the Kestrel pedigree. She had known that the Kestrel family was not aristocratic, but hadn't realized that Sir Calleford's grandfather had managed to connect himself so neatly with the aristocracy. Was Gwen supposed to marry well—even into the aristocracy herself?

And what of Mrs. Tanner's comments about marriage? Were they aimed at old Jethro, who had married the last of the Marchands? At Sir Calleford, marrying the lovely but dim Miss Bronwen? At Gwen, finding an understanding husband despite any personal inclinations she had?

Or were they aimed at me? thought Franny. Her face involuntarily reddened at the thought of this elderly servant reading her.

My goodness, what a lot of information. But the pieces were floating without connection.

She was still thinking, and hardly looking where she was going as she turned onto a pleasant country lane with a row of neatly kept houses. A sound roused her—and what she saw sent all thoughts right out of her head. It was the door closing at Mrs. Bellinger's cottage as a visitor left: Mr. Mehmet.

She didn't attempt to hide, just stayed her ground on the lane and waited for Mr. Mehmet to notice her. He did—and she saw both surprise and dismay on his face, but only for a few seconds before his debonair look came back. Her eyes then darted to the windows and she saw a curtain twitch. Mrs. Bellinger was watching.

"Lady Frances, how pleasant to meet you again." *Liar,* she thought.

"Good afternoon, Mr. Mehmet. I was just planning to visit Mrs. Bellinger on behalf of Miss Kestrel to thank her for attending Sir Calleford's funeral. But seeing you, I can thank you as well." She kept her tone bright and cheerful.

He bowed slightly. "The honor was mine, to show my respects to the Kestrel family."

"And to perhaps make some new acquaintances and renew old ones?" She raised an eyebrow. "I couldn't help but see you in conversation with my brother, Lord Seaforth, and Inspector Benjamin Eastley, from Special Branch of the Metropolitan Police Service."

Mr. Mehmet's smile was forced now. He was upset, perhaps angry, and trying to control himself.

"You are truly remarkable, my lady. Most English girls, indeed, most Turkish girls as well, would spend the time at a funeral offering sympathy to friends and family. But you found time to see so much."

She was dying to ask Mr. Mehmet what they had discussed, but knew it would be an outrageous breach of etiquette to ask. She would have to find a way to do so obliquely.

"I suppose the three of you share an interest in politics. I don't know about Turkish girls, but English girls, at least this one, enjoy political discussions." She gave Mr. Mehmet what she hoped was a sweet smile. "I tell you this so you won't have to hesitate to invite me to join any such discussions in the mistaken belief I would be bored."

He laughed. "Again, you are most remarkable. A remarkable lady from a remarkable family. Very well, Lady Frances, I will take you at your word that you have a great interest in the family profession of government and diplomacy. Perhaps, at some future time when the situation is more settled, you and I can have a discussion about politics over tea. Good day, my lady."

And with that, he tipped his hat and left.

He's a smooth one, she thought. But for now, it was off to see Mrs. Bellinger. She knocked on the cottage door and the lady opened it very quickly.

"Good afternoon, Mrs. Bellinger. Lady Frances Ffolkes. We met very briefly at the funeral today, and I wanted to extend the family's thanks for your attendance. May I come in?"

She saw emotions chase themselves over Mrs. Bellinger's face, as the woman was trying to think of a reason to refuse admission.

"Of course," she finally said. And stepped aside to admit her.

The cottage was small, but well-kept and cozy. The furniture was plain and old-fashioned, although in good condition. *The windows were clean and would've let in plenty of light*, Frances thought, *if the curtains had been open. Odd to see them closed in the middle of a sunny day.*

Mrs. Bellinger motioned for Frances to take a seat, and took one herself, sitting on the edge of a chair. Unlike with Mrs. Tanner, there wasn't going to be even a pretense that this was a mere social call.

"I know Miss Kestrel appreciated your coming. The number of people who came showed her how much her father was loved and admired."

"As you see, Lady Frances, I live in a cottage on the estate. It took no great effort to attend." She said nothing more, and didn't offer to serve tea.

"It must be nice, living on such a fine estate," offered Frances. "The quiet and beauty of the country, but in close proximity to others." She smiled. Frances knew that her comments, in the wake of Mr. Mehmet's departure, were right on the border of rudeness. But Mrs. Bellinger was a match.

"I make preserves as a hobby, as is well known in the neighborhood. Mr. Mehmet heard from one of the servants at the Eyrie. He inquired and I told him to send a servant around for a few jars of my strawberries." She paused.

"And in return, he tells you tales of his former life in the East? Life there must seem so exotic."

At that, Mrs. Bellinger gave a brittle smile. "Oh, just ask, Lady Frances. You want to know why a Turkish gentleman calls on an obscure widow. As if he had nothing more on his mind than provisioning his kitchen for something to put on his morning toast." Her voice became a sneer, and Frances was momentarily taken aback.

"I'm sure I don't know what you mean," she said.

"Oh come. Don't be so modest. Your reputation precedes you. Even in the country we've heard of Lady Frances, the women's suffrage ringleader, on a first-name basis with senior officers at Scotland Yard, and friends with people your late mother wouldn't have admitted to her servants' hall, let alone her drawing room."

This was something. Usually only close family—her brother and her many aunts—bothered to upbraid her like that.

"I take that as a compliment," said Lady Frances.

"Of course you do," said Mrs. Bellinger. "But tell me, for someone as busy as you, it must be more than idle curiosity that brings you to my door, inquiring about the society I keep." She used her noble face to full effect, cold and haughty. Frances wasn't offended. Rather, she admired Mrs. Bellinger for playing a grand lady, even in this simple cottage. But that didn't mean she was going to apologize.

Still, she tried smiling again to soften the tone. "You are right. I am too busy to come here simply to indulge myself. I am trying to solve a problem on behalf of a friend, to prevent a scandal. Sir Calleford's murder is part of it."

Mrs. Bellinger just blinked. She didn't say anything.

"As a result, I am looking for anyone with insights into Sir Calleford. Perhaps you were a friend, who can share some observations into the kind of man he was. I will keep your answers confidential."

"I am sorry then. Your trip was for nothing. He was just my landlord. I doubt if I shared more than a dozen sentences with him in all the time I've been here. Is there anything else I can help you with?" The tone said she didn't think there should be.

"Since we are being so frank with each other, you could tell me a little bit more about Mr. Mehmet, seeing as you're such good friends. It may have some bearing on my research."

The request was outrageous. And Mrs. Bellinger's reaction was not a surprise. She stood, and what little color was left in her pale face disappeared.

"It's been some years since I've lived in London. Perhaps such humor is now the fashion there, but it's not in these parts. Good day, Lady Frances."

Frances's late mother would forgive her daughter a lot, but not rudeness. Frances decided to end on a good note.

"I am sorry to have taken up so much of your time, on such a sad day. Good day, Mrs. Bellinger. I'll see myself out."

CHAPTER 12

That was . . . interesting. The key thing she had learned was that there was more mystery about Mr. Mehmet. *How had he struck up a friendship with a widow of modest means?* Charles had said he was dangerous, but perhaps that was just to discourage her.

She walked along the path to her next destination. Mr. Mehmet talked about diplomacy and politics. *Was he a spy? If so, for whom? European politics being as complicated as they were, there was no telling whose interest he was serving. Perhaps just his own. There was no lack of men selling themselves to the highest bidder in these turbulent times. Mr. Mehmet was hiding something.*

She hoped Mrs. Sweet would at least be more welcoming. Her cottage turned out to be similar to Mrs. Bellinger's, but all the curtains were open. And she didn't have to knock, as Mrs. Sweet was in her garden, tending the last few plants to survive into the English autumn. She turned when she heard Frances approach.

"Lady Frances. This is a nice surprise." She stood. "I hope you don't think it's disrespectful, my working in my little garden on the day of Sir Calleford's funeral. But I wanted to keep busy." She wasn't beautiful, but there was so much gentleness and warmth, Frances was inclined to think her attractive.

"Mrs. Sweet, I never met Sir Calleford. But I've seen enough of these magnificent grounds to know how important they were to him. So I think he'd be tickled to see someone tending to the grounds today."

Mrs. Sweet laughed at that, and pulled off her gardening gloves. "What a wonderful outlook you have, Lady Frances. Come in, and I'll put on some tea." And soon they were comfortably sitting in the bright room, drinking out of good china that Frances suspected was reserved for company. Mrs. Sweet also passed Frances a box of chocolates. "My besetting sin. It became something of a joke with my late husband, liking candy so much I even became Mrs. Sweet. The village here is small but boasts a very nice sweetshop."

"I'm afraid I like them too much as well—thank you. Anyway, I just wanted to thank you, on behalf of Miss Kestrel, for coming to the funeral today. I know she appreciated it. And as her friend, I liked what you said about how he talked about her. That gave her a lot of comfort."

Mrs. Sweet looked closely at Frances, who then realized she may have misjudged the woman. She may be pleasant and kind, but she wasn't stupid.

"That was a convenient lie, as you well know, Lady Frances. But if it brought a sense of peace to Miss Kestrel, I can truly say I'll have no qualms when I go to church Sunday."

"And now it's my turn to praise your outlook," said Frances. "Your comment did more for Gwen than all the people who stopped by to tell her what a wonderful man he was. And he must have been, from the outpouring. I never met him myself. Did you know him well?"

She thought for a moment. "Do you know why these cottages are called the widows' cottages? There was a centuries-old tradition of making a handful of cottages available at nominal rents to gentlewomen fallen on hard times. The Kestrels kept up the tradition when they took over the estate. Mrs. Bellinger and I are two of the current residents."

"I visited Mrs. Bellinger before I knocked on your door—she was not as welcoming."

Mrs. Sweet smiled and shook her head. "That doesn't surprise me. But perhaps some Christian charity is in order. She's had a hard life. Did you know she's the granddaughter of the old Earl of Orran? Her mother married badly and she did as well. The marriage quickly soured. The man drank himself to death and she was left badly off, and out of embarrassment, the rest of society shunned her. She was too proud to ask her noble family for help and they were too hard-hearted to offer it."

Frances nodded. That explained the prickly personality and the aristocratic arrogance.

"At least she's made a friend. I've seen her with Mr. Mehmet, the Turkish gentleman visiting at the Eyrie."

"Ah yes. Mr. Mehmet is a frequent visitor to the Eyrie from London. I believe he engaged Mrs. Bellinger to help improve his conversational English. She could use the extra money."

That was different from making preserves as a hobby. But perhaps Mrs. Bellinger was embarrassed to admit she was earning money as a tutor.

Now Mrs. Sweet gave her a wry smile. "I know who you are, Lady Frances. It was your brother, Lord Seaforth, who spoke so well at the funeral. A very distinguished family. And as a well-bred young woman, you're being too polite to ask me my story."

Frances laughed. "You give me too much credit. If you hadn't brought it up, I would've."

"Well, I'm afraid it's nothing as dramatic as Mrs. Bellinger's, although the results were the same. But you wanted to know how well I knew Sir Calleford. My husband died when we were fairly young, and I was awkwardly living with a distant relation in London. I met Sir Calleford through a mutual friend and he mentioned these widows' cottages."

"So you had a friendship with him?"

Mrs. Sweet hesitated. "Not a close one. He wasn't unfriendly, just a very private man. He kindly saw Mrs. Bellinger and I were invited to dinner parties. He liked taking walks after breakfast, and if we came across each other, we'd talk. I understand he was a great diplomat, but I found him shy and intellectual. He would've made a fine professor at Oxford."

Frances nodded. "I wish Gwen could've known him better. She's feeling somewhat at sea, especially now, as she's finally realizing that she's mistress of the Eyrie."

"A great responsibility," said Mrs. Sweet. "She's no doubt very wealthy now, but the house comes with a lot of work. Of course, she could always sell it."

"Nowadays, very few people have the money to buy an estate like this."

"How true," said Mrs. Sweet.

Frances thanked Mrs. Sweet again for being frank and for coming to the funeral, and began walking back to the Eyrie. Two women, rather commonplace really, who had been dependent on husbands, with no way of earning any kind of living as a man would. England was full of such women. Two widows. They should be living simple, dull lives.

And yet, for some reason or other, both were lying to her.

Mrs. Sweet clearly had been more than a casual acquaintance of Sir Calleford's. The footman, Owen, had seen his late master breaking a rigid habit for a nighttime conversation with her. *She was a little too shrewd*, Frances thought. That lie she told to Gwen about her father caring for her was a great kindness, it was true, but only a woman with some knowledge of the family would've thought to tell it. Where had Mrs. Sweet come by that knowledge? Had she drawn it out of Sir Calleford?

She walked back to the Eyrie, visited briefly with Gwen and Tommie, then headed to her room, where Mallow had already laid out her dress.

"Because of the elaborate funeral luncheon, my lady, there will be a simple buffet dinner tonight. Nevertheless, I laid out your usual evening dress." Quite right. The simplicity of dinner was no excuse for anything less than a full-fledged dinner dress.

"Good. Any more gossip from below stairs?"

"Not as such, my lady, although there is talk about the Turkish gentleman's valet."

"I didn't know he had a valet. Also Turkish?"

"Yes, my lady, name of Adem. Looks a little sullen, and very quiet, so there's much curiosity about him. He speaks English, though. He's been seen outside talking and smoking with the head gardener, also sullen. Cook says she heard Adem was the son of a gardener back in his country, and they talk about plants whenever Mr. Mehmet visits."

Frances was annoyed at herself for not thinking that Mr. Mehmet might have a servant—but of course, he was a gentleman of means. She was also annoyed at Inspector Eastley and her brother for not mentioning it. If Mehmet was some sort of spy or even criminal, Adem the valet might be more than a valet. He might be a junior in whatever Mr. Mehmet was up to.

Mallow got Frances into her dress and began touching up her hair.

"By the way, there will be a visitor tomorrow. Just for the day, most likely. Mr. Wheaton is coming down from London to see Miss Kestrel."

"Very good, my lady."

Her tone was even. Frances never knew just what Mallow thought or suspected about how deep their relationship was.

"I'll put out your rose dress for the morning, my lady."

Frances turned. Her maid's expression was bland. "Why the rose dress?"

"It brings out your eyes very nicely, my lady. But if you would rather—"

"No. Thank you, Mallow. The rose dress will be most suitable."

"Very good, my lady."

CHAPTER 13

In the morning, the Rolls-Royce was dispatched to Morches-ter station to pick up Henry "Hal" Wheaton, Esq., and Fran-ces was in the foyer to greet him. He wasn't wearing one of the smart, elegant outfits he favored in his off hours, but the old-fashioned black suit from another generation. "My older clients seem to expect it," he always said with a sigh. But today, his hair was a little ruffled by the wind and there was no disguising the merriment in his eyes.

"I am very pleased to see you, of course," she said. "But I am sorry to interrupt your busy schedule. When I called you yester-day, I assumed you'd offer to send a junior."

"But this sounds like a fascinating situation, and you know my interest in architecture, so I always wanted to see Kestrel's Eyrie." He looked around to see that they were alone. "And I've missed you."

"Then let's take care of business," she said with a wink. "And just maybe we'll have time for a private walk around the gardens."

Gwen and Tommie were waiting for them in the solar, and a maid was just serving tea and sandwiches.

"Miss Kestrel, Miss Calvin, this is Mr. Henry Wheaton, the Ffolkes family solicitor and advisor to the House of Seaforth."

"A pleasure to meet you, and my deepest sympathies on the loss of your father, Miss Kestrel."

Hal sat down and put his case on the table. He gave a reassuring smile to Gwen. "Now, Miss Kestrel, did Frances explain to you why she asked me to come?"

Gwen looked a little hesitant. "She said you could help me— that is, with my money and things. But I was a little unclear, because Mr. Small has always been our solicitor. . . ." Her voice trailed off.

Hal began to explain things immediately. That was one of the wonderful things Frances liked about him. He was always clear but never condescended.

"Yes, Miss Kestrel. Mr. Small represented the estate. That is, Mr. Small is in charge of the house, the lands, and all the money your father has left you. It is yours, but Mr. Small manages it. However, Miss Kestrel, I will represent you personally. I will not replace Mr. Small, but I will make sure that he is managing the estate in your best interest and represent you in discussions with him. I will charge a fee, but you are allowed to have your own solicitor, and Mr. Small must pay my fee out of your estate."

"I see. Thank you." She paused. "Is it acceptable for me to ask my friends for their advice?"

"I hope you will. That is why I asked Frances to make sure she and Miss Calvin were present while I spoke with you."

"Oh! Thank you." She looked around. "Is this a good idea?" she asked her friends. Tommie smiled.

"Yes. Franny knows about these things, and Mr. Wheaton is very distinguished."

"Very well then, Mr. Wheaton." She gave her golden curls a toss, and tried to look sophisticated. "You will be my personal solicitor."

"Excellent. There are just a few papers to sign, which I have here." He showed her where to sign. "And for now, to make it official, money must change hands. I just need a small coin—do you have a shilling?"

Yes, she had a shilling, and Hal slipped it into his waistcoat pocket. "And that should be all for now. I am ready to pay a call on Mr. Neville Small and obtain an accounting of the estate you've just inherited."

"Do you need me to attend, Mr. Wheaton?" asked Gwen a little fearfully.

"You may attend, but do not have to. As your solicitor, I have the power to examine any documents on your behalf and report back to you."

"That will be fine," said Gwen, relaxing again. "But oh, why don't you take Franny with you? She's so clever, and I know you have to return to London soon, and this way Franny could discuss it with me at her leisure."

For the first time, Hal's face fell. "I see your point, Miss Kestrel, but by law, only you or I, as your solicitor, can view the documents."

"But that's not entirely true, is it?" said Frances. "In London, you have your clerks reviewing documents."

Hal felt a mix of admiration and annoyance at that. "True, Frances, but you're not a clerk at my firm."

"But she could be, Mr. Wheaton. Franny is so smart and has been to university. Everyone admires her in our suffrage group and she knows all about money—" Tommie laid a gentle, restraining hand on Gwen, but Frances beamed at the compliments.

"You could make me a clerk, couldn't you, Mr. Wheaton? And I could help you?" She smiled sweetly.

"Your logic is irrefutable," said Hal, giving in with good grace. He pulled Gwen's shilling out of his pocket and handed it to Frances. "Congratulations. Welcome to the firm."

Frances was thrilled. First she was engaged as a consulting translator for the Metropolitan Police Service, and now as clerk to one of the most distinguished firms in London.

Hal sighed, taking another sandwich, and Gwen smiled. "If you'd like, Mr. Wheaton, I can have a maid show you to where you can refresh yourself before you call on Mr. Small."

"Thank you. I will do that and then, Franny, you and I will go." Gwen rang for a maid, and a few moments later, the three women were left alone to finish the tea.

"He is very, very nice, your Mr. Wheaton," said Gwen.

"Yes, he is," said Tommie. Frances looked up. There was something in her friend's tone, and those gentle eyes of Tommie's looked amused. "He is . . . a friend of yours? He called you 'Frances,' not 'Lady Frances,' and once he even called you 'Franny.' But I'm sorry—I'm prying."

But Frances had to smile. "Well, yes, he is more than a solicitor. He is a friend . . . and I suppose by way of being a suitor." She blushed.

"Well, he is very handsome," said Gwen. "I don't blame you."

"Neither do I," said Tommie. "Even briefly, it was clear that he's a man of intelligence and sensitivity and kindness. But I daresay there are those in your family who had hoped that as the daughter of a marquess you'd make an aristocratic match."

"By this point, much of my family would be so grateful that there's a man left in London whom I haven't offended or scandalized, they'd forgive him for—horrors!—being of the middle class."

And they all laughed.

After Hal returned, the chauffeur drove them to the office of Neville Small, Esq. His suite was handsome in an old-fashioned way, much like Hal's office in London, with lots of dark leather, wood, and well-shined brass. *What was it about solicitors that made them feel that they were stuck in the 1860s?* wondered Frances.

Hal handed the secretary his card. "I'm a solicitor down from London, recently engaged to represent Miss Gwendolyn Kestrel, and wish to speak with Mr. Small. As you can see from these papers, she has signed over full power of attorney to me." And a few minutes later they were ushered into the inner office, where a very surprised Neville Small greeted them. Surprise for Henry Wheaton, that is, and irritation for Frances.

"Since I have long represented the Kestrel family and am sole trustee of the estate, I cannot think why she thought she needed additional representation."

"Lady Frances suggested that I review the estate papers on Miss Kestrel's behalf." Hal smiled, but Mr. Small looked daggers at Frances. He shuffled his papers, checked the power of attorney letter, then cleared his throat.

"Very well, Mr. Wheaton. I will show you to an office and have my clerk give you the general accounts. Will that be satisfactory?"

"Perfectly," said Hal.

"And you, Lady Frances? There's a pleasant tea shop in town for you to wait for Mr. Wheaton to complete his examination."

Hal cut in before she could reply. "Lady Frances will be staying with me. She is employed by my firm as a confidential clerk." He smiled blandly as the color drained from Mr. Small's face. *Was this a joke? Were they trying to make a fool of him?* He cleared his throat again.

"I understand that the most prestigious firms in London can boast of their many aristocratic clients. But your firm must be the most distinguished of all to actually employ members of the nobility. My secretary will see you properly set up."

"Excellent. And one more thing—I assume Miss Kestrel has a will, and it was deposited with you? I'd like to see that as well."

With little further ado, they were set up with pens, paper, and ledgers in what appeared to be an unused storeroom. The rickety table and chairs showed that this was not a room clients ever used.

"Let's look at the will first." Hal opened it up and began reading it. "These country lawyers may be old-fashioned but they're thorough. This will was drawn up as soon as Miss Kestrel came of age—not strictly necessary, of course, but very prudent. Of course, she was probably just living off an allowance from her father, but tell me, Franny, what do ladies from wealthy families have to call their own?"

"I'm not only clerk, but expert witness? Very jolly, Hal. We all have a little put by. An elderly cousin who knew you as a little girl leaves you a bit in his will. A favorite aunt sends you something on Christmas, and your godfather remembers you on your birthday. And don't forget—Gwen's mother was dead. That means it's likely all her jewelry came to Gwen, and with a rich man like Sir Calleford, that could be a very nice collection indeed."

"Shrewdly reasoned, my lady. Now this will is interesting. Our Mr. Small was careful. Everything is spelled out. Also, Miss Kestrel may have more of a backbone than we gave her credit for. Did you know anything about her will?"

"No, I just assumed that Mr. Small pushed some papers in front of her and told her to sign, and that Gwen didn't care or even remember."

"Come look at this, then." He passed the will to Frances, and she read it herself. Gwen had left one hundred pounds to the suffrage group and one hundred pounds to the soup kitchen where Franny volunteered and served as treasurer. All her jewelry was left to Tommie.

"I can't see our Mr. Small being thrilled with that," said Franny. "But Gwen must've insisted. I am surprised—and pleased."

"Yes. And note how it's worded. Those few pounds and her jewelry were probably all she owned when the will was drawn up. A lesser lawyer might've just done something like, 'all my property to Thomasina Calvin, except for these small sums to charity.' After all, it was very little. But Mr. Small had her specify it. Now look at that last line." Frances read it: all other property to Mr. Christopher Blake.

It was clear now. Without that line, a simple "all my property" might've made Tommie, with Sir Calleford's death, next in line to inherit the Eyrie. "All my property" meant nothing a few days ago—now it meant a vast fortune.

"So even then, when Sir Calleford was in good health, Mr. Small wanted to make it clear that even if he suddenly died, there was no chance the estate would accidentally end up outside the family," said Frances.

"Exactly. Christopher Blake was always to be next in line if Gwen had no husband or children. The eventuality was always taken care of. And I imagine that was common knowledge."

They thought about that in silence, then Hal folded the will and put it back in the envelope. "I'm just a simple solicitor," he said. "You'll want to consider those implications."

"You're not simple, and you know the implications as well as I do," she said. "I will talk to Gwen about that later."

"Very well, Lady Frances," said Hal heartily. "But now comes the boring part. You want to be a legal clerk; you are going to work like one."

"I am sure you will find me a most satisfactory employee," she said, and indeed he did. Frances had learned well from her work as a treasurer for her charitable group. Hal told her it would take a team of solicitors and chartered accountants weeks to check every detail of such a large estate, but meanwhile he told her how to look for a sign of something suspicious.

They worked in quiet, poring over the ledgers. Mr. Small unbent enough to send his secretary in with tea and biscuits.

"I think I've found something," said Frances eventually. "There's a spike here in the cost of cottage maintenance. See here, this entry for Lavender Cottage. I was there actually." She explained about the widows cottages and having tea with Mrs. Sweet, the current occupant.

"The thing is, that cottage looked to be in good condition with no recent work. And yet, this sum of money is almost large enough to build a new cottage, and it's just a few weeks ago."

"Good catch, Frances! I was beginning to despair—our Mr. Small may be pompous, but his ledgers have been predictable and ordinary, until now. If you're looking for a reason for Mr. Small to be reticent, this might be it."

He tucked the ledger under his arm, and he and Frances asked the secretary to see them back into Mr. Small's office.

"I trust that you found everything in order, Mr. Wheaton?"

"Very clean books, Mr. Small. I congratulate you."

Mr. Small looked pleased with himself. "We may not have your London polish, but we do our best," he said.

"Just one question," Hal said, and showed Mr. Small the entry for Lavender Cottage. "I don't think that's for repairs. It's too large, and major capital repairs should have been listed separately."

Frances watched him closely. He was thinking what it could be. No—he knew. He was thinking of an explanation. A lie.

"If you'll wait one minute, I can find the related disbursement slip." He left the office, and returned a few moments later with the counterfoil of a check. "It was paid directly to the tenant, Mrs. Genevieve Sweet."

"That's very unusual, isn't it? A personal payment hidden in a business account?"

"It's perfectly legal and regular, if unusual. Perhaps it was for household repairs."

"That much? You could almost build a new cottage for that fee."

Mr. Small shrugged. "I just followed Sir Calleford's orders. I have no idea what the money was for."

Now that's definitely a lie, thought Frances. Solicitors like this knew where every single penny went.

"Ah, well. I'm sure we can follow up with Mrs. Sweet herself."

"That's your right, of course," said Mr. Small. "It may seem to be large for cottage repair, but considering the size of the estate, this amount wouldn't seem worth your time."

Hal smiled. "You may be right. Thank you for your help. Until we meet again, then." Mr. Small looked unhappy about a future meeting, but politely said they could sit in the reception area until their motorcar returned. However, they said they'd rather wait outside, as it was a pleasant day.

"You'll have lunch at the Eyrie, before you go back to London," said Frances as they strolled along High Street.

"That will work nicely," said Hal. He looked at her. "You know something, don't you? About that payment?"

"I do, I'm sure I do." It made sense now, with the overheard conversation between Mrs. Sweet and Sir Calleford the day before he was murdered. She would face Mrs. Sweet with that soon. Why had Sir Calleford given so much money to a tenant?

"Dare I ask?" said Hal.

"Let's just say I doubt it was malfeasance on Mr. Small's part. It was . . . something else. And if you don't know, you won't have to lie to your client."

Hal laughed. "Very well. I'm just glad I could help." He gave her a sly look. "Speaking of which, it didn't go against your principles to have to bring a man in to assist you in whatever it is you're up to here?"

"You're teasing me, but no. I make use of whatever resources are available. If there had been a female solicitor, I would've hired her."

Hal gave her look of mock horror. "Are you telling me, dearest Franny, that you'll abandon a business relationship that has endured since your father's day as soon as a woman becomes available?"

She smiled sweetly. "Of course not. Because you'll be hiring the women solicitors in your firm—even making them junior partners."

Hal laughed again, and Frances joined him, as the Rolls-Royce pulled up.

CHAPTER 14

For the first time since Sir Calleford's death, a meal at the Eyrie approached something like normality, and the guest was probably the reason why. Hal was very much at ease in groups and fitted in nicely. He discussed art exhibits with Miss Hardiman, dogs with Gwen, and horses with Mr. Hardiman and Mr. Blake. Both Tommie and Mr. Mehmet asked several questions about the English legal system, and Mr. Mehmet's eyes landed briefly on Frances with what she thought was some amusement. And Mrs. Blake seemed pleased with the way the conversation went.

Frances saw him back to the car.

"Be careful," he whispered.

"I always am," she said. And Hal rolled his eyes as the car pulled off.

Back inside, Mrs. Blake was giving a few instructions to Pennington, but turned when Frances reentered the house.

"Lady Frances, if it's convenient, could I have a word with you?" The words sounded serious, but Mrs. Blake was smiling gently.

"Of course."

Mrs. Blake led Frances to her morning room, where she clearly felt most comfortable.

"As if running a household after a death, after a murder, isn't bad enough, I have to cope with the constabulary wandering around and that inspector asking questions and making reports."

"Do they appear to be close to finding the culprit?"

Mrs. Blake shrugged. "Inspector Bedlow, the local man, seems to think it's an outside gang of robbers, and perhaps a servant was bribed, although I find that hard to believe. Who knows? Meanwhile, they've asked for everyone to stay, except for the French guests, who were vouched for by the French embassy and allowed to leave. But to the matter at hand." She waved away the topic and then smiled. "I understand you have arranged for Gwen to engage her own personal solicitor."

"She's a woman of wealth and property. And I felt she could use someone for whom her well-being was his sole concern. Mr. Wheaton is one of the most distinguished solicitors in London." She studied Mrs. Blake closely for reaction. She gave away little, but again, Frances saw strain in her face.

"I'm sure. But Lady Frances, there is so much more than financial and legal issues. Mr. Wheaton can't help Gwen serve as chatelaine."

It was an old-fashioned word for the lady of a great castle, from the days when the Eyrie was new. Frances knew what Mrs. Blake meant: A lady hired and managed servants, both indoors and out. She made sure her house was the social center of the county and set standards for behavior and entertainment. Frances thought of the aristocratic Marchands, Gwen's ancestors. Frances couldn't think of anyone less suited to be lady of the castle than Gwen. But Mrs. Blake reveled in it.

"With her money, Gwen could hire the finest housekeeper in England."

"And you no doubt wonder why we don't have one? Because I couldn't find anyone who could do what I could. Even if Gwen hired one, there is so much more to be done than a housekeeper can do. This household is the envy of England. Sir Calleford was one of the finest diplomats in Britain, and he made history here. And I gave him a household worthy of his tasks."

So it was about purpose. The Eyrie was Mrs. Blake's reason for living. Frances couldn't blame her for that. So was this about fear that Gwen would send her back home to the small house she shared with her son? No doubt Christopher would marry someday, and Mrs. Blake would be sent off to a dower house, alone and forgotten.

"I'm sure Gwen won't send you away."

"Of course she won't," said Mrs. Blake with a touch of annoyance. "She needs me, and even Gwen has the wit to see that. I have to think about the years ahead. This house has been handed down to blood relations for more than three centuries, and I mean to see that that continues. Gwen will stay here. I will stay with her. She will marry and have sons or daughters who will themselves marry and have children, those who can run this when I'm gone."

"And if Gwen doesn't wish to marry?" asked Frances. She said it softly, and watched Mrs. Blake carefully. Red spots appeared on the older woman's cheeks—she was angry, but she kept herself under control.

"What she wishes? We can't all be like you, Lady Frances, with the money, intelligence, and wit to flout all convention. Gwen has no skills for that. Will you and Miss Calvin guide her for the rest of her life? I have a plan for her. I would've thought you realized it. She will marry Christopher. She has always had affection for him, and he has always been kind to her. I will stay on to manage things, and Gwen will be perfectly satisfied with that."

Gwen wouldn't mind her Aunt Phoebe looking over her shoulder, thought Frances. *But if the Eyrie somehow ended up in someone else's hands, Mrs. Blake would lose her place.*

"And Christopher wants to marry her?" asked Frances.

"Lady Frances, I wouldn't have thought that you of all people would need things spelled out. Christopher will have an obliging wife, mastery of the house he's always loved, and his mother to run the household."

Frances thought over her next sentence carefully. "Mrs. Blake, I don't think a married life with Christopher—with anyone—is something Gwen desires."

Mrs. Blake rolled her eyes. "I appreciate your delicacy, but I'm not a fool. You are not married, so maybe I have to explain to you that in a marriage, not everyone gets all they need from a spouse. Christopher will no doubt make only minimal demands on her. Please tell me I don't have to explain further."

No, she didn't. The couple would do what was necessary to get an heir, and Christopher would take a mistress. Many marriages in society worked that way, and the couples were content, even happy.

Mrs. Blake smiled, as if to soften her message. "Please understand I'm not trying to be cruel. I really want what's best for Gwen. Surely you can see how this works so well for her, for everyone. Life is hard for a single woman in society—yourself excepted, of course. And if she wants Miss Calvin to live here as a sort of companion, then as you see, we don't lack room. She'll have the life she wants, with the security she needs."

Frances nodded. Mrs. Blake wanted Gwen to have a place in the world, and there was no getting away from the fact that Gwen was now mistress of the Eyrie. But there had to be another solution, something besides what was essentially a forced marriage.

"Do you think that Sir Calleford would've wished this for his only daughter?"

"What an extraordinary question. But a fair one. Yes, I do. He was a pragmatic man. In this very house I saw him solve problems that prevented wars and saved lives. You have no idea what a great man he was."

"It must've been a great privilege to run a household for such a paragon."

Mrs. Blake stared at Frances, as if to see whether she was making fun of her.

"It was. But I think we've strayed from the subject at hand. Can I take it, Lady Frances, that you will use your considerable influence to see that Gwen follows my plan?"

"Let us say, Mrs. Blake, that we both wish to do what is best for Gwen, now and for the rest of her life."

It was not the answer Mrs. Blake had hoped for, but Frances saw she was gracious about it.

"Thank you for hearing me out, Lady Frances. Things will be difficult in the coming days, with Gwen still in mourning, and we can plot a course for her later on." She stood.

"Just one more thing, Mrs. Blake, on another topic. I assumed Mr. Hardiman was a representative of the American government. Did not his embassy also ask that he be allowed to return? I'm surprised to see he's still here."

"I don't know if he is a diplomat—he wasn't one of Calleford's friends. He was just introduced to me as Mr. Hardiman, from somewhere in upper New York state. You should ask Christopher. He's the one who invited him."

"He did? You mean, to the Eyrie?"

"Yes. He said he had met some Americans while conducting business in London, and could he ask them down to the Eyrie to see the great house. Christopher hardly ever asked for a favor like that, and Calleford was happy to welcome them. Anyway, they seem delighted with it—especially Miss Hardiman. Good afternoon, and I'll see you at dinner."

Frances knew what to do next. *So an arranged marriage was not just a wandering thought, but a definite plan, at least in Mrs. Blake's mind. Had it been in Sir Calleford's? And that was interesting about Mr. Hardiman. Why had he been invited?* The two Americans were ciphers and it was time to find out more.

A passing footman told her he had seen Mr. Blake outside, near the stables. She headed out—it was a fine day, if a little cool. If Mr. Blake was thinking of riding, today was a good day for it.

She found him inspecting the horses, in the company of a groom, and wearing solid walking clothes. Frances thought about her own male walking clothes, and wished she could be wearing them.

"Lady Frances, a pleasure to see you. Despite the tragedy, work calls, and I always made regular inspections of Sir Calleford's stables. He didn't ride much himself, but he cared for his horses and wouldn't want them neglected." He said a few words to the groom, and dismissed him.

"Of course. And I know Gwen appreciates all you do."

"And I appreciate all you and Miss Calvin do for her. I've always had a soft spot for my cousin. I heard how you—and Miss Hardiman, too—were keeping her company in this difficult time."

"You're welcome. And I enjoyed meeting Miss Hardiman. I went to school in America, and made many American friends. Where did you meet the Hardimans?"

"A dinner party in London. I was up in the city on business, and Mr. Hardiman was there with some business contact. He had built an enormous Great Lakes shipping empire out of nothing and had become extremely wealthy. And now, with his sons largely managing the business and his wife deceased, he thought he'd take some time and see Europe with Miss Hardiman, his daughter. He and I took to each other. In fact, the three of us are going for a walking tour of the grounds. Miss Hardiman specifically asked me. And if you'd like to join us—"

"Thank you, Mr. Blake. But actually, I just wanted to ask you a question. An entirely inappropriate question. But a friend's happiness is at stake."

Christopher grinned. "I've heard of you, Lady Frances. Ask away."

"Has your offer for Miss Hardiman's hand been accepted?"

His jaw dropped. "Lady Frances, Mr. Hardiman is a recent friend. I hardly know Miss Hardiman, it never occurred to me—" He stopped when he saw Frances's skeptical look and sighed. "How did you know? Did Miss Hardiman tell you?"

"No, but it made sense. You want the Eyrie. And Mr. Hardiman can buy it for you. You invited them up here—not to your house, but to the Eyrie, which I hear you've hardly ever done. And Miss Hardiman is obviously enchanted with the place."

Christopher leaned his head against a post and gathered his thoughts. "Yes. And this is going to sound like a terrible mess, but hear me out."

Yes, Miss Hardiman had come to London looking for a well-connected husband. Wealthy New York society would not open their doors to nouveau riche like the Hardimans, but in England, there were more possibilities.

"We got to know each other. I told them about my family—we have a slender connection to the aristocracy. And I told them about the Eyrie. Believe me, I meant no harm. Dear Gwen never liked this place. I had an idea that would satisfy everyone: Effie and I would marry. My mother could then retire, so to speak, back to the home she shared with my father. We'd move into the Eyrie. Effie would become lady of the manor. I'd continue to manage the estate. Uncle Calleford would stay involved in politics as he wanted. Eventually, he would go to his final reward and Effie's dowry would buy the estate from Gwen, who could live happily in London. I know it sounds mercenary, but everyone would get what they wanted."

"I'm afraid it rather does, Mr. Blake, but you're right about what everyone wants. You really want this house, don't you? Gwen has talked about how much you loved the Eyrie. There was even talk about your marrying Gwen."

He eyed Frances. "Is that some sort of joke, Lady Frances? Or a test? I love Gwen like a sister and would do nothing to hurt her, nor tolerate anyone else hurting her. I make no claim to sainthood, but I'd live in an estate cottage before using that girl like that. Believe me. Gwen isn't going to get married. I know that much."

Frances nodded. "I understand and agree with you. But from what your mother has said, however, you and Gwen would have the banns read starting next Sunday."

He flashed that so-charming grin again. "And if your mother had had her way, Lady Frances, you'd be married to an earl or duke by now."

Frances laughed. "Touché, Mr. Blake. Thank you for your frankness. I promise I'll be discreet."

"I appreciate that."

"Does your mother know?" Frances thought Christopher was being too optimistic about his mother's retirement. Was he doing that intentionally?

"No, not even her. I expected her to cut up rough, I'm afraid. An American girl of no background, even if she had money, and her hoping I'd marry Gwen and take over the Eyrie. Anyway, we were going to wait until the diplomatic meeting was ended, and break our news to Mother and Uncle Calleford. But so far, no one knows. I haven't even formally asked Mr. Hardiman, although I'm sure he's put two and two together." He hit his forehead with the heel of his hand. "And now look at this. If we got married now, my prospective father-in-law would buy us the Eyrie right away. Mother loves running the Eyrie—to be bundled out by what she'd call an American adventuress; I can't imagine what she'd say. And I don't need to be a police detective to know how bad this looks. In a horrible way, it gives me a motive."

Frances had to agree. There was no assurance that Sir Calleford would have agreed to Christopher's idea. He could've lived another twenty years at least, and Effie Hardiman was not going to wait forever to move into the Eyrie. But with him gone, Gwen inherited and would be only too happy to sell the estate and return to London.

"It does look bad," said Frances. Christopher appeared genuinely shocked. But was it that he was accused—or that he was caught?

He sighed. "Fair enough, Lady Frances. You don't know me well. But you must've heard Gwen talk about me. She'll tell you I've always been her friend."

Yes, Gwen's friend. But what about Sir Calleford's?

"You make a good point. But if you don't mind some advice, Mr. Blake, I'd keep your secret engagement just that—secret. Anyway, you're fortunate in that the local man, Inspector Bedlow, seems to think an outside gang is responsible."

"Bedlow," said Christopher sourly. "He's completely out of his depth. His limit is tracking down poachers."

"Then why doesn't your chief constable call in more experienced detectives from Scotland Yard?"

"I can see that you haven't spent a lot of time in the country. The gentry here—and that includes the chief constable—is a tight-knit bunch. No one wants strangers from London poking their noses into county business, even when there's a murder to solve. Things will have to get much worse for that to happen. We have influence here, especially Mother as the lady of the house, and right now the preference is to keep things local. Meanwhile, the chief constable asks all the guests to remain. I don't know why—the police have questioned everyone."

Because the chief constable knows that one of the guests may have committed the murder, thought Frances, *even though no one wants to say it.* As Christopher said, things would have to get much worse.

"Say, Lady Frances, I don't suppose you could have a go at the chief constable the way you did at Mr. Small? If anyone can convince him, you can." His look was so engaging in that handsome face, that Frances was inclined to think that Kestrel's Eyrie wasn't the only reason Effie wanted to marry him.

"It may come to that yet, Mr. Blake. Enjoy your walk—I have things to do."

Actually, it wouldn't come to that. She didn't need Inspector Bedlow and she didn't need the chief constable. She started walking back to the house, and came across Effie Hardiman.

"Why, Lady Frances, were you just out by the stables? Dad and I are going for a walk with Christopher—that is, Mr. Blake. You can join us, I'm sure. Dad will be along in a moment."

"Thank you, but I have previous appointments. I'm sure you'll enjoy your walk. You seem to really appreciate this house, this estate."

"Oh, I do!" She turned and looked at the Elizabethan masterpiece. Even from the rear, it was grand and imposing. The two women took in the house together in silence. Miss Hardiman, it was clear, was imagining herself in the great hall, presiding over a ball. But Frances just got a chill.

"Would your father do anything for you, Lady Frances? Mine would do anything for me, I know, and if you can keep a secret, just between us girls, I'm going to ask him to get me this. Miss Kestrel doesn't seem to want it, but oh, I do."

"What if he can't get it for you?" asked Frances quietly.

"But of course he can," said Miss Hardiman, as if Frances had said something silly. "He's gotten everything he ever wanted, and if we want the Eyrie, we'll have that too. Good day, and I'll see you at dinner."

She marched off to the stables. *Well*, thought Frances, *that explained why Miss Hardiman was in no rush to leave and there were no complaints about having to stay. Her father would do anything for her. And she wanted nothing more than the Eyrie. Sir Calleford was the only possible hindrance—and now he was dead. Effie Hardiman and Phoebe Blake—two women who were both strong and strong-willed. They would both bear consideration.*

CHAPTER 15

Frances found Tommie in her room.

"I encouraged Gwen to lie down again, and she's having a good sleep, so she'll be fresh for dinner. How did it go with Mr. Small? I bet he was horrified to see you there as a solicitor's clerk."

"I'm sure I created a scandal. They'll be talking about the 'lady clerk' all winter. Anyway, the books were in order, as far as we could tell. There was an odd payment to Mrs. Sweet—we met her at the funeral—but maybe it was just some quiet charity. I'll speak with her later. Meanwhile, I also had a frank talk with Mrs. Blake."

She summarized the talk, and Tommie nodded solemnly.

"I suppose, from Mrs. Blake's viewpoint, it would be the best thing. This house needs a mistress, and Gwen can't . . ." she bit her lip, and couldn't go on.

"But wait—this story has a sequel. There is a woman who very much does want to become mistress, and I think she'll do anything to get there . . ."

Tommie cheered up as the story went on. "But that's wonderful. Miss Hardiman will become the new Mrs. Blake and I know I speak for Gwen when I say they're welcome to this place."

Sweet Tommie, thought Frances. *She always thinks the best of people. And I always think the worst.*

"Tommie. A man was murdered here. And you've been threatened twice. This arrangement is much more likely to go through without Sir Calleford. And if someone thought you might have too much influence over Gwen, they might have reason to threaten you."

"But Franny, you can't mean Miss Hardiman would, I mean, it's absolutely impossible . . ." She put her face in her hands. "There is so much wickedness in the world."

Frances laid a gentle hand on her. "Tommie, I'm not accusing anyone, not yet. There's a lot I don't understand. There are personal and diplomatic problems all mixed together here." She hadn't forgotten about Mr. Mehmet. "But I have discovered some things and will discover more, I promise." Tommie gave her a hug. "You stay strong for Gwen, and I'll stay strong for you."

There was a knock on the door, and Gwen came in. "I had a nice nap—and I'm glad I found both of you here. Franny, I was thinking about the Eyrie. Am I really going to be mistress here? You will help me, both of you?"

"Of course," said Tommie. Gwen looked out the window. "There's a view of the back lawn. Every year my father would sponsor a village fete in midsummer and have a traveling theater troupe perform. A comedy, something suitable for families. I will want to continue that, if I stay here. The villagers liked it so much—we can do that, can't we Tommie?"

"Of course," said Tommie.

"Ladies," said Frances. "Here we are refreshed and at loose ends. It's too late to pay calls, so why don't we get a little suffrage work done? Tommie, let's have another look at that pamphlet manuscript, and Gwen, it would be delightful if you could organize some note cards."

Tommie instantly focused on the task at hand, and Gwen was pleased to have something to do.

In the servants' hall, Mallow was enjoying a cup of tea with Nellie, Amy Hopp, and some of the other maids. Although many ladies and gentlemen visited the Eyrie, it couldn't compete with the London home of the Marquess of Seaforth. Mallow impressed everyone with an account of the king's visit, as well as visits from the prime minister, the bishop of London, and various dukes and earls.

"And at Miss Plimsoll's Hotel, where we live, the great actress Mrs. Patrick Campbell once called on Lady Frances in her carriage, and they went out to dinner together."

That was the most impressive of all to the other servants—the glamour and raffish reputation of the London stage. But the cook was not one of them, saying that "actresses are not respectable."

"Lady Frances is the daughter of a marquess," said Mallow. "Everything she does is respectable." That settled the argument as far as Mallow was concerned, but the cook just shook her head.

A young maid, unfamiliar to Mallow and looking a little shy, broke into the circle. "Excuse me, Miss. Are you maid to Lady Frances Ffolkes? My name is Dolly and I was told to ask for you."

The other servants looked on with curiosity as Dolly and Mallow stepped into the hallway, where they could have a bit of privacy.

"You see, Miss, I work a bit part-time for Mrs. Sweet, in one of the widows' cottages, and she's been in her room for hours, and I think she's sick. She won't answer my knocks and her door is locked."

"I'm sorry to hear that. It's always a bit awkward when a lady does that. But we haven't met—why are you asking me?"

Dolly fidgeted. "Your lady called on my great-grandmother, Betsy Tanner, and she was very impressed. She said, 'That's a real lady, that is, Dolly. And you can tell from her dress and hair, she has a maid who knows what's what.' So I'd like to ask you, Miss, what to do, as you're a guest, you see."

Of course. If Dolly asked for help from a visiting servant, there was less chance word would get back to the butler or head housemaid that a problem had come up that she couldn't handle.

Mallow felt pleased with herself that this young girl was asking for her advice and guidance. The cottages were a short walk away, Dolly said, and as it was still some time before she would dress Lady Frances for dinner, she could walk over with Dolly and help her solve the problem. Mallow got her cloak, and they headed over to Lavender Cottage.

"The door was unlatched, as it usually is when Mrs. Sweet is home. But the bedroom upstairs is locked."

They walked upstairs. Mallow tried the door; it was indeed locked. She rapped sharply. "Mrs. Sweet. Are you unwell?" she called loudly. She put her ear to the door, which in this simple cottage wasn't nearly as thick and heavy as the doors in the Eyrie. She didn't hear a sound. She looked through the keyhole; there was no key. Mallow could only see the empty bed.

But Lady Frances had taught her a trick. She sent Dolly downstairs to get a thin knife from the kitchen. She looked confused, but did as she was told. When she returned, Mallow began working on the lock. Lady Frances knew how to do this, and once they spent an amusing afternoon practicing on their own door back in Miss Plimsoll's. After ten minutes, Mallow was rewarded with a click.

"How clever," said Dolly.

"Mrs. Sweet? We're very sorry to disturb you, but—oh!" Mrs. Sweet was slumped in her chair with her jaw and eyes open and a box of candy on her lap. Mallow could see a hole in the bodice of her dress, and what appeared to be dried blood surrounding it.

Mallow steeled herself, walked up to her, and gently placed her fingers on Mrs. Sweet's hand. It was cold. It was the second dead body Mallow had seen in a few days, but Mallow had become used to it. She had seen dead people before; that wasn't something that could be hidden in the crowded tenements where she had grown up. And this woman was certainly dead—and had been for some hours, at least. Mallow had never seen a gunshot wound up close, but she guessed that's what she was looking at.

Dolly started to whimper.

"Stop that," said Mallow sharply. "We have things to do. I will get my mistress. You will stay here."

"I can't stay in this house," wailed Dolly. *It was an old cottage,* reasoned Mallow. *Dozens of people had probably died here over the years. But that wasn't going to reassure the girl.*

"Fine. Stay outside. If anyone comes by, say that Mrs. Sweet is unwell, she's not receiving, and the doctor has been called." The girl sniffled and nodded.

Mallow saw a key on the night table. *So someone had an extra copy. And took it with them, apparently.* She locked the bedroom door on their way out and pocketed the key. She set up Dolly outside. Then started walking briskly back to the house.

Finding Lady Frances at work with her friends, she simply said that Mrs. Sweet was not feeling entirely well and would like it if her ladyship could stop by.

Frances excused herself from her friends, who sent their good wishes, and walked out with Mallow.

"She's not sick, is she?" asked Frances when they were alone.

"No, my lady. She's definitely dead." She explained how she came to uncover the body, and how she found the key even though the door had obviously been locked by a second key. Frances listened as she usually did, focusing carefully and not interrupting.

"Very good, Mallow. Nicely handled—again. You weren't upset by the body?"

"No, my lady."

"You didn't call the police, did you?"

"Certainly not, my lady. It's not my place."

"Very good, Mallow."

The miserable-looking Dolly was still sitting outside and jumped up when Lady Frances arrived.

"Oh, my lady. Shall I go for the police, now that you're here?"

"In a moment, Dolly. I just want to see for myself."

"But, my lady—"

Frances turned. "Now, Dolly. If Mrs. Sweet really is dead, a few minutes won't make any difference."

Once they were upstairs, Mallow gave Frances the key and they walked in. Frances also felt the body's temperature, then she turned her attention to the spilled box of chocolates. Mrs. Sweet had been eating them when she died.

"She clearly was shot, Mallow. And I guess by someone she knew. She was happily eating chocolates when she was killed."

"That is evil, my lady."

"Yes, it is, Mallow."

"What could she have done to anyone that they'd want to kill her?"

"Sometimes, people are not killed for what they've done. They're killed for what they've seen." She thought of Sir Calleford and Mrs. Sweet walking in the night. Was that the reason—they had seen something?

Mrs. Sweet had indulged her passion for candy in the privacy of her bedroom. A visitor came and shot her. Then the murderer had locked the door from the outside and walked away with the key, to ensure it would be a while before someone found the body.

Nothing more to learn here. Closing the bedroom door behind them, they went into the sitting room. Frances didn't find anything out of place. The room was neat and tidy, with just a few ladies magazines and a couple of popular novels. Then they walked into the little kitchen. Nothing out of order here either. It was simply set up. Perhaps Dolly, or some other local girl, prepared her dinner. The only things that caught Frances's eye were three small canisters of dried herbs: ginger, red raspberry, chamomile. "Come, Mallow. I think we've seen whatever there is to see."

Dolly was anxiously waiting outside.

"Dolly, just one more thing. Did you cook for Mrs. Sweet?"

"Not the dinners, my lady. Usually one of my older cousins, Katie or Sophie, did that. But I made her sandwiches sometimes for her lunch."

"There are herbs in the kitchen. Do you know if they were used for cooking?"

"Oh no, my lady. Mrs. Sweet liked her gardening, and said she made teas and things with those and we weren't to use them."

"I see. And one more question—did you help Mrs. Sweet with her clothes at all? Mending or anything like that?"

"Yes, my lady. Small things, torn hems and darning. But for the big things she had me bring her dresses to the village seamstress, Mrs. Copley."

"Really? Was that frequent?"

"Only of late, my lady. Mrs. Sweet laughed and said she ate too much chocolate and needed her dresses let out. Mrs. Copley is a very clever seamstress, I told her, and good at things like that."

At that, Frances sent a very relieved Dolly to fetch the village constable, while she and Mallow made themselves comfortable in the sitting room.

"I did not know her well," said Frances, "but I think I learned one thing about her. She was Sir Calleford's mistress."

Mallow's eyes got wide. She had seen a bit of life since going into service, but sexual immorality still shocked her.

"Really, my lady, a great man like Sir Calleford? And Mrs. Sweet seemed so pleasant. I saw her at the funeral lunch." But it was clear. The large sum of money Sir Calleford had given her and their conversation in the nighttime garden. That was the best explanation. The gentle, good-natured Mrs. Sweet must have reminded Sir Calleford of his late wife.

"She was pleasant, Mallow. I doubt if she was a simple prostitute. I can see how they truly enjoyed each other's company."

Mallow gave a little "hmph," the closest she came to a complete disagreement with her ladyship.

"You don't believe in romance?" teased Frances.

"Oh no, my lady. I like romance. The moving pictures with romance are the best. But one thing can lead to another, my lady; I've seen it too often. The man has his bit of fun, and he doesn't believe in romance anymore. He's gone, and as likely as not, the girl is in a family way and no respectable man will marry her, and no respectable place will hire her. What then, my lady?"

And Frances had to agree that Mallow made an excellent point.

Constable Dill, the one who had questioned Mallow earlier, came briskly up the path with Dolly—and Inspector Bedlow.

"Oh, Lady Frances, we meet again." Bedlow gave a thin smile. "Now, I hear there's a dead body?" Mallow produced the key, and the two officers went upstairs after telling the three women to wait in the sitting room. They both came down a few moments later, the inspector looking grim.

"Now, Dolly here was a little unclear when she came by the station. Can you two tell me the full story?"

Mallow explained her part, then Frances took over the story, both of them watching the inspector get more and more annoyed, as Constable Dill took notes.

"Miss Mallow, why didn't you come to get the police straightaway?"

"I wasn't sure it was a police matter yet, inspector. It was for her ladyship to decide that."

The inspector looked dubious and thought a moment. Then he told Dolly she could go home, and she practically raced out of the house. "Dill, stand guard outside. And Miss Mallow, I'd like a private word with your mistress—you can wait outside too, with the constable."

When they were alone, he said, "This is the second time you and your maid have found a body. That's quite a coincidence, my lady, don't you think?"

Frances ignored his tone. "I think that's very significant. Don't you? Mallow has wisely intervened where lesser servants were afraid. That tells me the killer deliberately created situations where bodies would go undiscovered for a while. This is someone who knows how servants behave. It was the murderer's bad luck Mallow and I were here."

Bedlow just glared at her for a while. "The killer's bad luck? And mine too, it seems. I would've thought that you, Lady Frances, would know enough to get the police directly if your maid reports a body that at least appears dead. Your maid may have been worried Mrs. Sweet was ill. But why did you enter the room?"

"I didn't want to be accused of wasting valuable police time and thought it best to check first myself. Anyway, I think it's obvious that this was a case of murder, inspector," said Frances. "Killed by someone she knew."

"This is very odd, Lady Frances. On one hand you didn't know enough to contact the police, and on the other you were able to deduce so much about the murderer."

Frances sighed. "You're missing the point. There were no disturbances in the room. Surely she admitted someone and sat down for a cozy chat in her bedroom. And then her guest shot her and locked up with a spare key afterward."

"I think this may be part of the same gang that killed Sir Calleford," he said, more to himself than to Frances.

"I doubt that. There's virtually nothing in these cottages to steal. And an outsider would be afraid a gunshot would attract attention. But a local would know there was only Mrs. Bellinger's cottage within hearing."

"So you're saying Mrs. Bellinger shot her?"

"I have no reason to think that. But anyone here knows Mrs. Bellinger keeps to herself. She probably wouldn't even notice a gunshot. She'd assume it was a gamekeeper shooting vermin, or a poacher."

Inspector Bedlow fixed her with a sharp look. "So, Lady Frances, murder is something you have wide experience with?"

"As a matter of fact it is," she said. "From time to time I have been of assistance to the police in London."

"Then you're welcome to go home and help the police in London. We don't need help from amateurs in this county."

Frances struggled to keep her temper. "Inspector Bedlow, Mrs. Sweet was not murdered by a robber. And if you don't accept that, I can assure you there will be more murders."

Chapter 16

Outside, it was getting a little cool, and Mallow's cloak was thin.

"If you're getting a chill, Miss Mallow, I'll lend you my jacket until your lady comes back."

"Thank you. But I will be fine for now." They heard the voices getting louder inside. "I think my lady is getting angry at your inspector."

"And I'm sure he's getting angry right back at her," said Dill, with a grin. "Just between us, the inspector is under a lot of pressure. It was hoped he would make an arrest soon, and the chief constable has been asking for progress reports. We've been looking into local gangs, but they all have alibis."

Mallow nodded encouragingly.

"In one case, he thought he knew who did it, only to find the gang was under lock and key in the next county on another charge when Sir Calleford was murdered. He was very angry at that, I can tell you," said the constable. "But he still thinks it's a gang. Although . . ."

Mallow looked up expectantly.

"I have also heard him mutter things about your lady's friend, Miss Thomasina Calvin—that she may have a reason to wish Sir Calleford dead. I can't see a quiet lady like that stabbing a man like Sir Calleford. I shouldn't really say anything, but I've

heard your lady knows important people. She was seen talking with that important inspector from London. If she has any
influence . . ." He let the thought hang.

"You don't like Inspector Bedlow much, do you?" asked
Mallow.

Constable Dill looked over his shoulder to make sure he
wasn't being overheard. "I don't seem to be getting on with my
career doing this," he said. "We're going in circles. I'm up for
sergeant, like I said, and I just found out there's a watch supervi-
sor position open. Again, Miss Mallow, just between us, helping
Inspector Bedlow chase his tail isn't going to raise my profile
with the chief constable."

"Well I'm sure that your skills will shine through," said Mallow emphatically, and Dill seemed surprised and pleased with his
compliment.

"Thank you very much," he said.

At that point, Frances came out of the house walking
very briskly.

"Come, Mallow, there is nothing more here for us." She had
that clipped tone that signaled great irritation.

Mallow quickly fell in line next to her mistress.

"That utter fool," said Frances. "Too stupid to see the obvious, too stubborn to call in help. I never thought I'd say this, but
I wish Inspector Eastley was back here. He's stubborn too, but at
least he's intelligent and competent."

"Yes, my lady." She paused. "I did hear some information,
though, from Constable Dill. He's the one who interviewed me
earlier." She told Frances what she had heard.

"Very interesting, Mallow. That goes along with what
Mrs. Blake told me earlier—they hate calling in Scotland Yard.
I never thought it was a gang, but this does show that someone
is getting desperate, and desperate people do desperate things.
We have to watch carefully because Inspector Bedlow will likely
arrest someone out of his own desperation. And we must be

especially careful for Miss Calvin—she could easily become a scapegoat."

"Yes, my lady." She paused. "You won't reveal that you found this out from Constable Dill, though? I wouldn't want to get him in trouble."

Frances smiled. It was not like Mallow to worry about a constable. As loyal as she was, she never liked getting mixed up with the police. *Had this one caught her fancy?*

"I'll treat it as confidential, of course, Mallow. We wouldn't want to mar a promising career, would we?" She shook her head. "Poor Mrs. Sweet. 'More sinned against than sinning.'"

"My lady?"

"A quote from Shakespeare. I only meant that whatever sins Mrs. Sweet committed, she didn't deserve this."

"Of course not, my lady. I will say a prayer for her in church on Sunday."

"Even though she was with a man outside of marriage?"

"I'm sure it's not my place to judge her for that, my lady. And if she was a sinner, all the more reason to give her our prayers."

───◆◆◆───

Back at the house, Frances broke the news quietly, saying Mrs. Sweet had been murdered but the police had no suspects yet. The accepted explanation, for now, was the "gang" that had supposedly killed Sir Calleford.

Mrs. Blake accepted the news calmly. Gwen teared up, even though she hardly knew the woman, and quickly offered to pay for funeral expenses—although Frances knew of course that Sir Calleford's substantial gift was sitting in the woman's account. Tommie caught Frances's eye—she knew there was more to this.

Christopher Blake accepted it calmly as well and said he would call the chief constable personally to see about his progress. But Frances could tell he didn't believe the convenient fiction any more than she did.

"Mr. Blake. All of this has been so upsetting for Gwen. I know I'm being shockingly forward, but she speaks of you with such affection. Could you invite us for a day at your estate? I think Gwen would enjoy the change of scene and it would give your mother a day of quiet here."

And most of all, it would give Frances and Mallow a chance to talk to Blake servants. They may have some insights into family workings.

"Splendid idea, Lady Frances. I'm sorry I didn't think of it myself. I'll make the arrangements. And there's good shooting not far on a neighbor's estate—that might give the gentlemen some sport while you ladies get a tour of my lands."

"Thank you so much. And no need to tell anyone it was my idea. I wouldn't want anyone to think I was being too forward." No need for anyone to think Lady Frances was more curious than she should be, either.

Frances caught the Hardimans and Mr. Mehmet before dinner as well. The Americans offered conventional words of sympathy. Mr. Mehmet said, "I wish you solace upon the death of your friend," and he seemed sincere.

But since no one knew her well, her death didn't seem to cast much of a pall over dinner. Mrs. Blake asked the Americans if they had had a good tour of the grounds, and Miss Hardiman gushed about the extent and beauty of the Eyrie estate.

"The estate was a long time in the making," said Mrs. Blake. "It was laid out more than three hundred years ago."

"Imagine that," said Miss Hardiman.

Mr. Mehmet said little, but Frances was not done with him yet. He was the one with an interest in the cottage right next to Mrs. Sweet. He was also the last of the dinner guests Frances still didn't fully understand.

After dinner, Mrs. Blake said if anyone was interested, the usual after-dinner reception would be held in the drawing room for the first time since Sir Calleford had died. "Gwen and I thought it was time," she said, including her niece—an acknowledgment of Gwen's role as the new mistress of Kestrel's Eyrie.

Frances thought this would be a good chance to speak with Mr. Mehmet again, and was disappointed to see him heading away from the stairs as the rest of the party walked up to the drawing room. She quietly stepped away from the stairs and into a shadow, to see him heading out the door. *Was he hoping for a breath of air?* It was quite cool outside. Frances thought for a moment, then quickly followed him out.

The cold air hit her, and she wished again she was in her male walking clothes and strong boots. From the little light leaking from the windows, she saw Mr. Mehmet head along the path to the widows' cottages. *Another visit with Mrs. Bellinger?* It was very late for a man to visit an unattached woman in a home without a live-in servant.

Confident she knew where he was going, she followed at a distance. She knew he wouldn't expect her to follow him anyway. Her heart beat faster and she forgot how cold it was. She'd catch him out now—there were no innocent explanations for this.

And suddenly he stopped, and she saw him with someone else, the shadowy figure of a man. Frances heard murmurings in a foreign tongue, probably Turkish. She heard the word "Kerem" more than once. They exchanged something, but she couldn't see what, then there was more talking in Turkish. She clearly made out one English phrase: "our friend in London." The second man disappeared into the darkness. Mehmet continued on his way.

They were almost there. There was a welcoming glint in the window of Mrs. Bellinger's cottage and she saw more light as the door opened. So she was expecting him, even eager for him. Frances increased her pace—she'd catch them now, right on the threshold. *What was going on here? Was the financially desperate Mrs. Bellinger working with Mr. Mehmet as a spy?*

And then she felt an arm going around her and she was lifted from the ground. She started to scream, but a cloth was stuffed into her mouth. A man held her tightly and tucked her under his arm, immobilizing her hands. Craning her neck, she saw they were heading toward the still open door. They stepped inside, and she heard the door close.

CHAPTER 17

Once inside, she was put on her feet, and she instantly pulled the cloth, a cheap handkerchief, out of her mouth. The man who had grabbed her was dressed as a manservant, but did not appear English—no doubt Mr. Mehmet's valet.

Without thinking, she smoothed her dress, then took stock of her captors: Mrs. Bellinger was giving her a look of pure hatred and Frances glared right back. Mr. Mehmet had the faintest look of amusement.

"Since it was obvious I was coming here anyway, it was unnecessary to have your . . . minion assault me like that."

Mr. Mehmet gave an ironic bow. "My apologies. It was feared you might stop and turn back to the house, and report what you saw. And Adem, while a fine servant, perhaps overreacted. Although I asked him to watch you, I didn't want him to kidnap you. Again, I am sorry." Mr. Mehmet said a few words in Turkish; Adem responded briefly and disappeared into the kitchen.

Frances watched a look pass between Mrs. Bellinger and Mr. Mehmet. She still didn't know his full story, but she knew what was happening here. Certain kinds of looks were only passed between certain kinds of people. The opened door, welcoming, made it all clear. And Mr. Mehmet's daytime visit—discreet, but still in the open. Frances guessed no spies would meet by day like that.

"I think we've had enough of her prying," said Mrs. Bellinger in that icy tone of hers. "Let's just dump her somewhere and be done with it."

Frances knew it was anger talking—anger and fear. Mrs. Bellinger just wanted to get a rise out of Frances, but she refused to give her the satisfaction of a response. She only spoke to Mr. Mehmet. "Tell me, did you know she was that bloodthirsty when you first fell in love with her?"

Frances delighted in the absolute astonishment on his face. And then he took a step forward and grabbed her hard on the shoulders. "Who told you? Tell me how you knew that?" he yelled.

She slapped away his hands. "Stop manhandling me. Once was enough. And there's no need to yell. It was the way you two looked at each other, the easy way you visited. And you were seen at the Eyrie lands in a romantic moonlight walk." That last was a bit of a guess, but Mme. Aubert had seen them and Frances felt it was a reasonable conclusion.

"Let's lock her in the root cellar until we decide what to do," said Mrs. Bellinger, still hoping for a reaction. Now, Frances heard even more fear behind the anger.

"Oh, do stop being so dramatic," said Frances. "I have no interest in any affair you two are having."

"We are not having an affair, Lady Frances," said Mr. Mehmet. "She is not my . . . lover. Mrs. Bellinger is my wife."

That did surprise Frances. She wouldn't have guessed their relationship was that close.

"Well then," she finally said. "I have no interest in your marital status. I'm here because of my friend. Now can we sit down? If you haven't forgotten everything you knew about hospitality, you will offer me a seat and a glass of that sherry I see on the side table."

Mr. Mehmet had regained his self-control. "I think you are correct, Lady Frances. Although considering your behavior, you are perhaps not in the best position to lecture us on hospitality.

Please, take a seat. And you, too . . . my wife." He poured three glasses of sherry, and a few moments later they were all in a somewhat mellower mood.

"You say you are here for your friend, Lady Frances?" asked Mr. Mehmet. "That would be Miss Kestrel? You are trying to find her father's murderer?"

"Yes, but that is not my main reason. Miss Kestrel was the subject of vicious rumors—and she doesn't even know about it. I came to find out who started it, and why. Sir Calleford's murder is probably related. And now your neighbor, Mrs. Sweet. I assume you told your wife about that. And your behavior, Mr. Mehmet, has been suspicious."

"Of course. But now you see. I visited Sir Calleford a number of times on business in past months. On my first visit, I met Mrs. Bellinger over dinner. And recently she gave me the great honor of becoming my wife, quietly in a registry office where no one knows us." He smiled at her, and she smiled back. Years fell away from her, and for a few moments she looked like a beautiful bride. "But we must be secret because of my work and the need to avoid gossip—a Muslim Turk marrying a Christian English-woman. It could provoke extreme reactions from my associates and family. And I wanted to protect my wife from any embarrassments regarding her family or social circle."

"And what is your work, Mr. Mehmet?"

He shook his head. "That too is secret. But please know I had no hand in Sir Calleford's death. Why would I do that? I don't want any attention called to myself, at least not until sometime in the near future when my wife and I can leave."

Mrs. Bellinger finished her sherry and stood. "This is difficult for me. I am going to my bedroom. I imagine you will talk a little while. Good night, Mehmet. Good night, Lady Frances."

Mehmet stood too and kissed his wife. "We won't be long, and I'll look in on you before I go." As she turned to head up the stairs, Frances spoke.

"You may not believe me, but I wish you the greatest happiness in your marriage," she said.

Mrs. Bellinger just looked at her. "Thank you. But you don't understand, do you? You can't imagine a well-born English-woman marrying a Turk. But then, you can't possibly imagine what my first marriage was like—the emotional and physical pain I endured. I don't like you, Lady Frances, but I don't wish you the marriage I had."

"You're right about that. I can't understand. But my greatest wish, all my work, is to make sure no woman has to endure what you had to."

Mrs. Bellinger smiled coolly. "You have a reputation for giving pretty speeches. I see it was well-deserved. Do you know what you do not understand? The importance of kindness from a man. For all our differences, Mr. Mehmet is a kind man. So much kinder than the so-called Christians who turned their backs on me after the humiliation I suffered at my first husband's hand. Someday, when you are older, you will realize what I mean about the importance of kindness. For now, I appreciate your wishes for my recent marriage and bid you good night." She headed upstairs. Frances glanced now at her host, whose wet eyes were following his wife up the stairs. She felt a pang in her heart and felt momentarily like an intruder.

Mr. Mehmet quickly wiped his eyes and finished his sherry.

"Lady Frances, if there were anything I could tell you about Sir Calleford's death, or if there were any rumors about his daughter, I would tell you. I don't see how I can help you further—except with this: In my faith, hospitality is sacred and inviolable. It is no doubt clear to both of us that it was a guest who murdered Sir Calleford, a man to whom he offered hospitality, a sin that defies description. Such a murderer must have a black heart."

Frances nodded. She was not of his faith, but his words made sense to her.

"When Adem carried you in here, I saw anger in your eyes, but not fear. You are fearless, Lady Frances, and intelligent. I think you will find what you seek. In a strange way neither of us can understand, you will be Allah's instrument in uncovering a murderer."

"I find it odd that your God would pick a woman—a Christian woman—for his plans."

He smiled. "You mock me, but it is not for us to question his ways. As a woman, you cannot begin to plumb the depths, but it is true. You will be Allah's sword in this. He will use you to uncover this great sin. I am convinced."

Frances thought that one over. *What could she say? At some level this was a compliment, but "thank you" didn't seem right, somehow.*

She was saved from trying to find an answer by a knock. It wasn't at the front door, but rather the kitchen door. Mr. Mehmet jumped up, alarmed. No one was expected. They heard Adem open the door.

"Excuse me," came Mallow's strong London accent, with the superior tone she used for fellow servants. "I believe my mistress, Lady Frances Ffolkes, is here."

Frances started to talk, but Mr. Mehmet silenced her with a glance. "Please, I don't want anyone else to know," he whispered. Frances could've told him it was a lost cause, but said nothing for the moment.

"Your lady isn't here, please go home," said Adem.

"I don't believe you. She went down this path and there are no other cottages with the lights on. Now please show me to her at once."

"All I can say is that your lady is not here. Now please go—"

"How dare you lay hands on me!" said Mallow. Frances rushed to the kitchen—if Adem had hurt Mallow . . .

Before she could make it through the door, there was a crack and Adem cried out. When Frances and Mr. Mehmet entered the kitchen, Adem was sitting down, clutching his left shin, and

Mallow—looking very pleased with herself—was holding a rolling pin.

"My lady, I hope you are well. This . . . person dared to lay hands on me. It was necessary to strike him." She was affronted that such a thing had come to pass. Frances bit her lip to stop herself from laughing at her diminutive maid laying into a manservant who probably had eight inches and one hundred pounds on her.

"Mallow, what are you doing here?"

"I was concerned, my lady, when I couldn't find you after dinner. A maid saw you leave, and when an assistant gamekeeper said he saw a lady along the path to the cottages, I assumed it must be you." She glanced down at the rolling pin. "I borrowed this from Cook, my lady, in case of any eventuality." She stopped to glare at Adem, who was scowling at her. "And I brought a wrap for you, my lady, so you wouldn't get a chill."

Mr. Mehmet sighed, but there was a hint of a smile. "This little cottage has become too crowded, I think. All our business has been concluded, has it not, Lady Frances?" Then, with irony in his voice, he continued. "And now, with your maid here, you may go home accompanied by her and thus avoid any damage to your reputation."

"Thank you for your kind observation," Frances shot back. "I do agree we're done here. Your secret will be safe with me."

"So you trust me then?"

"I didn't say that, Mr. Mehmet. I said I'd keep your secret. You still haven't told me what you're doing here—that is, what your occupation is. Acceptance is one thing. Trust is quite another."

He laughed. "I appreciate the distinction. And now, I suggest we return."

The path was only wide enough for two abreast, so Mr. Mehmet walked with Frances, while Adem and Mallow followed behind—the two servants eying each other with suspicion.

Even in the dark, the Eyrie was imposing, filling the sky as they approached it.

"Have you been to India, Lady Frances?"

"No, but I would very much like to someday. Have you?" She wondered where this conversation was going.

"Yes. There is a great building there, I'm sure you've heard of it, called the Taj Mahal. It looks like a palace, but it's a tomb for a queen. And looking at the Eyrie, I think of that. I know it's a home, but it feels like a tomb. I cannot imagine actually living there. I hope I make sense, Lady Frances, and that I don't give offense?"

"Not at all, Mr. Mehmet. In fact, I agree. It's a beautiful house to visit, but I wouldn't want to reside there. Even less to be its mistress. Your comparison to a tomb is apt. It makes me think of the line, 'The grave's a fine and private place, but none, I think, do there embrace.'" Mr. Mehmet laughed.

"An amusing line. Where is it from?"

"A poem by Andrew Marvell, an English poet of the seventeenth century. It's called 'To His Coy Mistress.'"

"My wife has promised to recommend English writers for me. I shall ask her to add this Andrew Marvell to the list."

Frances had a vision of the stiff Mrs. Bellinger—now Mrs. Mehmet—sitting by the fire with Mr. Mehmet, reading English poetry. You just never knew.

"One more thing, Mr. Mehmet. May I ask whom you were speaking with before your servant Adem seized me? You were speaking in Turkish, so it was clearly one of your countrymen."

"What a curious girl you are, Lady Frances. But there was no other person. It was Adem I was speaking with, then he turned back and grabbed you. He is more comfortable conversing in Turkish."

"That's impossible. If the man were Adem, he couldn't have slipped behind me that quickly after talking to you. There was another man there, and seeing all that has happened here, and how you're depending on me to solve this crime as 'Allah's agent,' I think you should tell me."

"Distances in the country, at night, are hard to judge. I assure you, it was just me and Adem."

"Who is your 'friend in London'?"

She couldn't see his face clearly in the dark.

"I have lots of friends in London, Lady Frances."

"You are lucky I'm not with the London police. They'd have constables checking every person in the village, every coming and going."

"I suppose I am lucky. But I still have nothing to hide. Or, I should say, nothing more to hide."

"Very well, don't tell me. But I know I'm right. And I still don't trust you."

Back in the house, they said a quick good-night. Adem studiously ignored Mallow as he followed his master up the stairs. He still had a slight limp—Mallow must've hit him pretty hard.

Frances quickly stopped by Gwen's and Tommie's rooms to say good-night and apologize for not being able to join them earlier in the drawing room, citing "personal business." Then she had Mallow help her undress and get ready for bed.

"I hope you don't think I overstepped by coming to fetch you at the cottage, my lady, or by assaulting Adem."

"Not at all, Mallow. I should've taken you with me in the first place." She smiled at her maid. "You're quite handy with that rolling pin."

"Thank you, my lady. You should've known my old gran, my lady. She was a head taller than me and was famed in the neighborhood with her rolling pin. No one took advantage of her. Not twice, anyway."

"I'm sorry we never met." She sighed. "I had expected, even hoped, that Mr. Mehmet was involved in these murders. It seemed so . . . obvious. There is still something there, I'm sure, but this is really a family affair, I'm afraid."

"You mean someone in the family killed Sir Calleford and Mrs. Sweet, my lady?"

"It would seem so. But why? That's what I can't figure out. What did they hope to gain from it?" She shook her head. "I thought it might be to gain the Eyrie, but everyone knew Gwen Kestrel would get it anyway. Mrs. Blake knew that, and so did her son."

"Miss Hardiman seems to want to be mistress here, my lady."

"Exactly, very good. But she can buy it, and if she marries Mr. Blake . . ." She frowned. There were too many motives. Greed. Desire for power. Love and lust. "If Gwen died, everything would go to her nearest relation, Mr. Blake."

"Oh, my lady, do you think Miss Kestrel is in danger? Mr. Blake seems like such a good man, my lady."

"I agree. But there is some danger to Miss Kestrel—although not for her life. Another kind of danger. More to her reputation than her life. Does that sound strange, Mallow?"

It did, but Mallow just said, "I'm sure you'll figure it out, my lady."

"Mr. Mehmet says I'll figure out it. He said he's convinced I'm the sword of Allah."

Lady Frances had always been very patient in explaining things to Mallow, and the maid had no doubt she would explain this if asked. But sometimes—and this was one of them—it was just easier to say, "Yes, my lady. Will that be all?"

CHAPTER 18

The next morning, it was ladies only at breakfast. Mr. Mehmet was off on another walk—at least Frances knew with whom he was having breakfast. Mr. Hardiman and Mr. Blake had also risen early to go riding. *Little could pull a man away from a woman he was wooing—unless he was trying to curry favor with the father,* Frances observed.

Miss Hardiman seemed very eager to talk with Gwen, Tommie, and Frances. "Good morning, ladies. I assume you heard that Christopher—Mr. Blake—thought it might be a good idea for a change of scene, to spend a day at his house. We'd make a party of it, all of us going, early tomorrow before breakfast."

"Yes, I haven't been in years. I'm so looking forward to it," said Gwen.

Mrs. Blake laid a hand on Gwen's arm. "You were always happy visiting there as a girl, and a change of scene with Christopher might do you some good."

"Are you coming, Aunt Phoebe?"

"No dear. I would prefer a quiet day here. There are some things I'd like to take care of. Old General Anstruther has invited Mr. Hardiman and Mr. Mehmet to shoot at his place."

Mr. Hardiman must be loving this, thought Frances, *this self-made American riding and shooting with the English gentry.* Interesting he was spending time with Mr. Mehmet—she wondered what they made of each other. And Miss Hardiman? This was another opportunity to be with Christopher—and away from Mrs. Blake.

"I agree it would be good to go," said Tommie, grasping Gwen's hand.

"Mr. Blake has to meet with some of the tenant farmers for much of the day," said Miss Hardiman. "But that will give us girls a chance to get to know each other better. My late mother always said that at times like these, a woman wants the company of another woman."

"What will you ladies be doing today?" asked Mrs. Blake.

"Tommie thought a healthful walk around the grounds would be good for me," said Gwen.

"I agree," said Mrs. Blake. "As you're now lady of the manor, it would be good for you to familiarize yourself with the place. You haven't really been around the grounds since you were a little girl."

That didn't seem to sit well with Gwen, but she forced a smile.

Frances suddenly had an idea. "Miss Hardiman, I was going to visit Mrs. Tanner, an elderly woman who used to be in service here. Would you keep me company? It's not a long walk, and she's a rather interesting character."

"Mrs. Tanner? Really?" Mrs. Blake seemed surprised and amused.

"I paid her a call after the funeral, and found she knew my great-grandmother, who visited here. Family lore says she was a 'notable personality,' as my mother gingerly put it, and I'd like to hear some more stories."

Miss Hardiman said she'd be delighted to walk with Frances. And Mrs. Blake said that she would ask Cook to pack some delicacies to bring to Mrs. Tanner—she'd let the ladies know when the basket was ready and they could go by motorcar.

"Splendid suggestion," said Frances. "I just have a few letters to write after breakfast and then we'll go."

It wasn't completely the truth, however. After making sure Miss Hardiman had gone to her own room, she quickly headed for Gwen's room, where Gwen and Tommie were discussing the path of their walk.

"Gwen, I just have a few questions for you, from some discussions Mr. Wheaton and I had after our talk with Mr. Small." Gwen nodded. "We found out that when you came of age, your father and Mr. Small had you sign a will. Do you remember?"

"Oh yes," she said brightly. "Mr. Small said it was just a formality, of course, because I was so young, but the law required it." Not quite true, of course, but the easiest way of explaining it to Gwen. "I had to say where I wanted everything I owned to go if I died. I said whatever money I had would go to the East End soup kitchen and our suffragist group. Mr. Small made a face at that, but Father shrugged and said it was my money; I could do what I want. Oh, and all my jewelry to you, Tommie."

Tommie looked astonished. "But that's all your mother's jewelry—it's very valuable. That's very sweet, of you, of course . . . I don't know what to say . . ." She seemed deeply moved.

"Who else should get it?" asked Gwen. "And anyway, nothing is going to happen. But Father said it was important to make sure the house and estate stayed in the family, and so should be left to Christopher. Until—" Gwen suddenly broke off, and her eyes lost their focus. It's what she did when she didn't understand something, and didn't know how to proceed.

"Until what?" asked Frances gently.

"Until I had a husband, and children," she said, so quietly it was hard to hear her. She turned to Tommie. "I wish I could just walk away from the Eyrie, just shut it up and go back to London with you. But that wouldn't be fair. So many servants put out of work. I asked Aunt Phoebe if we could sell the Eyrie and have everyone work for a new master and mistress, but she said no one could afford it, except people who already had their own estates."

So Mrs. Blake was unaware that Hardiman gold was available? Or maybe she didn't want Gwen to know, didn't want to see an American woman presiding over tea. Of course, the forthright Miss Hardiman wasn't going to be as compliant a daughter-in-law as Gwen would.

"You grew up here, Gwen," said Frances. "You really don't want to live here? And if we could sell it, you wouldn't miss it?"

Gwen shook her head. "My mother died when I was so little. I hardly remember her. And then, it was just me and various nannies in this huge, empty place, and the only fun I had was when I could visit with Christopher—" She burst into tears and fell into Tommie's arms. "Please, I don't want to stay here. Please."

"I'm so sorry," said Frances.

"We'll be all right," said Tommie as Gwen whimpered. Her eyes asked if they could tell Gwen about selling to the Hardimans, but Frances shook her head. She didn't want to involve Gwen with that yet.

"Gwen, I promise we'll work this out. I can't tell you more now, but trust me."

Gwen made an effort at drying her tears and smiled.

"You're so clever, Franny. I knew you'd come through." She turned to Tommie. "Didn't I say that?"

And Frances left Gwen in Tommie's care, so she could work to keep her promise. Mrs. Tanner held more secrets, and maybe a second visit would pry them from her. She already trusted Frances, and might like to show off in front of the eager American visitor.

Downstairs, they found that Cook did them proud, packing a full basket at Mrs. Blake's orders. Frances decided to take Mallow along to help young Dolly set up the food. Miss Hardiman seemed pleased with the outing, and to Frances's practiced eye, was a bit overdressed for the occasion. If she did become lady of the manor, she'd need a lesson in proper dress.

"Is this something commonly done by ladies in England— visiting the local tenants and retired servants?" she asked.

"To be mistress of a great house is to be responsible for everyone. For the servants in your house, the staff tending the grounds, the tenant farmers, and their families. My father and his father before him always said it was a sacred duty."

Miss Hardiman seemed rather startled at that and frowned. *So it wasn't all balls and parties among the elegant gardens.*

"My father missed Easter at home once, when I was a girl, because he said he had to oversee the building of some canal locks. He said it was his canal, his boats, and thus his responsibility— and that sometimes came before family. Is that what you mean, Lady Frances?"

"Yes," she said. "That's exactly what I mean." *Perhaps*, thought Frances, *there was more to Effie Hardiman than I had realized.*

After the short trip to Mrs. Tanner's, the chauffeur parked alongside the small path that traveled around the cluster of cottages. The appearance of the Rolls-Royce caught the attention of everyone in the hamlet, especially the children who clustered around while the chauffeur attempted to shoo them away.

Dolly seemed pleased and surprised to see them.

"We thought we'd come for another visit, since Mrs. Tanner seemed to enjoy our visit so much last time. I brought my American friend, Miss Hardiman, who would like to hear more about the estate. And Mrs. Blake packed some treats for Mrs. Tanner."

"Do come in, Lady Frances, Miss Hardiman, Miss Mallow. My great-gran, that is, Mrs. Tanner, will wake from her nap soon. Come in and we'll set it out."

Once inside, Mallow quite overawed Dolly. As a housemaid, Mallow had helped set the table for the most formal occasions for the Marquess and Marchioness of Seaforth, and she provided the same critical eye to Mrs. Tanner's rickety table. The base metal forks and earthenware plates were laid out as if they were sterling silver and the finest bone china.

"Thank you, Miss Mallow," said Dolly humbly. "Gran is sleeping rather late this afternoon. I'd best go see." And Mallow said she'd finish laying out the table while Lady Frances and Miss Hardiman unpacked.

It took Frances a few moments to think about what Dolly had said. *"Gran is sleeping rather late . . ."*

Oh God. Frances raced by the startled Dolly and up the stairs. The door wasn't locked, and it took her only a moment to get inside. Mrs. Sweet had been cold, but Mrs. Tanner was still warm. She hadn't been dead long.

Frances glanced around the room. No sign of food, but her habits were probably well-known. Someone gave her something and then sent her to bed. Dolly probably wasn't around every moment; it was easy to remove all traces.

Frances turned her attention back to the body. Mrs. Tanner's face was a deep red. The result of a heart attack? Yes, she was very old, but Frances was inclined to be suspicious in the wake of two other murders. That red face meant something. . . . Frances leaned over the woman and sniffed close to her face. Then she stood up again, and smiled grimly. Bitter almonds and red complexion—the sure signs of a cyanide-based poison, as she learned during a most entertaining afternoon with Sir Arthur Conan Doyle.

Frances closed the door behind her and headed downstairs, where the other women were all staring at her.

"Dolly. I'm afraid your great-grandmother has passed away." The girl put her face in her hands and started to sob. Mallow firmly, but gently, led her to a chair in the corner.

"Lady Frances, shall I send the chauffeur for the doctor or police?" Miss Hardiman didn't seem particularly upset, and there was no tremor in her voice.

There was no reason for a delay, but she did want to question Dolly.

"Thank you. Yes, tell the chauffeur to fetch the village constable."

Miss Hardiman stepped outside and Frances turned to Dolly. "This is very upsetting dear, especially after what happened to

Mrs. Sweet, but your great-gran was very old, and it's no surprise she was called to God. Now, the constable may have some questions, because that's the rule, so let's just get them out of the way. You've probably been in and out today, but who else was here?"

It was a busy little hamlet, populated by retired servants and the families of the ground staff. No stranger could sneak in here easily. Everyone knew each other.

"Just family, my lady. Everyone was related to great-gran. They were in and out as usual, asking advice, gossiping. I didn't really take any notice, my lady."

Miss Hardiman came back and headed straight to the kitchen. Frances watched her put out some tea and then, without any self-consciousness, take down more plates. She found a bottle of cheap wine and put it on the table with a motley collection of glasses.

As she set the table with the additional places, Frances caught her eye.

"People come by after a death," said Miss Hardiman. "There will be many of them, no doubt. You said she was well-known here. That little girl Dolly is in no fit state and your maid Mallow is calming her." She gave a half smile. "We didn't have servants when I was a girl. I learned to take care of things myself."

"You may not have always had servants, but I believe you've always had common sense," said Frances, and began helping her. "Mrs. Tanner's death doesn't upset you?"

Miss Hardiman shrugged. "I am sad for her and her family, of course. But as you said, she was very old. You went to school in New York, in the Hudson Valley. You know what winters are like there. Well, think of a winter with ten times the snow and twenty degrees colder, and that's Buffalo." She began to unpack the basket. "In the early spring, we'd find the bodies of those who didn't make it."

Frances glanced over her shoulder, at Mallow doing an effective job of soothing the child. Mallow had grown up with younger siblings.

"I imagine you don't want to go back," said Frances.

Miss Hardiman gave her a shrewd look. "There's nothing I'd rather do less than return."

"So you'll stay here and marry Mr. Blake?"

Miss Hardiman didn't answer right away, just completed laying out the food. "You're a sharp one, Lady Frances," she finally said. "Do you disapprove?" She seemed concerned about that, despite some bravado.

"Why should I?"

"Because he's one of your English gentry. He had an ancestor who was a lord. I'm just a social-climbing American heiress."

She wants reassurance, thought Frances. "Those things don't matter the way they used to."

"They do to Mrs. Blake," said Miss Hardiman. "I think she'd like him to marry Gwen. I don't think she'd like me to be the mother of her grandchildren."

And Frances was saved from responding by the arrival of Inspector Bedlow and Constable Dill.

"Well, well, Lady Frances," said the inspector. "Every time someone dies, I find you." His tone was jovial, but there was a hint of anger behind it.

"I was paying a visit. But she died quite recently."

"How do you know? Are you a coroner too, my lady?"

"When I took her hand, she was still warm."

"Ah. You were quite right to call me, but I know she was very old, and with the shocking death of Sir Calleford, it probably wasn't much of a surprise. Constable, secure the scene as a formality until the coroner's men can come from Morchester."

"You aren't going to investigate further?" asked Frances. She suspected no one would seriously consider the woman was poisoned, as she was so old.

"Why should I? This was not a murder, and I don't want you to start anything by saying otherwise."

"You don't think this is too much of a coincidence?"

"The only coincidence I see is your ability to keep finding dead bodies."

"Two of which were people I was about to speak with."

"From what I hear, you're speaking with everyone. A coincidence is all it is, Lady Frances, and I'll thank you not to interfere further. An old lady has died. That's it. Now I think you ladies should head back to the manor house."

"People will be coming. And we're going to greet them, at least until other relations arrive."

He looked as if he might argue the point, but finally said, "As you wish."

By that point, the many relations of Betsy Tanner began arriving. Mallow turned over Dolly to one her aunts, then joined Miss Hardiman and Lady Frances in serving, until various grand-daughters and grandnieces could take over. They eventually left the makeshift wake quietly, and the chauffeur drove them home.

CHAPTER 19

Frances was pleased the next morning that they were all going to the Blake estate, a thirty-minute drive in the Rolls-Royce. Gwen had, predictably, cried when hearing about the death of Betsy Tanner, but Tommie had soothed her: the woman was extremely old and no doubt in pain from crippling arthritis. "It was her time," said Tommie, but she looked at Frances.

Blake Court was built of mellow local stone, nicely proportioned and substantial, although of a much more manageable size than the Eyrie. Mr. Blake had returned the previous day, and was on hand to greet them with his housekeeper, Mrs. Pear, who greeted them warmly.

"I scolded young Master Blake for not bringing you over earlier. Poor girl, stuck in that huge drafty place." She gave Gwen a hug, while Christopher just grinned. It was clear this housekeeper had known Mr. Blake—and Gwen—since they were children.

There was a full breakfast laid out in the dining room, which was more cheerful than formal—the furniture was good but scuffed in places, Frances noted, as if generations of careless, happy children had run through it.

"Mrs. Pear, I brought my maid, Mallow. We've descended on you with quite a few people, and she can help out, if you need."

"That's very thoughtful, my lady, but we can manage—although I daresay your Mallow will be a welcome face below stairs. Not many new faces around here nowadays."

Gwen seemed very happy, and Frances hadn't seen her eat so much since they had left London, although the food was better at the Eyrie.

"Now ladies, I thought I'd take you on a tour of my grounds and then we'd have lunch. I have to meet with a farm manager after lunch, but will see you at dinner."

"There will be no walk around the estate without a chaperone," said Mrs. Pear, and Mr. Blake laughed.

"Dear lady, it's 1907, and we're a group."

"None of your lip, young man," said Mrs. Pear, and Mr. Blake laughed again.

They fell into three couples. Mr. Blake led the way, in close conversation with Miss Hardiman. Arm in arm, Tommie and Gwen followed, as Gwen pointed out places she played as a child when she came on visits.

Frances hung back with Mrs. Pear, congratulating herself on her good fortune. Here was another servant who knew something of the family and seemed inclined to talk. In fact, Frances didn't even have to prompt her.

"If I may say so, my lady, I'm very glad to see Miss Gwen with good friends like you and Miss Calvin. Mr. Christopher has mentioned she has friends in London, and I'm glad of it. She had a rather lonely childhood. Mr. Christopher was her only real friend."

"It was a pity she lost her mother so young," said Frances.

"Oh yes, my lady. She so loved her little girl. Lady Kestrel's death was very sad."

"I never met her, of course. What was she like?"

"Bless you, my lady; Miss Gwen is just like her, sweet and gentle."

Frances then led the conversation to Lady Kestrel's younger years, when she and her friend Phoebe had made a foursome with Sir Calleford and his cousin, Captain Jim. It was much the same story as Betsy Tanner had told. But Mrs. Pear had some further insights: they were all friends, it was true, but it was clear to Mrs. Pear that the young Calleford had worshipped young Miss Bronwen, and she was delighted with his attentions, while Miss Phoebe was destined for Captain Jim.

"I've heard some family tales that the four of them were so close that although marriages were expected, no one was sure who would marry who."

"It was a long time ago, my lady. I'm sure I couldn't say." The housekeeper had said enough, but Frances suspected Mrs. Pear knew a lot more and decided to push. She was clearly a born gossip.

"Discretion is very important, Mrs. Pear. It's only that Gwen hardly knew her mother, and now has lost her father, and if I had a little more knowledge of family history, I could better understand Gwen and help her through these trying times."

"I see, my lady. But I'm not one to gossip."

"Of course not. You wouldn't have risen to a high position as housekeeper of such a fine place as Blake Court if you lacked discretion. It's only old family . . . history I'm after. Not vulgar gossip about what is happening today."

"Well, if you put it like that, my lady. More than one person was surprised at the way things fell out, I don't mind saying. Even as young men, their way in the world was marked. Calleford Kestrel would become a great man in London, we all thought, with an important position, dinners at the palace. And Captain Jim Blake would hunt, breed his horses and dogs, do his turn as a deputy lieutenant for the county, and give away the prizes at the local school. That would've suited Miss Bronwen just fine, and Miss Phoebe would've made a gracious London hostess. But that's not the way it happened." She sighed.

"Calleford Kestrel proposed to Miss Bronwen, not Miss Phoebe?" prompted Frances.

"It would seem so. But looking back on it, it may not be so strange. For all he was a great man, Sir Calleford could be a little . . . nervy . . . I may say. There are those who say that Miss Gwen was all her mother's daughter, but she was her father's, too, and Sir Calleford was not disposed for a lively London life. But if you could've known Miss Bronwen, my lady. The gentlest creature the good Lord ever created. Her quiet ways soothed him when he fretted. It was a great love."

Frances asked if Miss Phoebe, who became Mrs. Blake, had as strong a romance with Captain Jim.

"Ah, my lady, now that was a little different." She lowered her voice. "Captain Jim had to woo her rather hard, so we all thought. Oh, I think she liked him well enough, my lady, but he was a bit of a lively lad, and she wanted to make sure he'd settle down—and sure enough, he was a good master and became much admired for the way he ran the estate. It turned out to be a fair match. Captain Jim needed a strong wife." She laughed. "Someone to tell him no, he couldn't give his favorite dogs the run of the house, and yes, as the squire he had to do the reading Sunday morning at church, never mind he was out late on Saturday."

Frances smiled. "There is more than one Captain Jim in my family, with the same arguments. But it sounds then like Mrs. Blake ran a strict household when she was here?"

Now Frances had pushed too far. Old memories were fair game, but Mrs. Blake was still mistress of Blake Court, and there would be no criticism there. A few set words on what a fine lady she was, and that was it.

But Mrs. Pear wanted to gingerly sound out Frances. After all, the death of Sir Calleford affected her as well.

"I didn't want to bother the family during these trying times, my lady, but seeing as you're such a good friend of Miss Gwen's, I was wondering if you knew what would happen? If Mrs. Blake would come home now, and what would happen with the Eyrie?"

Frances lowered her voice as well, to a conspiratorial whisper. "I don't believe things will change much. I think it is Mrs. Blake's intention to stay on at the Eyrie indefinitely and help Gwen manage the estate."

Mrs. Pear nodded. "That's what I thought, my lady. There's nothing for her here. Mr. Blake, as you see, runs a somewhat informal house. He'll marry soon, I imagine, and we'll have children running around, God-willing." She seemed pleased at the prospect. "No real place here for Mrs. Blake then, however."

Mrs. Bellinger. Mrs. Sweet. Mrs. Blake. No matter what their class, single women had a hard time finding a place in society, reflected Frances—not for the first time.

Mrs. Pear broke into her thoughts. "Speaking of marriage, my lady. I know it's not my place, but might my next mistress be an American, my lady?" It was only half a question. It probably didn't occur to her that anyone could actually purchase the Eyrie from the Kestrel family and settle there. If Christopher Blake would marry, his wife would be mistress of Blake Court, and that's all. Frances was also amused that Christopher might think he was keeping his romance with Effie Hardiman a secret. Servants always knew first.

"I would not be at all surprised, Mrs. Pear. But think on this. What if, as a wedding present, Mr. Hardiman bought his daughter the Eyrie, and Mr. Blake and his wife lived there?"

"Mr. Hardiman could do that, my lady? My goodness." She thought about that, and Frances feared she might refuse to discuss it more, but she was clearly surprised. "I don't suppose Miss Gwen wants to be a great lady. But what would she do, my lady?"

"Continue to live in London. She has many friends, Mrs. Pear. She will be well-looked-after, and I'm sure Mr. Blake would have her up to visit often."

"And Mrs. Blake would come back here? It's not my place to comment, my lady, but I think she's rather used to the Eyrie.

I mean, we still think of her as mistress of Blake Court, but I doubt if she's spent a night here in ten years."

"She must've thought that someday Gwen would marry," said Frances, looking closely at Mrs. Pear. "And that her husband would not expect his wife's distant aunt to be part of their household. Certainly not running it."

The housekeeper sighed. "But if . . ." and then she stopped.

"You were about to say, 'but if she married Christopher.'"

But Frances had gone too far. "I'm sure I couldn't say, my lady," said Mrs. Pear, ending the conversation.

———————

Mallow, meanwhile, was sharing a nice cup of tea with the cook, Mrs. Bailey. Unlike the cook at the Eyrie and most cooks at great houses, Mrs. Bailey was fairly young, only in her thirties. As a bachelor in the country, perhaps Mr. Blake didn't entertain so lavishly that he required a more senior cook.

Mrs. Bailey was pleased to have someone new to talk to, and like the servants at the Eyrie, she was entertained by Mallow's stories of the great parties at the Seaforth house in London. Even more so, because at least at the Eyrie there had been a lot of entertaining, but not here.

"Oh, local gentry, with their unmarried daughters hoping to catch Mr. Blake's eye—the vicar and his wife, the doctor and his wife, but that's it. Mind you, Miss Mallow, I don't do any of your fancy French cooking, like what you're used to in London, but I do very nice roasts and have a good hand with game, if I say so myself."

"I'm a London girl and prefer solid English cooking myself," said Mallow. "Are these your scones? I haven't had better, even when I was housemaid for the late Marchioness of Seaforth."

Mrs. Bailey seemed tickled that a maid in a titled family liked her scones.

Lady Frances had told Mallow to find out if any of the servants knew about Mr. Blake's courtship of Miss Hardiman. But care was needed. Servants liked to gossip, but push too hard, especially with a senior servant like a cook, and they'd suspect something.

"Rather nice of Mr. Blake to show that American lady around the grounds. She's stuck here in the country not knowing anyone."

Mrs. Bailey smirked. "I could tell you, Miss Mallow, it's more than just kindness."

Mallow's eyes grew wide. "Really? He's courting an American lady? Well, I never."

Mrs. Bailey enjoyed knowing something that would entrance this London lady's maid, who was probably privy to scandals among the great lords and ladies in the city.

"Oh yes. The way we heard it, he was friends with her father, Mr. Hardiman, something about the American interested in horses and coming up to see the Eyrie stables. But it's the daughter Mr. Blake's interested in."

"Well fancy that," said Mallow. "So perhaps you'll get a new mistress here? What with Mrs. Blake always up at the Eyrie, it's been awhile since you've had a proper mistress here."

"Oh, I don't know about that," said Mrs. Bailey. She looked a little crafty. *Oh*, thought Mallow, *she knows something and wants to tell me, but can't decide.* Suddenly, Mrs. Bailey changed the subject.

"But tell me. Your Lady Frances must be ready to marry. She's pretty, and being in an important titled family must come with a very nice dowry. I daresay you'll be living in a great house before too long."

So Mrs. Bailey was going to give gossip, but she wanted some in return. Very well. Mallow would give her what she wanted— even if she had to make it up.

"There have been gentlemen callers, I can tell you. Now you must keep to yourself, Mrs. Bailey, but three times now Lady Frances has dined at the home of her brother and sister-in-law when they had Lord Lucas Brakeland, eldest son of an earl he is, and will inherit Brakeland Park. He is an equerry to the king. That means His Majesty himself will probably come to the wedding."

And that just amazed Mrs. Bailey. In recent years, Blake Court hadn't seen anyone more prominent than Canon Witherspoon, from Morchester Cathedral—an occasional visitor who tended to fall asleep over dessert. The cook couldn't top that. But she could come close.

"Well, perhaps we'll have a wedding here too, Miss Mallow, but Mrs. Blake won't be attending. I'll tell you, they just had a row the likes of which you've never heard. I was just coming up to discuss the menu, when I heard. She came back here to have a talk with Mr. Christopher. Oh, she really lost her temper she did."

"Mrs. Blake? She seems like such a great lady," said a wide-eyed Mallow. Great ladies didn't lose their temper.

"Oh, you should have heard it, Miss Mallow. She accused the master of romancing Miss Hardiman, and just as angry, he denied having made an offer. She told him an American lady of no background couldn't preside at the table of the gentry."

Mallow was surprised at that. She knew of several wealthy American women who had married into the aristocracy in London; Mr. Blake didn't even have a title.

"Miss Hardiman seemed very respectable to me," said Mallow.

"Oh, but it's more than that," said Mrs. Bailey. *Cooks were the worst gossips*, Mallow knew. Stuck in the kitchens all day, they weren't privy to the goings-on that even junior maids saw upstairs. So when they got something, they were thrilled.

Still, she was very free with her comments. *That's what happens*, thought Mallow, *when a house doesn't have a mistress to properly watch over the servants.*

"Mrs. Blake wants him to marry his cousin, Miss Gwen, then they'd live at the Eyrie. She said that the late Sir Calleford had wanted to share a grandchild with her, that they were Marchands too—that's what the family was in olden times—and you couldn't always do what you wanted when you were a noble.

You had responsibilities. And then Mr. Blake said the oddest thing." Mrs. Bailey frowned. "He said he would never force Gwen to have a child. He's usually a temperate man but then things really heated up, I can tell you. Mr. Blake said he owed his uncle a lot, but he'd be damned—yes, he used that word, Miss Mallow—he'd be damned if his gratitude to his uncle meant being tied to Gwen for the rest of his life. And then his mother said, and I remember these words: 'I gave him everything. And you will too.'"

"Everything?" asked Mallow.

"I guess, giving up her home and keeping house for Sir Calleford." She shrugged and they sipped their tea, lost in thought. Miss Gwen was a pretty girl and possessed a huge estate. Why not get married? No accounting for the behavior of the gentry.

"Ah well, he's the master and can make his own decisions," concluded Mrs. Bailey. "It's all right for some, but for me, I have to see about luncheon."

⬦

The walk put color in everyone's cheeks, and they enjoyed it, despite the cold. A fire was waiting for them in drawing room and hot tea was served. Gwen was chatting away, and her black dress was the only sign that she was in mourning. Tommie had noticed too and seemed so pleased with Gwen's mood.

Miss Hardiman, meanwhile, was hanging on every word Christopher Blake was saying. Frances recalled what her own mother had said at the start of her first season: "Men like to talk about themselves and what they find particularly interesting. You would do well to appear fascinated." At this point, Mr. Blake was talking about dairy cattle, and Miss Hardiman was indeed looking fascinated.

But Miss Hardiman had grown up on a farm. Her interest in cows may have been genuine. Frances upbraided herself for not realizing that her interests were not everyone's. Indeed, a really good Stilton cheese was the extent of her dairy interests.

After lunch, Mr. Blake apologized for having to leave the ladies to attend to business and promised to be back for dinner. The ladies, meanwhile, played backgammon and cards and took turns reading to each other.

"My father was very much looking forward to his hunting with the general," said Miss Hardiman. "In fact, he went into the village yesterday, and bought some scotch whiskey for the general and some chocolates for us this evening. I remember from an earlier chat—you liked the crèmes, Miss Kestrel; and you liked nuts, Miss Calvin; and white chocolates were your favorite, Lady Frances."

Frances suppressed a shudder. She loved chocolate, and it was very sweet of Miss Hardiman to remember everyone's favorites. But the memory of the dead Mrs. Sweet, with her chocolates spilled over her, was still fresh. It was funny how she indulged herself—well, everyone had their fancies. And yet she was careful in other ways, painstakingly cultivating dried herbs. But herbs weren't going to prevent her from becoming quite stout if she kept eating chocolate like that—Dolly mentioned the dressmaker having to let out her clothes. Still, something about those herbs tickled Frances's memory, but why? Frances had never had much interest in gardening—yet another exasperation for her mother. Who had ever heard of a well-born Englishwoman not making at least a show of pottering about a garden?

It would come later, no doubt.

Christopher returned just as dinner was served. Miss Hardiman's eyes glittered when she saw him, and he greeted her warmly. He was gallant to all the ladies, in fact, and Frances was pleased to see him particularly solicitous for Gwen.

As everyone enjoyed the plain roast and potatoes with good country mustard and cheese made on the Blake estate, Christopher held court among his guests. He was a natural-born storyteller, and had amusing anecdotes about the old county families, from pompous squires to the workmen who had managed the estate for generations. This wasn't tedious provincial gossip, but genuinely funny stories. Gwen seemed to delight in them, and among her giggles, Frances reflected on the nature of jealousy. Someone might be unhappy to see someone else amuse their beloved, but not Tommie, who was just pleased that Gwen was cheerful.

When it was time to go, Christopher saw them into the motorcar, and said he hoped to see all of them again soon, looking meaningfully at Miss Hardiman. Once they were driving, she took out the chocolates to share, and everyone reflected on what a nice visit it was. But Frances had to force her merriment. She still couldn't get chocolates and Mrs. Sweet out of her mind. And the horrible, illiterate note left for Tommie, the second threat made to her.

The ladies all said they were tired and would head to bed, but Frances said she wanted a word with Tommie and went with her to her room—she motioned for Mallow to join her.

Once the door was closed behind them, Frances turned sharply to her friend. "Tommie. I keep thinking of that awful note left for you. Someone wasn't just threatening you, but accusing you of being a killer. And we've been gone all day. If someone wanted to make you look like a murderer, today would be the day to do it. You're in danger, but I don't know how."

"What? From whom? Whoever has been threatening me?" Her eyes grew big, and she licked her dry lips in fear.

"From those who want to separate you from Gwen. Now, we see one stabbing murder. One shooting murder. And one poison murder—Mrs. Tanner, I'm sure."

"Am I next?" whispered Tommie.

"Not directly. I think someone wants to ruin you. I keep going back to that line in the note—someone says they know you're a killer. And look, no one wanted to call in Scotland Yard to help that incompetent inspector. He's made no arrests, but he's going to have to. Arresting you, Tommie, would solve two problems—ending your friendship with Gwen and solving Sir Calleford's murder. No one cares about an ancient servant or a poor widow, whose death can be laid to a chance robber. But Sir Calleford was wealthy and important. Someone has to be arrested, and you've been accused twice already—one in the cathedral and once here. Someone has to be convicted." She smiled. "But not you, Tommie. If someone is setting you up, we're going to stay one step ahead of them. Come, the three of us are going to search this room, right now. It shouldn't take long."

It wasn't a big room and Tommie didn't have a lot of baggage. Tommie and Frances went through her things and Mallow began searching drawers and little corners, as only a good servant knew how.

It was Frances who found what was out of place, a dress stained on the sleeves.

"Mallow, what does this look like to you?"

Mallow looked it over under the light. "That's blood, my lady."

"But that's my traveling dress, what I wore here and haven't worn again since. I didn't get any blood on it."

"It's the perfect way to make it look like you killed him. Someone poured blood on it. This is farm country—there is always blood around for anyone who wants it. The inspector will find this dress thanks to a tip and figure you killed Sir Calleford because he wanted you away from his daughter."

"Oh, dear God." She put her face in her hands.

"Don't worry. Mallow, can you get another stain out today?"

Mallow was affronted her ladyship should even ask. "Of course, my lady. I'll have it out in a matter of minutes. I'll take it back to my room, wait until later when the laundry room will be empty, and have it back up to your room in the morning, miss."

Tommie collapsed on her bed. "Why?" she asked.

"Sir Calleford was either killed because someone wanted the Eyrie, because of Gwen, or because of something having to do with the diplomatic meetings here. Someone calculated this very neatly, killing him when there were so many motives. But only one of them could have led to all three murders."

"But you know, don't you, my lady?" asked Mallow.

"Almost, Mallow. Come Tommie, we'll save the day yet." And Tommie forced a smile.

Mallow liked her ladyship like this best of all—cheerful and brisk, with unshakable confidence in her own abilities.

"Tommie, get a good night's sleep. We're going to be busy. We'll talk more about this tomorrow." She turned, but then stopped. "Tommie, your room and Gwen's are at the end of this hallway. But I saw a door beyond—do you know where that goes?"

"Oh, yes. I was curious myself. Gwen said it goes to the original house, from the mid fourteen hundreds, which the Elizabethan portion eventually encompassed. It hasn't been lived in for more than a century, and it's now just used for storage. But there can't be anyone there—the door is locked. Gwen said Mrs. Blake always wanted to make sure the servants didn't get up to anything."

Frances nodded, and went back to her room with Mallow, who would help her get ready for bed before heading to the laundry room.

Once Frances was in her night clothes, Mallow took a look at the dress and frowned.

"Are you in doubt about the stain, Mallow?"

"Oh, no, my lady. No trouble with that. But I see there was a tear in the seam here, and the repair stiches are not as even as they could have been."

Frances smiled. Very little needlework met Mallow's high standards.

"You learned from an order of Anglican nuns, didn't you, Mallow?"

"Yes, my lady, as a young girl. They would teach any girl who had a mind to so she could live a virtuous life by her own hand. The sisters made money for their order by taking in sewing. Mostly for gentlewomen who were with child, my lady, and needed their clothes let out."

That was it. Frances hit her forehead with her hand.

"Mallow, Mrs. Sweet wasn't letting her dresses out because she was getting stout. Mrs. Sweet was with child. The herbs she had, ginger and the rest. I remember now—they provide comfort to pregnant women. She was having Sir Calleford's child. Her passion for candy—common with women in her condition. It all makes sense."

"So you know who killed her, my lady?" whispered Mallow.

Frances didn't answer for a moment. "I thought this was just about marriage and control. But this is darker, and deeper, than I realized. I need to think . . . actually, what I need is a good night's sleep."

"Yes, my lady. But before I go, my lady, you might want to hear what the Blake cook told me." She related the gossip about Mrs. Blake arguing with her son.

"Well done, Mallow! That shows what I'm beginning to suspect. There is a level of desperation there. This helps us move forward. But you have something else?"

"There's just one more thing . . ." Mallow seemed hesitant. "It seems I had to tell a little tale to the cook to get some gossip in return. I had to say you were about to get engaged . . ."

"Indeed. And to whom?"

And in a small voice, she said, "Lord Lucas Brakeland."

"You told the cook I was about to marry the stupidest, most offensive peer in England? And she believed you?"

There was a moment of silence, then Frances burst out laughing, with Mallow immediately following. "Oh dear Mallow, you and I are wasted. With our talents, we should both be in the Foreign Office with my brother. Good for us. We're going to need all our wits about us these next few days."

CHAPTER 20

Frances got up early and found herself first down at break-fast, although Mr. and Miss Hardiman joined her soon after. *Had Gwen and Tommie slept in? Had Gwen had another bad night? Mr. Mehmet wasn't there either. Had he wandered off somewhere—to his wife?* But no, he came down next, and bowed to everyone before getting himself a plate.

The Americans filled their plates, and Mr. Hardiman joined Mr. Mehmet, his hunting companion of the previous day. It seemed they were reliving their shooting. Meanwhile, Miss Hardiman joined Frances, who didn't think she had ever seen anyone look as pleased with herself as Effie Hardiman did at that moment. She looked like she was about to explode with mirth.

"You seem to have had some good news, Miss Hardiman?" The girl nodded, not even trusting herself to speak. "Let me guess. Mr. Blake asked to speak to your father, didn't he, when we were at Blake Court?"

"Oh, Lady Frances. I'm not supposed to say anything to any-one yet. But it seems—"

Frances just motioned for Miss Hardiman to be quiet. "Things are a little different here, my dear. I take it this house will be your dowry." The house that Christopher had craved since childhood.

"I haven't asked him, but I'm sure Father would make an offer to Miss Kestrel's lawyer. Christopher says she doesn't want to live here."

"And his mother?"

"Oh. I guess she'll go back to her house." Blake Court. But she no doubt thought of the Eyrie as "her" house now. So Christopher couldn't wait. Maybe he felt Miss Hardiman would take her dowry back to London and find herself the son of an earl if an offer didn't come through soon. She'd do anything to avoid another winter in Buffalo.

"Yes. I'm sure he'll work it out. But this is a very big change. These are important families, and you aren't just getting married. You're rising to a highly visible position. And it must be done very carefully and delicately if you want to get off on the right foot. Now, do you know if Mr. Blake has told his mother?"

Miss Hardiman looked a little shifty at that. "Christopher said his mother was a little . . . well, being as Christopher is her only son and I'm an American. As we discussed earlier, I may not be exactly what she wants. He said he'd ask my father in a week, as the police investigation should be done by then. And then we'd tell his mother."

"That sounds very wise. Just be patient. I know all will be well, but don't rush things, don't let the word out too soon. It could make your life difficult for a long time."

Frances felt bad then, spoiling Miss Hardiman's good news. "I'm sorry. I don't mean to dampen your enthusiasm. Your news is great indeed, and I'm sure you'll be very happy here. I just want to guide you in English ways." She spread some marmalade on toast. "You and I will be friends. So I should think, by this point, we can be a little less formal with each other? My friends call me 'Franny.'"

Miss Hardiman turned pink. "Oh, yes, I entirely agree. I'm Euphemia, but only my mother called me that. My friends call me 'Effie,' as you've no doubt heard from my father." Across the room, Mr. Hardiman looked up from his talk with Mr. Mehmet to smile benevolently at the two young ladies.

"We'll talk later, I promise. Remember, Effie. Discretion."

She stepped over to Mr. Mehmet and Mr. Hardiman.

"Good morning, gentlemen. Mr. Mehmet, I recalled last night some friends we have in common. Do you remember the Dowager Countess of Fairhaven?"

Mr. Hardiman took the hint. Or perhaps he just didn't want to get involved in a discussion of the English aristocracy. He excused himself to sit with his daughter.

Frances lowered her voice. "I want you to know, Mr. Mehmet, I've realized it's clear the buffoons in the local police seem completely out of their depth. My family has connections with Scotland Yard. I think I can bring London pressure on the local chief constable to turn this over to some professionals."

His face fell. "Are you sure that's wise, Lady Frances?"

"Wouldn't you welcome that? So much suspicion in this house. But then again, you were the one who warned me about secrets. We all have them, and they're not all criminal. Of course, I know one of your secrets. But you have more, don't you? You were friendly enough with Special Branch. And my brother. But you still don't want regular London detectives here, do you? And why? Your marriage may be private, but it's hardly illegal."

She took what she knew was a childish satisfaction in seeing Mr. Mehmet concerned. But he wasn't upset for more than a few seconds, and he gave her his debonair smile again. "I said you were the sword of Allah. And I must bow to the will of the Prophet."

"If you bowed to the will of your Prophet, you wouldn't be eating bacon, which is forbidden to your people."

And he laughed, but to Frances's ear, it sounded forced. "I keep forgetting how much you notice. I will need to be more careful."

Frances smiled and excused herself. She looked around and began wondering where Gwen and Tommie were—or Mrs. Blake, who never failed to oversee breakfast.

And then Mallow came into the dining room. It was startling—a lady's maid did not bother her mistress at a meal, and Mallow was practically running. Frances met her for a private word near the door.

"I beg your pardon, my lady, but I think you should come at once."

Frances excused herself from the surprised Hardimans and stepped into the hallway with Mallow. The maid's eyes were wide. It took a lot to disturb Mallow's equilibrium.

"A footman mentioned that the police arrived early this morning, even before you rose, my lady, and they were going at it hammer and tongs in the solar. I thought you'd want to know immediately. The door is closed but you can hear them."

"You were right to get me, Mallow. Come with me—I was expecting this after breakfast, but Inspector Bedlow has no sense of propriety. You took care of the dress, didn't you?"

"Of course, my lady. The dress looks completely new."

"Excellent. Now, let's come to the aid of our friends."

Mallow knew that look. Her ladyship wore it when she was planning to deliver a speech in the park or corner a government minister in his office. She scrambled to keep up as Frances shot up the stairs and headed to the solar door. She walked right in and took stock of the situation.

Tommie and Gwen were sitting on a couch looking stricken, as Inspector Bedlow stood over them talking loudly. Mrs. Blake sat in another chair, watching, and in a corner, Constable Dill stood at attention, looking unhappy.

But that was just for a second: Everyone turned to Frances as she entered. Gwen and Tommie looked deeply relieved. Bedlow looked up, angry at the interruption, and Constable Dill seemed almost scared. As for Mrs. Blake—she looked amused.

"May I ask what is going on?" asked Frances.

"Oh Franny, the inspector is coming to arrest Tommie!" Gwen wailed.

"Is this true, inspector? May I see the warrant?"

Inspector Bedlow hesitated. *He's losing control of the situation and he's trying to save face*, Frances concluded.

"I'm not here to arrest Miss Calvin. But she is needed to help the police with their inquiries, and that would be better done at headquarters."

"May we know what the conversation would be about?"

"The deaths of Sir Calleford Kestrel, Mrs. Genevieve Sweet, and Mrs. Betsy Tanner."

"That's beyond belief, Inspector. Surely you have some sort of evidence."

"In a moment, Lady Frances," he said, looking smug. *What a fool, to go out on a limb before the evidence was even in hand.* A moment later, another constable entered the room, carrying a dress—Tommie's traveling dress from the night they arrived. So someone had tipped him off after all. Frances had to control herself when she saw the inspector vainly look for the blood-stains. He had quiet words with the constable—this clearly was the traveling dress in question.

"Well?" asked Frances.

The inspector just stared at her. Then he realized what had happened, and his face filled with rage.

"You did this. You destroyed police evidence. That is a major felony."

"Evidence? What evidence?" She was wide-eyed innocence.

"You washed the blood from the sleeve, the blood Miss Calvin got on her when she killed Sir Calleford."

Tommie and Gwen were clutching each other now, too stunned to speak further.

"Don't be silly. Why would Miss Calvin kill the father of her dearest friend?"

"So her friend would inherit . . . and because . . ." He looked the around the room. *You wouldn't dare*, thought Frances. *You wouldn't dare say what you're thinking.* "Anyway, until you interfered, Lady Frances, I just wanted to have a simple talk with Miss Calvin at the station. But now that you had your maid clean the dress—" He turned on Mallow, but she wasn't scared. There were worse things in the neighborhood where she had grown up than a stupid rural inspector.

"Accuse my maid without proof and you will regret it, I promise you," said Frances. "Mallow, did you help Miss Calvin take off her traveling dress at the end of that evening—hours after Sir Calleford had been killed?"

"Yes, my lady," she said loud and clear.

"Was there any blood on her dress? Indeed, you helped Miss Calvin unpack. Was there any blood on any of her clothes?"

"No, my lady. I unpacked everything. I would've noticed."

Frances gave a triumphant look at the inspector.

"Your maid would swear the sun rose in the west if you asked her. But never mind. The dress isn't all I have." *I bet it is,* thought Frances. *Except for rumors about Gwen and Tommie. But unfortunately, that might be enough.* "So understand me. Miss Calvin comes back with me now, civilly, or I'll be back with an arrest warrant and take her away in chains."

"You will not!" said Gwen, and everyone stopped at that. No one had ever seen Gwen angry before, but there was that sweet face, set in rage. *My goodness,* thought Frances, *love gives us all courage.* Tommie smiled warmly at Gwen, and gripped her hand.

Mrs. Blake spoke first, softly but firmly. "Gwen. Your loyalty to your friend does you credit. But you are the lady of the manor now, and you cannot thwart the inspector on a whim. Miss Calvin is sensible, and I know she will go with the inspector to answer his questions."

So this was how it was going to end. Frances had known Inspector Bedlow was desperate, but hadn't counted on him coming down so hard, so fast. *Well, I'll give them a real reason to call me Mad Lady Frances.*

"Actually, the truly sensible thing would be to wait for an arrest warrant. And inspector, if you do somehow manage to get one, I will have my solicitor, Henry Wheaton, up here on the next train with a barrister, and you will regret this."

Her eyes darted around: Pride from Gwen and Tommie. Surprise from Mrs. Blake. And rage from the inspector.

"You are encouraging Miss Calvin to withhold cooperation," he said. "That's a felony."

"I doubt it. Go talk to your superiors," said Frances. "Do whatever you want, inspector. But you have no right to be here anymore. Leave this house. Or I'll have the footmen throw you out."

"I am warning you—"

"No need to shout," said Frances mildly. "Your anger is just a cover for your stupidity, stubbornness, and outright incompetence."

So, thought Frances, *this is what they meant when they said "so quiet you could hear a pin drop."*

The inspector turned to his constable. "Come, Dill. We're leaving. But we'll be back, this time with an arrest warrant, and you will be the one to regret this, Lady Frances, when I put your friend in jail." He started to leave quickly, with Constable Dill at his heels.

There was a good chance he could convince his superiors to issue a warrant, and there was no way Frances was going let the inspector go after the already frightened Tommie. *How hard will I have to push him to arrest me instead?*

"So, inspector. You're not going to arrest me? Do you mean on top of all your faults, you're also a coward?"

Frances felt almost dizzy with what she had just said. She couldn't even focus on the other people in the room, and she felt her heart about to explode out of her chest. She had never gone this far.

The inspector said in an even voice, "If you thought your title and connections and wealth would protect you, Lady Frances, you thought wrong. You are under arrest for interfering with police duties. Constable Dill, escort Lady Frances outside. Ladies, good day."

With a look of deep sorrow and reluctance, Constable Dill approached her. "I am terribly sorry, my lady, but—"

"No need for apologies, constable. I won't give you any trouble. Mallow, call Mr. Wheaton and explain what has happened. Gwen, Tommie, stay here until I come back and please allow Mallow to attend you."

Tommie met her eyes—she knew what Frances meant. Mallow would be their protector in Frances's absence.

And with chin up, and Constable Dill and Inspector Bedlow behind her, Frances marched off to the police station.

There was no talking in the police coach on the way to Morchester. Constable Dill sat next to her and Inspector Bedlow opposite her. He was looking grim. *I hope he's regretting what he did*, thought Frances. She was curious about what would happen to her next. She had to drag him away from Tommie, and that was essential. But the repercussions would be substantial.

Oh God—what would Charles say? Could she and Mallow escape to France for a few weeks until he calmed down?

The desk sergeant in Morchester appeared to be on the far side of sixty, one of those men who thought he had seen it all—until today.

"Put her in a cell, sir? You must be joking."

"Do I look like I'm joking? Find a place for her."

It seemed reasonable to Frances that there would be a place for women. In London, women could be hauled off for disturbing the peace. *Also, men were men all over*, reasoned Frances, *so why shouldn't Morchester, like London, have its ladies of the evening?* My goodness—she'd be meeting them . . .

But a lively night at a local tavern plus the capture of a couple of poachers meant no cells were empty, and there was some discussion of whether Frances could be properly locked in an unused office.

"Oh for heaven's sake. Do you think I'm going to make a break for it? Or have members of my gang spring me?" She was pleased to see the sergeant hide a smile behind his hand. So she was shown into an office with nothing but a desk and pair of chairs. Realizing it could be some hours before Hal could get there, she asked for something to read. Constable Dill looked like he would say something, then left and came back with a couple of issues of the *Morchester Tribune*.

Making sure the two of them were alone, he said, "My lady, if there is anything you want me to tell your maid, that is, Miss Mallow . . . I mean, it's not strictly regulation, but I'm going back to the village anyway . . ."

"Thank you. That is very thoughtful, constable. However, that won't be necessary." She could swear he looked disappointed. "Tell me, constable, just between us—have you become attached to Mallow?"

Constable Dill reddened. "Well, my lady, that is to say, we have managed to speak, that is—"

"I'll take that as a 'yes.' Mallow is difficult to impress, and she seems to trust you. And you appear to have some common sense. Indeed, you look like a bright young man who wants to make his way in the world. I will give you some information. Someone connected with the Kestrel estate killed Sir Calleford, and Mrs. Sweet, and Mrs. Tanner. Your Inspector Bedlow is absolutely wrong about outside gangs, but he knows that—and I think you do too. That's why he turned his attention to Tommie Calvin, who is about as likely to commit murder as the Archbishop of Canterbury." She paused. "You and I will talk later." *This man could be a useful ally.*

"Thank you, my lady. Whatever I can do to help." And then he left her before they could be overheard. Frances, quite pleased with herself now, proceeded to make her way through the back issues of the *Morchester Tribune*.

The newspaper kept her occupied for a while, and later the sergeant came back with lukewarm tea and sandwiches for lunch. Then she sat back and closed her eyes, weaving the threads of what she knew into one pattern after another. She felt so close.

She was startled when the door opened again to admit Hal. He looked down at Frances, then started to laugh.

"Oh, I am so sorry, dear Franny. I promised myself all the way down here I wouldn't laugh, but seeing you here . . ." He sat down.

"I suppose it has its ridiculous aspects," said Frances a little stiffly. "Do you laugh at all your imprisoned clients?"

"How wide do you think my criminal practice is? I'm occasionally sent to make arrangements for young bloods who come up to London from Cambridge or Oxford and have a too-lively night in the big city. But you're my first lady."

"And probably the first of my family," she said with a sigh.

"You would think so," said Hal. "But in the seventeenth century, Sir Reginald Ffolkes was personally arrested by Oliver Cromwell during the Civil War. Your brother pointed that out to me."

"My brother? Surely you didn't tell Charles?" She had thought she'd have a little more time. But telephones and trains made sure gossip spread far more quickly than it used to.

"Oh no. He found out on his own. All your aunts are up in arms and it was all I could do to talk your brother out of coming down himself. My God, Franny, you really did it this time. Now, the local justice is waiting to see us, so a quick summary, if you please."

She described the situation succinctly, as Hal took notes.

"So let me understand this. You deliberately provoked a member of His Majesty's constabulary to keep him from arresting your friend Miss Calvin?"

"Yes. That's exactly it. I didn't really lose my temper—although I was close to it. I had to do something to derail his attempt to arrest Tommie."

"You know he'll come back."

"But not for a while. He's made too much of a scene arresting me. Whatever I did, the chief constable and local justice will be very unhappy with a daughter of the House of Seaforth in the dock. I did it to save Tommie. Things would come out . . . I couldn't bear that for them. Gwen would be destroyed. But they won't dare create more of a fuss bothering anyone at the Eyrie until they have a lot more evidence, so I bought myself some time. I know Bedlow will be back and he'll use whatever information he's gathered about Gwen and Tommie, twist it, and use that to humiliate Tommie and drive her away, even try to arrest her again. But I'm almost there—I only need a day or two. Just get me off."

She looked into his eyes, then leaned over and softly kissed him on the cheek.

"Well if you put it like that." He blushed. "Franny, I reviewed the details of the arrest. It was vague enough to topple over on its own weight. But as for your brother—you're on your own."

Hal told the sergeant they were ready, and they were ushered into the office of the justice. Like so many justices in rural areas, he was a local squire with a manor to run and other things on his mind. The last thing he wanted was a problem with a highborn lady from London and her well-connected solicitor.

The justice invited them to sit. "I understand you are her solicitor, Mr. Wheaton. Have you briefed a barrister to come up should there be a trial?" Only barristers, not solicitors, could represent a defendant in a trial.

"Yes, your honor. Sir Edwin Culpepper has told me he's prepared to travel down here."

The justice looked startled. Even in these rural parts, they had heard about him. One of the finest barristers in England, he was frequently mentioned in the press. The great Sir Edwin would no doubt make the local crown prosecutor look like a fool.

"However, I see no need for that," continued Hal smoothly. "The charges would not stand up to strict examination. And Lady Frances was a bit overwrought. I was hoping she could quietly apologize, here in chambers. And then she'll resume caring for her close friend, Miss Kestrel, who is still distraught about her father's murder."

Frances bit her lip. She hated apologizing, but it was for the greater good.

"That would seem to be a satisfactory solution. What say you, my lady?"

"I am sorry if I inadvertently thwarted the police in the exercise of their duties," she said.

"You also deeply insulted the inspector, Lady Frances. You publicly embarrassed him."

Frances took a breath. "I am also sorry for losing my temper and calling the inspector an imbecile and coward." She paused. "It was rude of me to publicize those facts."

She felt Hal tense up next to her, and the justice glared at her.

"I suppose I'll have to accept that, my lady," he said dryly. "Case dismissed."

They were escorted out to the street, and Hal just looked at her.

"Franny—"

"Yes?" She looked at him with wide-open eyes.

"Never mind. Anyway, I called the house and asked the butler to send the car for us."

"Excellent. When does your train leave?"

"In about thirty minutes."

"Then I will keep you company until it leaves."

When the car arrived, Frances told the chauffer to take them to the train station. He clearly strove to remain as passive as possible, and Frances smiled to herself. *He's doing his best to pretend he doesn't know that I was just arrested.*

Hal was the only one heading to London, so they had the waiting room to themselves.

"What next, my lady? As I said, they will be back for Miss Calvin, even if they have to use her friendship with Miss Kestrel against her. I told you that someone had to be convicted for this. I'll come back with a barrister if it comes to that, but it's going to be unpleasant."

She turned her gray eyes on him. "I know, Hal. But what I've been learning is that someone is desperate. And desperate people overreach and make mistakes. I have some ideas about what to do next. But don't worry, Mallow will be there to protect me." Hal laughed. "Also, I'll be under the care of Special Branch. I need to get Inspector Eastley back down here. He knows who Mr. Mehmet is. And that may be the key."

"You think he may have killed his host? The Muslim believes hospitality is sacred."

"I'm not sure that Mr. Mehmet is a very good Muslim. He secretly married a Christian woman who lives on the estate. He drinks alcohol and eats pork. The sultan is not just the sultan, you see. He is also the caliph, the supreme religious leader in Islam. One wonders if Mr. Mehmet has any respect for him, if he is so irreligious. And there's more: I do know Sir Calleford was murdered. I know a gossipy old servant was killed. And a widow who lives next door to Mr. Mehmet's secret wife, who may've heard something. Mrs. Blake wants Gwen as a daughter-in-law so she can keep running the Eyrie, and that means getting rid of Tommie. But why kill Sir Calleford? She had what she wanted. Christopher Blake would kill for the Eyrie. Mr. or Miss Hardiman might, but his gold could buy his daughter another husband with a grand estate. And did you know Sir Calleford had a pregnant mistress?"

"He isn't the first. I'm just glad that I'm not representing any of the suspects."

"Or prosecuting. There's so little evidence. I wish I had half a dozen constables to check alibis."

Hal laughed. "I can see you, Inspector Ffolkes of the CID," he said, referring to the Criminal Investigation Division. "I'm not making fun of you, believe me. I'd pity any miscreant you were chasing."

"First the vote. Then the police service," said Frances. "I'll live to see women detectives at the Yard. But getting back to Mr. Mehmet—he's friendly with my brother and Special Branch."

"Surely that speaks well of him?" asked Hal.

"Not necessarily. I learned something growing up in a diplomatic family. You are cheerful and charming to those you distrust the most. And England and the Ottoman Empire are not on good terms right now. Does Mr. Mehmet serve his sultan—his caliph? He was vague about that. But this is the interesting point: he doesn't want me to bring in Scotland Yard. He was upset when I said I could use my influence to bring London detectives to the Eyrie, professionals who would go over everyone's movements. But not all secrets are criminal."

"That's it!" cried Hal theatrically. "Mr. Mehmet didn't commit a crime, but he saw something which he can't reveal without implicating something he was doing."

"Bravo," said Frances. "That's what I've been thinking. He encouraged me to solve the crime, hoping no doubt I could do so as an 'insider,' someone who already knows the players. Someone who wouldn't—who couldn't—check alibis and locations. But I need leverage to get information from him. That's why I want to visit Inspector Eastley. Also, there is another slender clue." She related to Hal her near kidnapping and the overheard English phrase, "Our friend in London." "Maybe Inspector Eastley knows who this 'friend' is. If I knew who this friend was, I think I could convince Mr. Mehmet to tell me what he knows."

Hal just grinned. "My God, Franny, how your mind works." He gave her a sharp, lawyerly look. "You know who killed Sir Calleford, don't you? And you can't prove it yet, can you?" Frances just raised an eyebrow.

Hal nodded. He put his hand on hers. "Be careful."

"I told you, Hal. I always am. But to change the subject, I see you are wearing one of your modern, new suits. Why not your formal black one? Magistrates are very old-fashioned in the country, you know." She had a teasing tone.

"I no longer own a suit like that. I gave it to a junior clerk with the same build as I have. He was very pleased to have it. I have fewer clients who expect me to dress like that; more captains of industry, modern men. Times change, and I change with them."

"When I first met you, I wouldn't have expected it."

Hal leaned over. "And when I first met you, I never would've thought I'd be spending a country house weekend painting you half naked, or extracting you from a jail."

"Touché," she said.

She felt an unexpected pang as she heard the train roll into the station. *Did I miss him more than I thought?*

"I'm afraid I have to board the train, my love. Good luck." Those liquid green eyes of his held hers for a moment, then he stood and headed out of the station.

Lost in thought, Frances slowly headed out to the back to where the motorcar was waiting for her. Then she stopped and turned, and gathering her skirts, she ran out to the platform where Hal was boarding.

"Hal!" He turned. She stepped up to him, threw her arms around him, and kissed him hard. He started to say something, but couldn't speak.

"Dear Hal. Astonishing men is my raison d'etre."

She waved him off as the train began chugging, then turned to face a rather astonished stationmaster. Between her arrest record, and public and passionate kissing, she knew she was going to be gossip fodder throughout the long country winter.

CHAPTER 21

Frances got back into the car, and told the chauffer to take her back to the village police station.

She caught Dill just as he was entering after walking his beat around the village. He seemed surprised and a little embarrassed.

"Please, my lady, come inside." They entered the small front room, and Frances looked around with satisfaction. Mallow would certainly approve of how neat and clean Dill kept it.

"Please, take a seat. And again, my lady, my apologies for having to arrest you. I trust, seeing that you're out, that charges were dismissed?"

"Of course they were, constable, and no need for apologies. But I'm afraid there is going to be more . . . unpleasantness. I was hoping you could help me."

"Yes, my lady." But he sounded a little uncertain.

"I just prevented the arrest of Thomasina Calvin. I think the real murderer wanted to frame her. That has failed for now, thanks to me. But someone is going to be very angry with me." She took great satisfaction from that.

"I assure you, my lady, I will personally take care of watching over you while you remain in the Eyrie. I will patrol extensively around the house grounds in the coming days."

"Thank you." It was a noble gesture, but a single constable couldn't even patrol a house of that size, let alone the grounds.

"I do appreciate that. And I know Miss Kestrel will as well." She paused. "And so will Miss Mallow." She watched him blush. "And if you do uncover anything unusual, report to Mallow. No one will think a constable calling on a maid is anything unusual." He blushed even more. "Now, as helpful as you are, we're going to need additional police assistance from London."

"But my lady, only the chief constable can request help from the Yard."

She smiled. "I'm not without influence. May I use your telephone?" She had the exchange connect her with a London number—Inspector Eastley.

"Inspector? It's Lady Frances Ffolkes. I hope you are well?" She heard his sigh over the line.

"What is it now, Lady Frances?"

"I am very close to uncovering the murderer. But I am going to need your help. Can you and Constable Smith make an excuse to come down here for a few days?" She listened to quiet static along the line, and she thought for a moment they had been disconnected.

He eventually started to talk. "Lady Frances. I don't know where to begin. I can't just walk away from London to take care of a crime outside of my jurisdiction. I came at Foreign Office request. That particular . . . incident is closed."

"But inspector, surely a man with your skills can make an excuse—some loose ends, some final files belonging to Sir Calleford that you need to review and collect. That was your initial job, wasn't it?"

Another sigh. "I must admit you do not have a history of wasting my time."

"Inspector, that almost sounds like a compliment."

"Oh very well. I'll be down tomorrow. Let's try to keep my arrival quiet, shall we."

"Just you and me and Constable Dill, who is being very helpful. I look forward to your arrival."

She rang off. What was that look on Dill's face? Worry, confusion, astonishment? *Perhaps I've been a little overwhelming. But I have gotten a lot done today.*

"As you gathered, constable, Inspector Eastley of Special Branch, whom you've already met, will be coming down tomorrow. It is his great wish no one else know about his arrival. Something is going to happen. I don't know how, or from where, but I'll want him standing by. Good day. We'll talk again soon."

And with that, she turned and walked out of the door.

Constable Dill stepped outside and watched the Rolls-Royce drive along the main street on its way back to the Eyrie.

"What just happened?" he asked himself.

―――――◦•✕•◦―――――

Like the chauffeur, Pennington gave no sign he knew that Frances, a guest of the house, had just come back from the Morchester police jail.

"Do you know where Miss Kestrel is?" Frances asked him.

"She had tea in the solar, my lady, with Miss Calvin and Miss Hardiman."

"And Mrs. Blake?"

"The mistress is in her room," said Pennington.

But Mrs. Blake was not the mistress of Kestrel's Eyrie, not anymore.

The three women were chatting, but descended onto Frances with questions and sympathy as she entered the room. "How are you . . . are you hurt . . . how dare that inspector . . ."

Over their shoulders, Frances saw Mallow in a corner, working on her knitting. A maid did not sit and have tea with ladies, but Frances had told Mallow to stay with them and she had taken that seriously.

Mallow also knew not to make a fuss. While the ladies besieged her, her maid quickly poured a cup of tea and placed the kinds of delicacies her mistress liked on a plate. "Please take a seat, my lady, and have some tea."

"Thank you so much." She eagerly sat deeply into the soft chair and sipped the hot, fine tea. Frances closed her eyes. An arrest, threats, bringing Special Branch back . . . Hal. It had been quite a day.

She opened her eyes to see Gwen, Tommie, and Effie looking at her.

"Effie, are you and your father leaving to go back to London?"

"Dad would certainly like to. He says enough is enough. Mrs. Blake called the chief constable and said there was no reason American guests should be subject to such a dangerous environment. And now we have permission to return to London. But I told Dad I'm staying. And I am."

A sense of adventure? Love for Christopher? Desire to be mistress of the Eyrie? All of the above? Of course, Mrs. Blake would love to see the back of the Hardimans, her rivals for control of the Eyrie. Frighten them away and use her influence as lady of the manor to get them released. But Effie Hardiman was made of sterner stuff.

Frances took Effie's hand. "Very good. We'll see this through together. Now, Tommie and Gwen, we've managed to thwart the police for now, but they'll be back. We need to be ready for them. I've been making plans. All three of you are to stay together as much as possible. Don't leave the house."

Gwen looked fearful, but Frances took her hand now. "You will be fine, my dear. I saw you defend your friend when you thought she'd be arrested. You have more courage than you think. Just hold onto that." She then looked into Tommie's eyes, for just a moment: *This will end very soon.*

"Now, tell me about Mrs. Blake. Pennington said she's in her room?"

"We haven't seen her at all since you left," said Gwen.

"I see. Mallow, I need to refresh myself. Again, the three of you stay together. I'll see you all at dinner, if not before." She smiled. "We'll be strong together."

Frances and Mallow didn't speak until they were in Frances's room with the door closed.

"I know it's not my place to say, my lady, but to arrest the daughter of a marquess—it's simply outrageous."

"The inspector is desperate, so we will make some allowances. But for now, let's look ahead and not backward."

"Very good, my lady."

"Have you seen Mr. Mehmet since I departed?"

"No, my lady. The ladies had lunch and tea in the solar, and Miss Kestrel was kind enough to make sure I was served as well. I heard he and Mr. Hardiman were served in the library for lunch. I don't know about tea." *When it came to tea, you just never knew with foreigners.* "You must be tired, my lady. You have some time to rest before we dress for dinner."

"Excellent idea. I could use a little rest." The next couple of days would likely be busy too, and she let Mallow help her out of her dress.

"Miss Kestrel indicated she and the other ladies would be in the solar until it was time to dress for dinner, and with your permission, my lady, I will stay with them." Mallow picked up her knitting bag.

"That bag looks very full. What are you knitting, a tapestry?"

"Oh no, my lady. I'm still carrying the rolling pin." And with that, she left, to sounds of Frances's chuckling.

But Frances's nap was postponed by the arrival of Mrs. Blake, shortly after Mallow left.

"I just wanted to welcome you back, Lady Frances. I am sorry for the indignities you had to undergo."

"Thank you. But I was actually treated very well. And I must admit I did provoke him."

"Yes. I'm curious to know why a lady of your background and intelligence thought it was necessary to provoke a local police inspector."

"I lost my temper when I saw him bully one of my dearest friends."

"I find that hard to believe. I'm sure you're capable of great rage. But you strike me as someone who always controls it, always channels it."

Frances just shrugged.

"The inspector will be back for Miss Calvin in the next day or two."

"And my family solicitor will be back as well. With a barrister. I think you will find it hard to separate Tommie from Gwen. Or Effie Hardiman from Christopher. We will all stick together until the end."

"You will stand up to the police again? The crown prosecutor? The courts of assize?"

Frances just smiled. "Oh yes. You have no idea what I'm capable of."

Mrs. Blake matched her smile. "Actually, I think I do."

Dinner in the servants' hall was somewhat unusual. All everyone had clearly been talking about was the arrest of Lady Frances, but no one was going to discuss it in front of Mallow. Indeed, with three murders and an arrest, the only safe topic of conversation seemed to be the blacksmith's daughter, who was seen walking out with a corn chandler.

Upstairs, conversation wasn't much livelier. Frances felt that even local gossip would've been preferable to endless discussions about gardening and what flowers to plant where.

Over dessert, Mrs. Blake asked everyone what their plans were for the following day.

"I called the vicar," said Tommie. "I asked if there might be any good works we could do to keep ourselves busy while we are here. He said he will come by with some donated yarn, and we can knit socks for poor children to keep them warm this winter." Gwen seemed cheered by that. Effie did not look like it was the most exciting prospect.

"If anyone would like, there are several pleasant walks."

"Now that sounds like fun," said Effie. "Do you think Christopher, that is, Mr. Blake, would be free to join us?"

"He's busy on estate work," said Mrs. Blake. That wasn't a surprise. Mother and son would not want to spend a lot of time together, considering Christopher's attraction to Effie.

"It's out of the question," said Mr. Hardiman. "Too many funny things going on around here. If you want to stay with your friends, Effie, we'll stay. But inside, until things are more settled." *Mr. Hardiman was no fool*, observed Frances. The scene with the inspector and the attempted framing of Tommie had made it clear that not even the police believed some vague "gang" was responsible for the deaths. "I have some letters to write, business to attend to," he said, and Effie pouted.

"I have commitments as well," said Mr. Mehmet. "Will you be taking a walk, Lady Frances?" His smile seemed challenging. She turned to Mrs. Blake.

"Thank you, but I'm sure Gwen would still like the support of her friends," said Frances. Gwen gave her a grateful look. "We'll all gather to knit."

CHAPTER 22

Frances had breakfast with her friends. Mr. Mehmet and Mr. Hardiman appeared to be discussing hunting, and as usual, Mrs. Blake made sure breakfast was up to Eyrie standards. She then sat down with the gentlemen, leaving the young ladies to themselves.

Tommie's face showed strain. She was no doubt wondering when and how someone would come after her again. Gwen was cheerful though. *In her mind*, Frances realized, *the problems were all solved when Frances stood up to the inspector.* Effie seemed lost in thought, perhaps dreaming of the day when she would preside over meals here and wondering how recent events might affect that. A private engagement was just that—if her father dragged her away from the Eyrie, her dreams could dissolve.

"So I understand that knitting is on the agenda," Frances said.

"I'm sure I'll be hopeless at it," said Gwen. "But it will be good to have something useful to do."

"Good works are among the responsibilities for English ladies," said Frances with a meaningful look at Effie.

"I take your point," she said with a sigh.

"I'm putting Mallow in charge of all of you. She excels in knitting and can help you get started and through the rough spots."

"You're coming too, aren't you, Franny?" asked Gwen.

"Of course. I just have a letter to write to Mrs. Elkhorn—committee work." She looked at Tommie and held her eyes. *Don't worry. I'm on the case.* "In fact, let me get started now, so we won't be apart too long. I'll have a word with Mallow to make sure she meets you in the solar."

She had a final sip of tea and met Mallow just outside the dining room.

"The vicar will be here soon, Mallow. Stay with the ladies in the solar. I'm going to be doing a little reconnaissance work, but that's just between you and me."

"'Reconnaissance,' my lady?"

"Searching and exploring. Armies have whole units devoted to doing this. We've seen how large this house is—in fact, much of it isn't used. Now, someone on this estate committed murders, and tried to plant evidence on Miss Calvin. They'd need a base of operations, so to speak, and there is a part of this house that's empty. I'm going to have a look through that locked door at the end of my hallway. No one is to know but you."

"Very good, my lady."

"I knew I could count on you. Of course, Constable Dill said he will also be keeping an eye on the grounds." And she hid a smile as Mallow blushed slightly.

"That is very reassuring, my lady," she said. She cleared her throat. "The vicar will no doubt be here soon. I'll make sure Mr. Pennington is aware he is to be shown into the solar."

Frances headed back to her room, where she selected a nail file from among her toiletries. Then she walked down the hallway, past Gwen's and Tommie's rooms, to the locked door at the end of the hallway. It was a better lock than the one in Mrs. Sweet's cottage, so Frances took a little longer than Mallow to pick this one, but in about twenty minutes it gave way, and Frances entered.

The hallway was dimly lit from a window at the end, so Frances could see the dust. No housemaid had swept here in a long time. There were other contrasts with the rest of the Eyrie:

No tapestries or oil paintings on these walls, which were bare and in need of painting. A series of rooms lined the hallway, and Frances tried the first of the doors. It opened easily, and inside she saw some old, cheap furniture probably kept in storage for servants' rooms. She prowled around for a while, but there were no clues here.

The next room was the same. She opened all the drawers in a cracked dresser and even looked into what appeared to be an old sea chest. It contained some faded clothes, perhaps used for a fancy dress party when the Marchands still held sway in the house.

But the third room she tried was a surprise. On a much-battered and stained table that might have once graced the Eyrie's kitchen, Frances saw what was clearly a fresh addition to this forgotten wing—a chipped bowl. She wrinkled her nose at the metallic smell that cut through the pervasive musty odor, and waved away the flies that supplied the only noise and movement in these halls.

The bowl's inside was stained deep red, and Frances gingerly touched the bottom. It was still a little sticky—the blood that ended up on Tommie's dress had been stored here. Convenient, and yet hidden.

Perhaps there was more to see. She continued along the hallway, which turned sharply left. She guessed she was on a gallery surrounding the great hall below, and would eventually come to another door on the other side.

There were a dozen more doors—should she check all of them for more clues? She was thinking what to do, when she thought she heard a creak. Was it her imagination? Her own feet? Frances stopped, and held her breath. *Definitely a creak.* She hoped it was just a field mouse, but even a cat didn't weigh enough to make that much noise. It came more steadily, from the turn in the hallway ahead of her.

Frances froze. Then from around the corner came a stranger, a man of middle years. His clothes were a gentleman's, but scruffy. He didn't say anything, and they stared at each other for a few moments.

And then Frances turned and ran. She heard his footfalls and was under no illusions: he had a longer stride and wasn't impeded by skirts. *But I'm smarter.*

Realizing she'd never make it to the exit before he caught her, she turned suddenly into one of the storage rooms and slammed the door behind her. It took just a moment to push over an old wardrobe. It fell with a crash against the door, and she heard her assailant try to force his way in.

He'd get in eventually, Frances knew, but she had slowed him down, and meanwhile she let her eyes adjust to the dark. She reached around for something to use as a weapon. Her hands found a small stool—it would have to do.

The man pushed again and again. Frances slid a chair behind the door, hopped onto it, and waited for him to get in. His eyes would be used to the relatively well-lit hallway and he wouldn't see her right away. She raised the stool and patiently waited for him to appear. And then, with great satisfaction, she brought it down on his head as hard as she could.

He collapsed on the floor.

Frances just stood there looking at him. He began to groan, and she realized he'd get up soon. She stepped over him, ran to the doorway leading back to the living quarters, and opened the door. Turning, she saw the man stumbling after her. She didn't want to let him get away, but knew she couldn't fight him. Reaching into her pocket, she produced the silver police whistle she always kept with her and blew it once, then again and again.

The vicar had dropped off the donated yarn, offered more words of comfort for Gwen, and praised the ladies for their charitable works. Mallow set them up and observed their progress. *Effie was surprisingly good,* she observed. But her ladyship had said that Miss Hardiman had been born poor—knitting wasn't an acceptable hobby for farm girls, but a necessity. Tommie was a little slow, but competent.

Gwen, however, did not seem to be able to manage.

"Why don't you read to us," suggested Tommie. "You have such a nice reading voice."

"That might be best," said Gwen, looking forlornly at the tangle of yarn. Mallow began to straighten it all out while Gwen looked for a suitable novel on the solar bookshelf. "How about Dickens? He tells such good stories," said Gwen. She sat back down on the couch and began to read aloud from *Great Expectations*.

Rachel, one of the housemaids, came in with a tea service. "Mr. Pennington asked me to apologize if you've been disturbed, Miss," she said to Gwen. "Apparently, the bootboy has been practicing his penny whistle, even though he was told not to."

"Quite all right," said Gwen. "We couldn't hear it here anyway."

It only took Mallow about ten seconds to make the connection.

"Rachel. Never mind the tea. Run downstairs at once. Grab every maid you see and look for Constable Dill, who is somewhere on the grounds. And send him and any footmen to the ladies' wing immediately."

Rachel just stared, and the ladies stopped what they were doing, looking back and forth between the two maids.

"Well what are you waiting for? Go!" said Mallow. And Rachel turned and left as fast as she could without actually running. "Miss Kestrel, Miss Calvin, Miss Hardiman. Lady Frances needs us now." And single file, they unquestioningly followed Mallow out of the solar and toward their wing.

On their way, Mallow glanced out of the window, noting with satisfaction that housemaids and kitchen maids were fanning out of the house, no doubt seeking the constable.

Then, up the stairs, and along the hallway. As they got closer, they could now hear the whistle, clearly not a penny whistle, but her ladyship's prized silver police whistle. Mallow felt relief flood through her—her ladyship was safe if she was blowing.

They turned the final corner, and there she was, standing in the open doorway to the empty wing. She had blown herself breathless, and just pointed down the hallway. Mallow peered into the hall and saw a man sitting on the floor and holding his head. The other ladies gathered around.

"I've sent for Constable Dill, my lady. And more servants should be coming."

"Thank you," gasped Frances. She motioned for Tommie to step forward, while she turned to her attacker. "You," she said. "Look at me." The man looked up, as he continued to rub a growing bump.

"That roman nose and high forehead—that's him. That's my attacker from London. Except for the addition of a mustache."

"Very good," said Frances. People started to arrive—Mr. Pennington, a footman, Mrs. Blake, and finally Constable Dill, panting almost as much as Lady Frances from his running.

Mallow pushed her way past everyone to the constable. "There's a man in there who has attacked her ladyship. He needs to be arrested, right now." He seemed a little stunned. "Well, constable. What are you waiting for?"

Dill strode into the hallway and grabbed the man by his collar. "Come with me, my man. You are in big trouble."

Frances remembered the bloodstained bowl. *But no. That had nothing to do with this man. He wouldn't have done that.* She'd keep quiet about that, especially with so many people in the hall. She told Dill to follow Mallow to the solar.

Frances then peered over everyone's heads to Mrs. Blake. Her expression was a perfect example of self-control. Frances couldn't help but admire her.

Mr. Pennington quickly sent all the servants back to their tasks. Tommie looked upset—no, angry. *But she'd get her justice,* thought Frances. Gwen was more confused than anything. Effie seemed—amused.

"Tommie, why don't the three of you go to Gwen's room and order some more tea from the kitchen."

"I don't understand," said Gwen. "Who was that man?"

"No need to worry, dear. Probably some tramp looking for a warm place," said Tommie. "The police will take care of it. Now, let's get some tea." She put a comforting arm around Gwen and led her away, leaving Frances and Effie alone.

"I guess Dad didn't hear from all the way in his room. We're going to have some fight when he finds out. He'll want to go back to London right away." She sighed. "Is it always like this in great English houses?" asked Effie.

"Not typically," said Frances.

"Too bad. It's kind of exciting. So what did you do to him anyway?"

"Slammed a stool on his head."

Effie laughed and gave Frances a hug. "You're my kind of girl, Franny Ffolkes."

"I'm glad you approve," said Frances, smiling back. "But don't worry—things will soon be back to the normal, predictable world we English so love."

CHAPTER 23

When Frances entered the solar, she saw that Mallow had gathered up the knitting and was serving tea, which was probably getting cool by now, to Mrs. Blake and Constable Dill. The culprit was cuffed and sitting in a chair with his head down. The bump was now very obvious. *I really hit him hard.*

"Are you all right, Lady Frances?" asked Mrs. Blake, as if Frances had done nothing more than lightly trip on a wrinkled rug.

"Quite. Thank you."

"I am sorry you were assaulted in this house." She paused, and her eyes seemed to drill right into Frances. "That door is usually kept locked."

Mrs. Blake then turned to the constable. "I have no idea who this . . . person is, or how he got into this house. I will have Mr. Pennington and the footmen carefully check all the doors and windows, and hire carpenters and locksmiths to make any necessary repairs. Please remove this man as soon as you can."

"Very good, madam. I do need to call for a police vehicle."

"If it would get him out of here more quickly, my car and chauffer at your disposal. I will give the necessary instructions." She swept out of the room.

"Come on," said Dill, dragging the man along. "You're going to jail on some very serious charges. Now let's start with your name."

"Silas Watkins," he mumbled. He had a London accent, but Frances remembered what Tommie had said—it was too exact.

"We'll be asking you more questions, Mr. Watkins. Now come along peaceably, and don't make it worse."

"I'll be coming too, constable," said Frances. "Do you know where Inspector Eastley will be staying?"

"He called me early this morning to say he was at the Three Bells in Morchester, my lady."

"Excellent. Mallow, go to the telephone and call the inspector at the inn. Tell him to meet us at the village station. Then look in on the ladies."

"Very good, my lady."

Mallow was about to leave, when Frances saw her pause to give Mr. Watkins a look of absolute hatred. It was clear Mr. Watkins was lucky he wasn't going to be left alone in some windowless back room with Mallow and her rolling pin.

Dill half led, half dragged Watkins downstairs and out the front door, under the eyes of curious servants. The chauffer admitted his odd group of passengers to the Rolls-Royce with the same attentiveness he gave to all who rode in his car, before getting behind the wheel.

"The village police station," said Frances.

"Very good, my lady."

⊙•◦•⊙

Constable Dill led his prisoner through the front reception and into a larger room in the back with a table and chairs. He pushed Watkins into a chair.

"An inspector will be coming for you. From Scotland Yard. Be prepared to tell him the full story." Watkins just groaned and buried his face in his hands.

They didn't have long to wait before Inspector Eastley and Constable Smith arrived. Dill jumped up and stood at attention.

"Good morning, sir. This man, Silas Watkins, was arrested trespassing at the Eyrie and attacking Lady Frances Ffolkes."

"So I heard from Miss Mallow." He seemed very amused. "From the look at that bump, maybe you should've arrested Lady Frances for assault."

"Sir?"

"That was a joke, constable."

"Yes, sir."

Dill remained standing, while Eastley sat next to Frances and Constable Smith stood behind the prisoner, casting a shadow over him. Watkins looked up nervously at the huge constable.

Eastley didn't say anything right away to Watkins, just studied him for a while. So Frances also looked at him, seeing what she could deduce. *Yes, gentleman's clothes, but they were even more uncared for and worn than she had first realized, as if he had bought them used. And how did he grow a mustache so quickly? There was something funny about it.* She suddenly leaned forward and ripped it off his face. It was just held on with some sort of adhesive, as she had suspected.

The man reacted to that, shouting out profanities in pain. So she had been right. Yes, he was city born and bred—but that was a Manchester accent, not a fake London one.

"See here, watch your language. There's a lady present," Dill said.

"Indeed," said Eastley dryly. "Lady Frances, it seems you were wise to invite me back to the country, and I was wise to come. But let's avoid any further physical contact with the prisoner. After all, that's Constable Smith's job." Watkins looked up again at the huge policeman and seemed to shrink into his chair.

"Dill, did you search the prisoner?"

"Yes, sir. And I found this rather odd instrument." He produced from his pocket what looked to Frances like a knife handle.

Eastley picked it up. Then suddenly, with a snap, a nasty-looking blade shot out of it.

"Dear lord."

"Dear lord indeed, Lady Frances. It's called a switchblade. Not very common in England. The Italians seem to like them, I heard. Used for street fights among the lowest sort of criminals."

"I think a low criminal is what we have here, inspector. That man, under disguise, has threatened my friend Miss Thomasina Calvin and now me. She has already recognized him." She summarized the incident with Tommie in the cathedral and then how she had trapped the man, and was pleased to see Inspector Eastley look impressed. "I am sure that this is related to the murders at Kestrel's Eyrie."

"You may be right. Let's see about that." Inspector Eastley started in his peaceful voice that somehow made what he was saying even more frightening. *This is a chance to learn about how to question a suspect*, thought Frances.

"You have committed a very serious offense. Attacking a lady. And not just any lady—the sister of a marquess, a powerful and wealthy man with a lot of influence. I'll be long-retired, in a comfortable cottage in the country, while you're still rotting, forgotten in some prison cell."

Watkins hung his head even further as if he wanted to disappear.

"So let's be a good boy and be as cooperative as possible, so we can avert needless unpleasantness."

"I'll tell you the whole thing, and you'll see it was just supposed to be a joke." He had a pleading voice, willing the inspector to believe him.

"We've been speaking for less than a minute and you've already lied to me," said the inspector. "That's not a good sign. Maybe you need to spend some time alone with Constable Smith, to consider your position. I am patient. Constable Smith is not. He doesn't like working into the evening. And he hates having to come to the country. He might try to persuade you to tell the truth. Constable Smith can be very persuasive."

"Yes, sir," said Watkins, who looked like he was about to pass out. "I won't lie. I knew it was wrong. I'm an actor, you see. I think you guessed that, my lady. Mostly regional touring companies. Well, a couple of weeks ago, you see, I got a letter, with a ten-pound note, from someone saying he had seen me perform and wanted to play a joke on some woman, a Thoma-sina Calvin—"

Rage rose through her and she was about to rise, when East-ley laid a restraining hand on her arm. *He was right*, Frances realized. The interrogation would have to remain calm if it was to be effective.

"Please continue, Mr. Watkins," he said, still quietly.

The story was simple. The letter, written in block characters and unsigned, told him where he could find Miss Calvin, and in whose company she'd be. It took him several days, but he did what was asked and thought no more about it—but then he read the accounts of the murders at the Eyrie and recognized the names. He began to think there was more to it than a joke—and then another letter arrived, with another ten pounds, asking him to threaten Lady Frances at the Eyrie. "I know you won't believe me, but it was Mrs. Blake. She let me into the house through a back door late in the evening, set me up in a room. I was going to get more instructions, but then Lady Frances sur-prised me. I was just going to threaten her with the knife—I'm not a killer, I swear. Just to scare her, to let her know she wasn't safe and should go back to London."

He put his face in his hands.

"You are accusing one of the most prominent women in this county," said Eastley. "Do you have any proof that Mrs. Blake invited you in? That you're not just making this up? Did you save the letters and envelopes she sent you?"

"No. I was afraid of getting caught with them and burned them."

"How did Mrs. Blake even find you?"

"Our theater company played at a lot of great houses. This was one of them."

Inspector Eastley tapped his fingers on the table. Frances looked up at Constable Dill, who seemed astonished at the accu-sations against Mrs. Blake.

"There's more to this story than you're telling me," said East-ley. "Why did you do all this for Mrs. Blake? Don't you dare lie to me again."

"Oh God, sir. You won't believe me."

"Try me."

"When I was here with the theater company, I may have helped myself to a couple of spoons. Mrs. Blake caught me, but said she wouldn't call the police if I did something for her. Oh dear God, I knew you wouldn't believe me." And again he buried his face in his hands.

"I'm not sure you've given us all the details," said Frances, "but oddly I do believe you've told us the truth. Or most of it. I doubt if you're good enough an actor to pretend to be as stupid as you are."

Eastley chuckled at that. "You have a point, my lady."

Watkins saw a thread of hope. "I wasn't going to hurt you or the other woman, my lady, just scare you. There wasn't anything I could do," he whined. "I was stuck."

"Mr. Watkins. You will be charged, but we will keep in mind your cooperation today," said Eastley. "God help you if I find later that you've lied to me about any of this. Because, as I said, I'd then have to have Constable Smith here help you with your memory problems. And you don't want that."

Watkins looked again at the huge constable and decided to take the threat seriously.

"Smith. Take the prisoner into the front room and remain there with him until we're ready to leave for London."

"Sir," said Smith. And pulled Watkins out of the room.

"Constable Dill," said Eastley.

"Yes, sir!"

"Today's meeting hasn't happened. Do you understand? There will be no record of this arrest. No mention to your superior. I am taking Watkins to London and you will forget you ever met him. I don't want local men muddying the waters until this is settled, and no one in London should know I came here either. Is that clear?"

"Yes, sir."

"Now, tell me. Even in London we heard about Lady Frances's arrest." He spared a quick smile for Frances, who gave him a cool look in return. "Dill, do you believe that a gang has been responsible for the . . . incidents here? Or do you agree with Lady Frances that there might be a more accurate explanation."

Dill slipped his finger inside the neck of his tunic. "There seemed to be some serious doubts about the gangs, sir."

"And you saw fit to bring Lady Frances to an interrogation? Is that the way policing is done here?"

Frances started to talk, but Eastley motioned her to stay silent. She frowned and folded her arms across her chest.

"Her, ah, approach and ideas seemed sensible, sir." Frances saw the poor man sweating despite the coolness of the day.

Eastley nodded, reached into his pocket, and pulled out a card. "Sensible indeed, constable. Well done. Take my card. If you ever decide you want to advance your career in London, I invite you to call on me."

"Thank you, sir!"

"Now I want to talk with Lady Frances. Go wait with Constable Smith."

Dill saluted, and left.

"Thank you again for coming, inspector," said Frances. "And for that nice vote of confidence. I know you took a chance trusting me and I'm glad it has worked out."

"Credit where credit is due," said Eastley.

"What happens now? Can you arrest Phoebe Blake?"

"Be reasonable, my lady. It's the word of this actor against one of the most distinguished women in the county. An admitted thief, arrested while attacking you. No judge would even allow charges to be presented. You have established a connection between the threats against your friend, even if we can't prosecute. But nothing to connect these threats with murder. You are a judge of character. Do you see Mr. Watkins as a murderer?"

"No, I suppose he's innocent of murder. He worked for Mrs. Blake to separate Gwen from her friends for his own reasons. But I feel I'm close to making a provable case. Now, I've done you a good turn. I'm giving you a criminal to bring back to the Yard. I need something from you. Who is Mr. Mehmet? And what is his role at Kestrel's Eyrie?"

"You tell me why you ask, and I will see what I can do."

"I'll tell you what I think. I think you know who Mr. Mehmet is, inspector. You and my brother were very friendly with him at Sir Calleford's funeral. I think Mr. Mehmet is a spy. For whom or why, I don't know. But he was doing something at the Eyrie, and he doesn't want Scotland Yard detectives looking into the murder."

"You think he's the murderer, Lady Frances? Because of the Turkish dagger?"

She shook her head. "I admit I once did. But not anymore. I think he knows something or saw something. It makes sense. A spy is always looking around, over his shoulder, beyond the turn in the hallway. Or so I imagine. If anyone saw something, he did. Anyway, he asked me to solve the murder quietly and tried to discourage me from using my connections to bring in the Yard—not politically minded Special Branch types like you, but murder investigators who'd want to know what he was doing and when. He doesn't want that, and will let a murderer go free before he tells me. I don't think he's even told you. Who knows? The detectives even might ask him about—" She looked intently at the inspector. "About his 'friend in London.'"

His mustache hid a small smile, and he nodded before speaking.

"It's interesting, my lady. A skill for analysis and reasoning must run in your family. Your brother thinks the same way."

"But my brother has one thing I don't. He has access to the official story, and Charles will never tell me. I know you have it too. I need a way to force Mr. Mehmet to cooperate, or I don't know if I can stop the killer. I am asking you as a police officer to help me."

"I can trust you, or so you say—but you want to use the information to blackmail Mr. Mehmet into cooperating with you. Do I have that right?"

"Blackmail is a very ugly word," said Frances, as if she were correcting a naughty child. "I just want to improve my negotiating position."

Eastley chuckled. "Nicely put." Frances wanted to look calm, but she could hardly breathe. She felt a sheen of sweat on her brow. Mallow would be horrified, and would jump in with a delicate handkerchief. She couldn't read the expression on Inspector Eastley's face.

"Why should I tell you what your own brother wants hidden?"

"Because my brother is charged with international policy, but you are charged with safety within the realm. And because I'm a bright and well-educated woman, not your little sister who still needs protecting."

That won her another smile. He thought for a moment.

"Let me make you an offer. I cannot intervene directly in this case. And you are right about Mr. Mehmet—he has a purpose here that will not be easily interrupted. But what if I use my influence to force the chief constable to accept Scotland Yard help? They may find the necessary evidence to charge Mrs. Blake. If she's indeed the murderer. You must admit you have no direct evidence."

Frances was thinking of a response when she heard yelling outside.

"What is going on here? Why have there been arrests without my knowledge?"

And Frances and Inspector Eastley said at the same time— "Inspector Bedlow."

Bedlow stormed into the back room and glared at both Eastley and Frances.

"They called me from the Eyrie," said Bedlow. *Of course,* Frances realized. *Mrs. Blake would've reported it.* "I should've been the one questioning him. You have no right to come from London." He then looked at Frances. "And you shouldn't be here at all."

"Do calm yourself," said Eastley quietly. "Take a seat."

Bedlow seemed to debate that, then roughly pulled over a chair and sat. "This is my patch, inspector. What are you doing here?"

"We heard word that a man wanted in connection with something Sir Calleford was working on was making his way here. Indeed, it turns out he was hiding in the house. We are bringing him back to London. That is all."

Bedlow's eyes narrowed. "That's ridiculous. This clearly has to do with Sir Calleford's murder. This man is my prisoner. He will be held in Morchester and I will question him."

But Eastley just smiled and shook his head. "These are secret matters for the Foreign Office. If you have a problem with my leaving and taking the prisoner with me, I will have the chief superintendent of Special Branch call your chief constable. And you'll live to regret your behavior."

Bedlow licked his lips and thought that over. "Very well. Take him and don't come back." He gave Frances a sly smile. "As long as you're here, my lady, I can tell you that we'll be coming back within twenty four hours with a warrant for Thomasina Calvin's arrest—for the murder of Sir Calleford Kestrel."

"I thought you held a criminal gang responsible. Or perhaps now Inspector Eastley's prisoner. Why will you be arresting Miss Calvin?" asked Frances. "And you have no evidence anyway."

"Never you mind. I think you'll find that Miss Calvin's very special friendship with Miss Kestrel will speak for itself—"

Frances stood up quickly. "If you dare say anything, I will—" She felt her hands making fists. *Striking men who threaten me is a habit I could develop.*

"What? Give me another excuse to arrest you again? Because this time—"

"Stop it. Both of you," Eastley said in the same soft voice that was nevertheless forceful. "Bedlow, you have no reason to be here. I suggest you leave."

"With pleasure. And Dill is a Morchester constable. He's coming with me."

Frances was now doubly annoyed. She wanted to talk with Dill. But Bedlow stalked out and ordered Dill to follow him.

Eastley shrugged. "I bluffed to get Watkins out of here, my lady, so the local men can't twist his story. You were waiting for something like this, weren't you? But there's really nothing more I can do until we have more evidence. If he can arrest Miss Calvin, even on flimsy evidence, it's a local matter."

"I can't sit back and just watch. It'll destroy both of them."

"I sympathize. Give me a week or two, and we'll figure out how to get Scotland Yard up here."

"But I can't wait weeks. You heard him. Very well—I'll have to make my own plans."

"Lady Frances—oh never mind. You won't listen to me anyway."

"Oh, but I will, if you tell me what I need to know. Before we were interrupted, you were telling me about Mr. Mehmet. Tell me more. Tell me the whole story."

Eastley sighed. "God help us if what I told you gets out. I'm only telling you because you're going to do what you're going to do and this will make it a little easier."

Frances pulled out a handkerchief and mopped her damp brow. She leaned back and prepared to listen.

CHAPTER 24

"There is a high-ranking Turkish diplomat in London," said the inspector. "His name in his language is difficult to pronounce, so we normally just referred to him by his title—the pasha. He is wealthy and well-connected, which is how he came to his post, but he is arrogant and stupid. One of the pasha's jobs is keeping track of Turkish nationals in London. With your knowledge of politics and history, you probably know what is going on in Istanbul right now, Lady Frances."

"I know the sultan is deeply unpopular," she said. "There are rumors that some young army officers and others may even be plotting against him."

"Yes. And Mr. Mehmet is one of them. Under the cover of working for the British interests of his family's business, Mr. Mehmet was in reality working to get important but unofficial support from His Majesty's government—from elements within the Foreign Office who would very much like to see the unstable sultan removed. But it had to be quiet—the government could not be seen as openly supporting rebels in these difficult times. It could precipitate a diplomatic crisis, even lead to war. So Mr. Mehmet worked very secretly, with no other partner but his cousin, Kerem, an officer in the Turkish army temporarily working out of the embassy in London. He often ran messages between London and Mr. Mehmet when Mehmet was visiting

Sir Calleford, who also unofficially helped Mr. Mehmet with his many contacts. It was convenient for Sir Calleford to arrange meetings with Mr. Mehmet in the privacy of the country—and Mehmet was supposedly just enjoying the hospitality of one of the great English houses. He was out of sight of prying eyes in London, and it worked well as long as Mehmet didn't stay here too long."

Frances smiled to herself. This confirmed that there was another Turk near the Eyrie working with Mr. Mehmet. He had been speaking to him that night she was kidnapped. "It was impossible to hide his work with the Foreign Office, but it was disguised as simple trade discussions, innocuous meetings about tedious shipping lane regulations. The pasha didn't like it, anyway, and we knew he likely considered forcing Mehmet back to Istanbul—or even having him killed—but for now accepted things as they were to avoid a possible scandal. If the pasha knew just what Mehmet was telling his secret contact at the Foreign Office, there is no doubt he'd have had Mehmet killed, never mind the repercussions. But Mr. Mehmet was careful. He had just one contact at the Foreign Office, a man only known as the 'friend in London.' This contact passed on information he wanted looked up or confirmed, and Mehmet and Kerem would send back intelligence they knew or had gathered from sources at their disposal."

"I see," said Frances. It was beginning to make sense. And no surprise Inspector Eastley knew so much—Special Branch kept many secrets. "Mr. Mehmet was risking a great deal, defying his government and working with this secret Englishman in the Foreign Office who was supporting him—the 'friend in London,' as you say."

She paused, then her eyes lit up. "Sir Calleford, being an unofficial diplomat, had secretly recruited Mr. Mehmet. He was quietly bringing in the French too, seeing if they wanted to be involved. And the 'friend in London' provided—I don't know—money, munitions, other supplies." It suddenly clicked.

"That's why my brother came to the Eyrie after Sir Calleford died. It wasn't just to deliver the eulogy—that was just his 'cover' so he could talk openly with Mr. Mehmet. I have that term right, don't I—his 'cover?' My brother is the 'friend in London,' isn't he?" The inspector toyed with his pen for a few moments before answering. Then he fixed Frances with a look, and gave her a half smile.

"Yes, Lady Frances. He's your brother. After the murder, he had to take me into his confidence. That's what Special Branch does, help clean up messes like that."

"I would've thought that my brother would find me as trustworthy as you," said Frances, feeling red spots grow on her cheeks.

"It's not a matter of trust. It's a matter of priority. The Foreign Office is your brother's only responsibility. He didn't tell you because finding Sir Calleford's killer was not a Foreign Office priority. A deep investigation could've made things very sticky at Whitehall. We all hoped the local force would turn up someone, but if Sir Calleford went unavenged, that was a price your brother was willing to pay for the greater good—for not revealing Mr. Mehmet as a spy, which might've happened if Scotland Yard detectives questioned him. He knew Mr. Mehmet didn't kill Sir Calleford—he had no motive. So it must've been someone else. Your brother trusts you. But he knew your goals were different from his. He wanted to protect the Foreign Office. You wanted to solve a murder and protect your friends."

"But you trust me," she countered.

"Because I want to see someone punished for that murder. That is *my* priority, Lady Frances. And much as I hated to admit it, I know you are the only one in a position to understand that. I am trusting you to use this information to get Mr. Mehmet to help you—nothing else. And I am trusting you to get justice without wrecking the arrangement your brother, Mr. Mehmet, and Sir Calleford set up."

Frances pondered that. "So, you trust me because you have to. And my brother doesn't trust me because he doesn't have to."

Eastley chuckled. "You want to involve yourself in men's affairs? Be my guest. But this is how men behave."

"Something else women can change when we get the vote," said Frances.

"Beyond my responsibility," said the inspector.

"I shouldn't harangue you. No, I am very grateful, inspector, and I will keep your secrets and not abuse your trust."

"Best of luck," he said.

She stood, and with her hand on the doorknob, she turned back to the inspector. "One more question. Is Mr. Mehmet married?"

The inspector laughed. "Don't tell me you've formed an attachment to him. Dear God, your brother would be appalled. In fact, I know he is unmarried."

"I asked because I wanted to make the acquaintance of his wife, if he had been married. As you said, inspector, women are also capable of analysis and reasoning." *Ha*, she thought. *I know something you don't.* Quite a man of secrets, this Mr. Mehmet. "Now tell me to be very careful."

"I might as well tell you just to stay home," he said. "But there have been vicious threats and murders here, my lady."

"And I've parried every attack," she said. Frances stood. "Thank you again. You'll be wanting to take your prisoner to London. Have a good trip." And without waiting for further reply, she headed out of the room. The chauffeur was waiting by the Rolls-Royce. Frances had plenty of things to think about. And plenty of things to do.

———◦•◦•◦———

Frances didn't see Mrs. Blake when she entered the Eyrie. Pennington said that Mrs. Blake was in her bedroom, and that Miss Kestrel and her friends were most likely in the solar.

Frances headed straight to the solar, where the ladies had returned to resume their knitting under Mallow's supervision. They instantly jumped all over her with questions.

"The man was arrested and will be questioned by the police—Scotland Yard police, in London. But that's not really important right now. All is going to be well, and I have some ideas. Now, Effie, where is your father?"

"Oh, somewhere talking about hunting again with Mr. Mehmet. Dad made another fuss about our leaving when he heard about that man who attacked you, but I told him to calm down; the police were taking care of it."

"Mr. Mehmet was apparently out walking this morning," said Tommie. "He seemed upset when he heard, and stopped by to make sure all of us were unharmed. He also asked if we knew whether more police would be coming."

"I see. Gwen, has your Aunt Phoebe been in to see you here since I left?"

"No. Right after you left, she told me she was going to her room and not to expect her for lunch. She said the man was just a tramp—and everything would be all right." Gwen looked confused and a little frightened. "I know I'm still in mourning, but can't we go back to London? I don't like it here. I don't like it here at all." She looked like she was going to cry.

Tommie put an arm around Gwen. "Soon—I promise." And she looked up to Frances for confirmation.

"Yes, Gwen. I have a few things to do, but I think we can go back to London soon. Now finish your knitting and I'll see you all at lunch. It's been a busy morning, and I'm going to lie down for a bit. Mallow, see the ladies to lunch. You and I will talk later."

"Very good, my lady."

Frances headed up to her room, but she had no intention of lying down. She had some plans to make, and pen in hand, started making notes. It was too bad that she didn't get a chance to speak with Constable Dill before Inspector Bedlow dragged him away. She had wanted to make plans for them to communicate. Frances was now sure the Eyrie was locked tight. But she'd find a way to work around that.

She knew she had little time; they would indeed come to arrest Tommie. Bedlow had told her as much, and she remembered what Hal had told her—someone had to be arrested. At this point, Mrs. Blake may have thought she'd won, but she'd be vigilant—she was no more asleep in her room than Frances was. She'd be able to see a lot from her room, and what she couldn't see her maid would uncover for her. Mrs. Blake's nerves may be close to the breaking point, but Frances had no illusions about her ability to watch over what happened at the Eyrie.

Pleased with her plans, Frances looked at the time. Lunch was soon—and she'd be ready.

The meal was certainly tense after the morning's events, and Mrs. Blake was conspicuous by her absence. Pennington said the same as Gwen had earlier—Mrs. Blake was feeling "tired," and would be having lunch in her room. Gwen sat uncomfortably at the head of the table, looking as self-conscious as she felt, while Tommie kept giving her supportive looks.

Mr. Mehmet was quiet and seemed almost nervous. The conversational ball was carried largely by the Hardimans, who discussed the gardens and grounds again and Mr. Hardiman's recent shooting at the neighboring estate. However, he occasionally glared at his willful daughter—and she glared right back.

"I trust your aunt will recover shortly," said Mr. Hardiman to Gwen.

"I am sure the strain of running such a large household, especially in the wake of recent events, has proved too much for even as competent a lady as Mrs. Blake," said Mr. Mehmet. "Doubtless she'll be fine after a well-deserved rest."

"Thank you both," said Gwen quietly, her mind clearly elsewhere. She glanced at Tommie, then Frances, as if looking for rescue.

As soon as lunch ended, Frances took charge. "Gwen, why don't you read quietly in the solar for a while? I need to have a few words with Tommie. Perhaps Effie will keep you company. Mr. Hardiman—" she gave him a smile. "I have some advice to ask from you. I am sure a man of your wide experience will be able to help me. I will meet you in your room in thirty minutes?"

"Any way I can help, Lady Frances," he said with a bow. *As always, no man could resist an appeal to his wisdom and intelligence,* Frances knew. "I also have some things to discuss with you." He gave another look at Effie, who was already departing with Gwen to the solar, and took his leave.

"Tommie, there is something I need you to do. Get everyone out of the Eyrie tonight before dinner. You, Gwen, Effie, Effie's maid Hopp, and Mr. Hardiman. It's time Gwen realized she is mistress of this house—and it's time the servants realized it too. She will ring for the chauffer and tell him to have the car ready. And she will give some instructions to Pennington— I've written them down." She handed the paper to Tommie, who looked them over and raised an eyebrow. "Have Gwen tell them not to discuss these events with Mrs. Blake—she's tired and overwhelmed. If you're with Gwen, I daresay she can get through this."

"If you say so . . . but where are we going?"

"To Blake Court for the night. Mallow will help you pack. But she is staying here with me. Christopher will be somewhat stunned at your arrival, but I'm sure he and Mrs. Pear will be up to it."

"I'm sure. But you didn't mention Mr. Mehmet."

"He also is staying here with me."

"I'll do exactly as you say," said Tommie. She hugged her friend and whispered in her ear. "God go with you."

Frances knew the ladies would follow Tommie's instructions. Now to make sure Mr. Hardiman did as well. She found him pacing in his room.

"I am glad to see you are doing well after the events of this morning," he said. "I won't subject my daughter to this any further. I don't want to sound rude, but I'm leaving with Effie tomorrow if I have to carry her out."

"I understand completely, Mr. Hardiman. I assure you that this house has probably seen more excitement in the past few days than in the past century. Why wait until tomorrow? I've made arrangements for the ladies to go to Blake Court shortly. I suggest you join them. As Blake Court is a bachelor residence, it would be appropriate for you to go along as a chaperone."

He rubbed his chin and cast a shrewd eye on Frances. "I didn't go to Oxford or Cambridge, but I can tell something is up here."

"Something is up, Mr. Hardiman. Among other things, I think Effie would like to see Christopher Blake again."

"I'm sure she would," he said. "But I'm not going to stay in the country if there's going to be more violence."

"Just until tomorrow," said Frances, offering him a smile.

"And what happens tomorrow?"

"Ah. Tomorrow is another day, Mr. Hardiman. Have a good visit at Blake Court. And if you see Mrs. Blake in the meantime, there's no need to mention this to her. She has enough to take care of. And I'll be sure to tell the staff none of you will be in for dinner."

And with that, she left before Mr. Hardiman could ask more questions.

Excellent. Everything was falling into place. She went back to her room, where Mallow was waiting for her. Her maid had the biggest role of all, and Frances closed the bedroom door firmly before speaking.

"Mallow. I have a very special task for you this evening. No one knows more than you how closely a lady works with her maid. I don't think Mrs. Blake is any different. But tonight, I need Mrs. Blake without anyone to assist her. Not even Miss Jenkins. Especially not Miss Jenkins. Mrs. Blake wants us to think she's unaware of what's going on, as she's been in her bed-room most of the day. But we need to be careful, and we need to see she really is cut off as much as possible."

The wide-eyed Mallow just nodded. Frances produced a vial of the sleeping draft that the doctor had given Gwen right after her father's murder. "So I need you to get rid of Jenkins." She went into the details.

"Don't you worry, my lady. I won't let you down."

"Good girl, Mallow! I knew I could depend on you." She smiled. "It isn't normal work for a lady's maid, is it?"

"Well, no, my lady, but—" started Mallow, turning a little red.

Now, Frances laughed. "You were about to say that I wasn't a normal lady."

"Well, not in those words, my lady . . ."

"But you're absolutely right, Mallow. Now, I must call on Mr. Mehmet, then when I get back, I'll need you to help me into my walking clothes." And she left before Mallow could object.

Now came the hardest conversation of all. She took a deep breath and sought out Mr. Mehmet in his room.

"Lady Frances? So glad to see you again. I hope you are well after the attack on your person this morning?"

"Quite, thank you." He motioned for her to take a seat, and he sat opposite her.

"I suppose, with the attack on someone from such an important family, police will surely come from London? Have you already, in fact, summoned them?" He tried to sound casual about it, but Frances heard the strain in his voice.

"No, I haven't. I can, but I have a better way of handling this. I need your help, Mr. Mehmet. I won't mince words."

"What do you need?" he asked a little warily.

"I need you to tell me what you know. I believe you saw something that could help me solve this murder."

"I assure you that you are mistaken."

"Why did you not want Scotland Yard here? Why do you want me to solve it—unofficially? You foreign affairs types put your concerns ahead of everything else. I've learned that much."

Mr. Mehmet stood, and his smile was gone. "This isn't profiting either one of us. I will be leaving soon—my wife and I. Whether or not we get official permission."

Frances stood too. "I know what you're doing here. There's no point in hiding anything from me. You're working to overthrow your sultan. From what I hear, why not? He sounds most unsatisfactory. Work with me and you're secret is safe. But if you stubbornly refuse to talk, then you'll force my hand."

"Lady Frances. I have no idea what you're talking about."

"Then I agree; this has been a waste of time for both of us," she said. "Good day. And before you can leave England, I'll have half a dozen of Scotland Yard's finest grilling you about every movement you've made. Not Special Branch, but regular Criminal Investigation Division men. Let's see if your Foreign Office friends can save you then."

She turned and opened the door. She knew this would work. Frances had played enough card games to know how far you could bluff.

Mr. Mehmet reached over her shoulder and slammed the door. "Lady Frances . . ."

She turned. "Come now, Mr. Mehmet. You trust your friend in London. You can trust your friend's sister."

He shook his head. "It was foolish of me to think you wouldn't find out. If you had been alive when this house was being built, you'd have been burned as a witch." He made that sound as if it was a prospect he relished.

"You're the one who said I'd be the sword of Allah."

"It serves me right for mocking the Prophet," he said. "Your Lord and mine both work in mysterious ways." He sighed. "So this is how it ends. With you blackmailing me."

Frances tossed her head. "My understanding is that this is the way men do business, and if I am to work in the world of men, I need to learn it. It's apparently called 'negotiating.' For a beginner, I think I'm doing very well."

"You're doing extremely well," he said. "What do you want to know?"

"The night of the murder, I think you saw something. You didn't tell the police because you didn't want to tell them why you were where you were. They'd want to know more—why you were gone so long, why you took a hidden door, with whom you were meeting. They'd make investigations. I won't. So just tell me. And I will do everything I can to leave it at that."

"Even if I told you, what would it do? I am a foreigner, not even a Christian."

"You are a man—a gentleman. Even as a foreigner, the police would have to listen to you. You have no reason to lie if it came to a court case—but I don't think it will. The threat alone will be enough."

He nodded. "It seems I have no choice. Very well. I saw Mrs. Blake entering the study, during the evening. I consulted my watch—it was five minutes after ten. That's all. I had slipped out a little-used side door. I couldn't have the police inquiring into what I was doing and when. I assume Mrs. Blake and Sir Calleford were having a liaison." He shrugged. "These things happen in English country homes, I know." He paused, and Frances saw the wonder in his face as he made the connection. "It was an affair, surely. You don't think—"

But Frances cut him off. She wasn't prepared to discuss her theories further. "By itself, it means nothing. She could've had half a dozen reasons to visit him there, including chiding him for neglecting his guests. But it's all clear now and I have what I need. Thank you. Again, I don't think we should need to publicize this. I just needed the leverage for Mrs. Blake."

"Like the leverage you needed for me," he said with a little bitterness.

"Oh, my dear Mr. Mehmet. You men invented the game. I'm just trying to play according to your rules. Oh, and one more thing. Later this evening, Mrs. Blake will be leaving her room to look for me. Could you do me a favor? Stop her. Just talk to her as long as you can. You're a talented talker; I'm sure you'll do well. Thank you."

And with that, she left. Her brow was covered in sweat. "*Oh my,*" she thought.

CHAPTER 25

She went back to her room, where Mallow had laid out her walking clothes with the same care and attention as if they were an elegant ball ensemble. Always, Frances had put on these clothes by herself. Now, for the first time, she had Mallow to help—but that made it worse.

"I am not sure why you need to dress in . . . these, my lady."

"I have to be secret. Mrs. Blake can't know I'm leaving. No servant can know I left, and I can't risk her seeing me. She'll be checking the exchange to see if I made a call. She needs to think she's safe. It's a trap, Mallow."

"Very good, my lady. I'll do my part. I just wish it didn't involve these clothes." She started to help Frances get dressed and approached the men's clothes with her usual attention to sartorial perfection.

"Mallow, I don't think it has to be perfect. I'm supposed to be a working man."

"My lady. When you promoted me to be your personal maid, Miss Garritty—maid to your sister by marriage, Lady Seaforth—made me promise that I would never let you leave your bedroom without being perfectly dressed. I will keep that promise. Even if you are dressed in men's clothes. Now I believe the shirt is tucked in like this . . ."

"Should the braces be tightened like that?"

"The braces are designed for a man's figure, my lady." Mallow had a point. It was one thing to dress like a man, quite another for someone with her rounded figure to pass as one.

"If I may say, my lady, we could use the services of a valet."

"It's too bad Randall isn't here to help," said Frances, referring to her brother's valet. Both women thought that over, then started to giggle. Although an excellent valet, Randall was a formal, humorless man, and the thought of him dressing his master's sister in men's clothes was really too much.

"Beg your pardon, my lady, but I think that's one place we won't get any advice."

"I agree with you there. Let's loosen the shirt a little and add this jacket, which will cover a multitude of sins. And help me tuck my hair under this hat . . ."

Frances admired the final results in the mirror. *Not too bad. This just might work.*

"How do I look, Mallow?"

Mallow sighed. "Again, begging your pardon, but I don't know how to answer that question, my lady."

Frances chuckled, then looked out her window: the workmen in the garden were breaking for the day. It was time to leave. "Now make sure the hall is clear and I'll be off."

Mallow gave her a nod and Frances slipped out. She had memorized the way to the back stairs, where she planned to leave through the servants' entrance at the back. She was almost out when she heard a voice from the stairs above her.

"You! What are you doing inside?" It was Pennington, the butler. Frances kept her head low to hide her face under the hat brim, and hoped a harsh whisper would pass for a man's voice. Fortunately, the stairwell light was dim.

"Beg pardon, sir. Won't happen again."

"You were all told the house was off limits. But wait a minute." His voice grew softer. "You're young Abel, aren't you? I heard you had started work. Good for you, my lad. No doubt here to visit your sister?" He chuckled. Frances concluded she had been mistaken for the young brother of one of the maids.

"Yes, sir. Just thought I'd say hello."

"Very well. But from now on, you call on your sister in the servants' hall and on your own time. Now be a good lad and go off with the rest of the men."

Frances almost went limp with relief. She didn't think she could keep up the charade much longer. She nodded and pushed her way out the door. The real Abel and his sister would be thrown into a lot of confusion later.

She was just in time to meet the crew of about a dozen men as they headed toward the road that led to the village. One man was clearly the foreman: he was older than the rest and they all deferred to him. The men looked up curiously as Frances approached, wondering if one of their number had gone astray. She walked up to the foreman, and only then was her deception apparent.

"I have to slip out of the house for reasons that are my own." She produced a purse. "Keep my secret and you'll all drink on me this afternoon."

The foreman laughed. "I'd like to know that story, but very well."

They all marched along together and Frances listened to their rough talk. Then she felt a heavy arm around her shoulders, as one of the men sidled up to her.

"So, sneaking out to meet your sweetheart? Where did you get so much money anyway—steal it from the mistress?"

"Get your arm off me," said Frances. The man just laughed, and she wasn't strong enough to remove it. She wished she had Mallow's rolling pin, but no matter, she had heavy boots on. Between Mr. Mehmet's servant, Silas Watkins, and now this man, she had had her fill of being assaulted by men. And so, she slammed her heavy boot heel down on his instep. The man quickly snatched away his arm and came out with a string of obscenities.

"Touch me again and you'll find there are worse places for me to kick you," she said, to much laughter.

When they got to the village, the foreman winked at her and grinned as he and his men went into the village public house, and she continued on. It was startling to be dressed as she was, not just like a man, but a working man. Her position as a woman—as a lady of quality—garnered respect and acknowledgement.

Now, she was invisible. And yet, she could easily have joined the rest of them in the tavern, something the daughter of a marquess couldn't do. *Something to consider*, she realized, as she came to the village police station.

Dill looked up from some paperwork and cast a frown. *Again*, noted Frances, *daughters of the nobility were treated much better than working men.*

She didn't need any interruptions, so she shut and bolted the door and pulled down the shade.

"See here, my man" said Dill. "That's police property. Do you want to spend the night in jail?"

"No, I've done enough jail time," said Frances, doffing her hat. "But I have a counteroffer. How would you like to solve a murder and earn your sergeant's stripes?"

"My—my lady . . ." he stammered.

"Exactly. Now I don't have much time. So listen carefully. You'll need to come by later this evening and you'll need another constable, someone obedient who doesn't ask too many questions." And the constable got out his notebook.

"I am under orders to have nothing more to do with you, my lady," he said.

"I'm sure you are. But you're too smart to pay attention to silly orders. Now, listen carefully."

He noted his instructions, and Frances was rather pleased he gave no arguments, just accepted his orders. So someone in this county had some common sense.

When they were done, Frances put her hat back on and strode out of the door. She felt a little wistful passing by the tavern: It was dim inside and she might be able to pass as a man for a while. She wondered what that might be like. But now she had the clothes, and rural England was well-populated with inns and taverns, so there would be a chance to try that again some other time. No need to tell Mallow.

CHAPTER 26

It was with relief that Frances heard the car leave with Mr. Hardiman and the ladies. At seven, Frances made her way to the great hall. She reviewed everything that had happened since arriving, and the realization that no one could've engineered all that had happened except for the mistress of the house. The coordination with servants, the knowledge of the estate. No one had as much to lose—the management of a house, an institution, really—that gave purpose to her life. Frances could understand that. It hadn't explained all the bloodshed though. That was something else entirely—it was love, love for a man who never loved her back.

There would be time enough for philosophy later. For now, she checked to see that the servants had done as asked. Indeed, as Gwen had ordered at Frances's request, a fire had been built in the great hall, which was most welcome because it had become quite cool. The footmen had put two wingback chairs by the fire, and on the little table between them were two glasses and a decanter of the extraordinary port Christopher had inherited from Sir Calleford. She was delighted he had not yet gotten around to removing it to his own house. Everything was perfect, and she wondered how Mallow was getting on.

Mallow made sure she had her sewing kit, took a deep breath, and headed to Miss Jenkins's room. As befitted the maid to the lady of a great house, she had a rather pleasant room for a servant. It was on a high floor, so there were a lot of stairs, but it was quiet. No one should be able to hear their talk. Mallow knocked.

"Come in."

Jenkins seemed surprised, and not particularly pleased, to see her. She put on her haughtiest face, however. Was she not a lady's maid to a daughter of the House of Seaforth?

"I beg your pardon, Miss Jenkins, but I seem to have run out of thread and need to repair my lady's hem. I was hoping you had some in a similar color."

Jenkins did not look like she wanted to help, but it would be an unforgivable breach of etiquette for one maid to refuse to help another.

"Come in, then. I'm sure I can match that color." Then, with a little malice, she added, "You might remember to bring your own next time. A proper lady's maid always travels with a well-equipped sewing kit." Mallow burned at that. But Lady Frances had told her she had to play a role.

"Oh, I did," said Mallow, feigning sadness. "But you don't know what it's like. Lady Frances is always running around. She never looks where she's going and is always catching her hems. I've repaired this one three times already and simply ran out of thread."

"Oh dear," said Jenkins, who seemed to relish Mallow's discomfort while seeing a chance for some gossip. "Busy girl, is she?"

"You have no idea," said Mallow mournfully. Jenkins smiled.

"You're welcome to sit here and repair the hem. It's quieter and the light is better than in the servants' hall."

"That is very kind of you," said Mallow. She sat and began sewing. Jenkins complimented Mallow's fine, even stitches, and soon they were talking like old friends. With just a little sympathy, Mallow started talking.

"I have to say, Miss Jenkins, that at first it was very exciting, being maid to a titled lady, but it has become very difficult—living in a hotel, not a proper house, with all sorts of unsuitable people calling on her ladyship. But worst of all is the way other servants look at me, being maid to a lady subject to so much gossip."

Jenkins clucked in sympathy.

"And she's not as high and mighty as she wants you to think," said Mallow. "She doesn't know that I know that she likes her bit of gin."

Jenkins was surprised. *Who'd have thought Lady Frances liked a nip at the bottle?* Then Mallow got a crafty look. "She can't even remember how much she's drunk. In fact, I have the bottle myself . . ." And from the folds of her dress she produced a small bottle of gin. "If you have a couple of glasses, Miss Jenkins, you can join me in a swallow or two. Don't know about you, but without an occasional gin there's no way I can get through the evening."

Jenkins looked greedily at the gin. No doubt Mrs. Blake ran a tight ship and even senior servants wouldn't have a chance to drink spirits. Jenkins produced a pair of mismatched glasses, but Mallow fumbled them; one fell and rolled a bit and then the bottle cap fell too. Jenkins bent to fetch them, and meanwhile Mallow filled the remaining glass.

"There we go. This one for you, and now I'll fill this one. Cheers!" And they downed their gin.

⬥⬥⬥

Mrs. Blake appeared in the great hall and found Frances looking at the old family portraits in the dim light.

"Lady Frances, what is happening? I heard the motorcar leave. What are you doing here of all places?"

"They left for Blake Court. Gwen, Tommie, and the Hardimans. They're going to spend the night."

"That's . . . so sudden. Cook was set to have dinner ready."

"Gwen told the staff there would be no need for dinner tonight. In fact, she gave them the evening off. She even ordered the fire in here. And why shouldn't she? Gwen is the mistress of Kestrel's Eyrie."

That struck home, and she saw Mrs. Blake flinch. Frances had caught her off balance. Mrs. Blake's plan was falling apart, but she didn't know why, or how.

"I'm glad to see you are feeling better. We all thought it was a miracle you kept going as long as you did. Running this enormous house, caring for Gwen, managing the funeral and all the guests."

Mrs. Blake pursed her lips, and Frances could see her try to figure out what she should say. "When I heard the motorcar, I decided to dress and come down immediately, but my maid Jenkins suddenly seems to have disappeared. And then that extraordinary Mr. Mehmet intercepted me in the hallway and I couldn't get away. I thought the police said everyone could leave—and yet he's still here."

Well done, Mr. Mehmet, thought Frances.

"Jenkins apparently became unwell. I believe she is sleeping in her room."

Mrs. Blake approached her, and Frances saw she wasn't composed as neatly as she usually was. Her hair was askew and her dress hadn't been adjusted properly. She had wanted to leave her room quickly, and her maid wasn't around to help her. Frances's eyes fell on a bag Mrs. Blake was carrying. *She had come prepared.*

"Needlework," said Mrs. Blake. "I was going to do some this evening. I've long enjoyed it, but haven't had the time recently. I was going to sit in the drawing room before dinner, but then I heard you were here."

Frances looked her closely in the eye. "We need to talk," she said.

"What would you like to talk about?" asked Mrs. Blake. She tried to look as controlled as always, but there was a line of moisture on her brow. *She knows why we're here. She wondered before*, concluded Frances, *but now she knows. No more fencing.*

"We can start talking about Tommie Calvin."

"Tommie? She's going to be arrested tomorrow. Running to Blake Court won't save her. Not even London. They'll bring her back here."

Frances just smiled sadly. "No, she won't be arrested. But you will be. For the murders of Sir Calleford, Betsy Tanner, and Genevieve Sweet."

The two women just looked at each other for a few moments. Then Mrs. Blake smiled—like a tigress.

"Even for you, that seems like an outrageous statement. Are you so eager to take revenge on that inspector who humiliated you that you would throw around such insane statements?"

Frances just shook her head. She knew Mrs. Blake wasn't going to surrender without a fight. "I accuse you because of what you did." Frances looked around the great room. "I learned from my mother how a lady should manage her household and supervise her servants. Only the mistress of such a grand house could have done all this. That much was clear early, but why? That took me a while. You see, I thought it was about who would inherit the Kestrel fortune—but the solicitor Mr. Small tied that up neatly. And then I thought it was about marrying off Gwen, to keep control of the Eyrie. That was part of it. But mostly it was about ancient, frustrated desires."

Mrs. Blake laughed, but it was tinged with hysteria. *She's been on the edge of breaking down for days*, realized Frances.

"Years ago, there were two men and two women," said Frances in a rhythmic voice, as if she were telling a fairy tale to a child. "They were all very close. And then they got married. Only, one of the women was unhappy. She wanted to marry a brilliant, intellectual man and become a great political hostess, propelling him to become foreign secretary, even prime minister. But he chose her friend—a sweet, childlike woman. And she settled for his cousin, a genial country squire, and a life of organizing dinners with the local worthies. But she never forgot what she might've had."

Mrs. Blake raised an eyebrow, but said nothing. Frances continued her story, and by keeping a close watch on Mrs. Blake, she could see how right she was.

"Eventually, the woman lost her husband. And her first love lost his wife. So she moved in. At least she could be with him. It was probably too late to push him into a London political career he never wanted anyway, but she could organize his diplomatic meetings and share his life—and running this enormous estate gave her purpose."

Mrs. Blake just stared, without denying anything.

"You were Sir Calleford's wife now, in all but name," said Frances, being deliberately provocative. "In his drawing room, his dining room—even, I believe, his bedroom."

Mrs. Blake should've struck her for saying that, but Frances had guessed right: She couldn't resist giving Frances a triumphant took. It gave it all away, but clearly Mrs. Blake felt it was worth it to show Frances how close she had come to achieving all her ambitions.

"I never met the late Sir Calleford, but clearly he was a passionate man. How furious you must've been when he took up with Mrs. Sweet. And a woman as sharp as you couldn't have failed to notice she was carrying his child."

"How did you know? Did the whore tell you herself?" asked Mrs. Blake, barely getting the words above a whisper.

"She was growing stout and had to send her dresses to be let out. A passion for candy. Preserves of red raspberries, ginger, and chamomile. There have been enough babies in my family for me to have learned which herbs give pregnant women relief. And scraps of a conversation she had one evening with Sir Calleford. Perhaps he was even going to marry her."

"A slut like that? Pay her off and send her away," said Mrs. Blake.

"Perhaps. But he was talking to her, making plans for the future. Maybe he would've married her, and had a son who could inherit. You would've been thrown out the day the banns were posted. The hurt and humiliation must've been overwhelming. No wonder you killed him. You did it perfectly. Killed him with a Turkish dagger to throw suspicion on Mr. Mehmet, during a political meeting where it would be so hard to narrow down the suspects or motives. That's what kept me guessing. I thought you had everything you wanted as mistress of the Eyrie. Sir Calleford was not very old and he was in good health. You could've stayed here for many years. But you wanted Sir Calleford's love."

Frances could almost admire her, she had done it so well. Mrs. Blake had been one of the most distinguished figures in the county as mistress of the Eyrie. She had no doubt been the leading voice in discouraging the chief constable from calling in Scotland Yard, guaranteeing the incompetent Inspector Bedlow would take charge.

"But that didn't end your problem. That only began it. Lord knows what Mrs. Sweet would eventually say. So you shot her. There must be all kinds of weapons tucked away here; this is sporting country."

"Really?" asked Mrs. Blake. "I'm just an angel of death. I suppose I killed Betsy Tanner too. Tell me why I killed an ancient servant who was practically senile."

"She wasn't senile. That was the problem for you. It was her remark that I should've paid more attention to—no one knew which man would pair off with which lady and how important it was to find the right spouse. I'll upbraid myself forever for not realizing how important it was right away—and for not visiting to question her again before you killed her. You were afraid of what she knew, that she would start reminiscing and tell me just how much you loved Calleford in the old days. Or maybe even that other servants shared gossip with her, and so she knew about Mrs. Sweet, and how you had been replaced in Sir Calleford's affections. Oh, she knew way too much. And she wasn't the only one—did you not say you had given Sir Calleford everything? By the way, the Blake Court staff was far freer with gossip than Eyrie servants. I must tell Christopher to keep a tighter watch on them. I thought you meant that giving everything meant giving your life. But you gave him your heart. All this, running this grand estate, was a gift of your love to him."

"What an interesting fantasy, Lady Frances,"

She was trying to sound cool, but Frances heard the tremor in her voice.

"You expected to live out your life as Sir Calleford's mistress, while running the Eyrie. All was well, until he abandoned you. That's when you decided to kill him. He probably never suspected a thing. Meanwhile, you bribed and blackmailed an actor to threaten Tommie. You had to get rid of her too, so you could marry Gwen to your son. You got him into this house, and God knows what you planned for him to do to me, to Tommie, even to Effie."

"No one will accept his word."

"Perhaps. But he's under lock and key in London by now, and will be questioned again and again by men who are very good at it. Who knows what he'll remember to prove your guilt. Meanwhile, you were seen entering the study by someone who didn't realize what was going on."

"Who? Who is saying that?"

"Someone, a gentleman who will testify in court that he saw you enter at five after ten. You won't be able to get away with that. But back to Gwen and Tommie. You needed to separate her from Gwen so you could marry her off."

"I needed to get her away from that revolting relationship."

"Revolting? How dare you," said Frances, trying to control her temper. "Can you imagine how broken Gwen would be, forced from her love into a marriage with your son, while you encouraged him to seek pleasure elsewhere? Dear God. You were the one who bloodied Tommie's dress. Too bad I was one step ahead of you. With your plan crumbling and Christopher all but engaged to Effie Hardiman, you were prepared to publicize Gwen and Tommie's relationship. You told Inspector Bedlow. You sent Silas Watkins to threaten me. You would destroy Gwen and Tommie. Gwen would be virtually forced into marriage with Christopher in the wake of a scandal, and Mr. Hardiman would take his daughter back to America. You'd have the Eyrie. And the shared grandchild with Sir Calleford everyone knew you wanted, a pathetic link to a love you never had. It wouldn't do to have Effie Hardiman running things, a brash, competent American who wouldn't have accepted an interfering mother-in-law."

"An American nobody, presiding over the table—"

But Frances waved away her objections. "And you involved your maid, too, although I am guessing she didn't even realize what she was doing. You had Jenkins leave that threatening note for Tommie—I could tell by the nearly illiterate writing. And Jenkins delivered what was no doubt poison to Betsy Tanner—I doubt if she even knew it was poisoned, though. She hasn't been buried long, and there are tests for poison. I'll have a Home Office exhumation order and the best doctors in London examining her for the cause of death, and you know full well what I'll find. I admit I was a fool for not realizing Jenkins had been there. Mrs. Tanner's great-granddaughter Dolly said that only relatives were around that afternoon, and I had already been told that Mrs. Tanner was related to almost everyone—Jenkins was no doubt a niece or cousin, so her presence in Mrs. Tanner's cottage was unremarkable to Dolly.

"There can be no forgiveness for you," said Frances, feeling the anger rising up again. Whatever mistreatment and disappointments Mrs. Blake had experienced, there was no excuse. "Gwen and Tommie have the purest hearts of anyone I know. They have a deep and real love for each other. What you did and attempted to do—"

"Spare me your university rhetoric," said Mrs. Blake, her voice rising in anger to match Frances's. "I had Gwen's interests at heart, and whatever else I may have done, that was my main goal. They have a sick, unnatural relationship, and if loyal servants and London sophisticates wanted to pretend it was nothing but an innocent friendship, then I had to do something to prevent Gwen's complete moral destruction."

Frances calmed herself, and in an even tone said, "There is nothing wrong with Gwen and Tommie. The only unnatural love I see here is your obsession for Sir Calleford, a man who ignored you for years, then used you as his servant and his whore and discarded you for someone else. And your only motive was to live out your life here in a fantasy about a love you never had and a position you usurped only because Gwen never wanted it."

The pain and hurt on Mrs. Blake's face was so deep, Frances almost felt sorry for saying it. Mrs. Blake started to speak, but nothing came out, and when she finally mastered herself, her voice was so low and quiet that Frances shivered. Ghosts were said to inhabit old houses like this, and that's what Mrs. Blake sounded like—a vengeful spirit.

"I thought you of all people, Lady Frances, would understand hatred for men, how they depend on us even as they humiliate us and take everything we do for granted. That you would understand, even approve, of why I had to kill him. Especially a woman of your astonishing intelligence."

"I was rather good, wasn't I?" said Frances with a smile. "After you failed to scare away Tommie, you tried to frame her by pouring blood on her dress. But I was there. You thought no one would notice Betsy Tanner had been poisoned. But I did. You thought Silas Watkins would take me by surprise, but I caught him. You're out of cards to play." *Go ahead, call my bluff.* "But I'm giving you one last chance. I sent everyone away to give you an opportunity to quietly surrender and avoid a family scandal. We'll call the chief constable now. Your servants and family won't see you taken away. I don't care about you. I'm doing this for Gwen and Christopher. It's over. Don't make it harder than it needs to be."

Mrs. Blake smiled right back. "You just gave yourself away. You're young. And arrogant. Pride goeth before a fall. I've taken on responsibilities you can't comprehend." She reached into her needlework bag and pulled out a dagger, the exotic-looking one with the wavy blade Frances recalled from Sir Calleford's study.

"It's called a 'kris.' Calleford loved talking about his swords and knives, and I was happy to listen. It comes from the Far East. I am going to kill you now, just as I killed him. You sent away my servants, my family, and now there's no one to hear you. You thought I'd just give up? I'm going to do what I should've done when you first entered my house. No doubt they'll arrest Mr. Mehmet, a foreigner of doubtful background."

She raised her arm with the blade, but paused when Frances just shook her head. "I'm not alone. The police are within shouting distance. While Mr. Mehmet performed his assigned task of delaying you outside your bedroom and Mallow was disabling your maid Jenkins, I was admitting two constables into the house."

"You're bluffing," she said. "You couldn't have assembled this plan until you returned just before lunch, and even in my room I knew you never left this house. No messenger was sent. The telephone was not used. There is no possible way you summoned Constable Dill."

Frances didn't answer. She just grasped her silver police whistle—she would enjoy using it again—and blew it loudly. A door slammed and Constable Dill, with another younger constable, came running up. Behind them, Frances saw a concerned-looking Mallow.

Mrs. Blake just stared stupidly, as if she couldn't believe what she was seeing. Constable Dill laid a gentle but firm hand on her arm, and with his other hand removed the kris.

"Mrs. Phoebe Blake, in the king's name I arrest you for the murder of Sir Calleford Kestrel, Mrs. Genevieve Sweet, and Mrs. Betsy Tanner, and the attempted murder of Lady Frances Ffolkes. More charges may follow. Anything you say now may be used against you." He turned to the other constable, who seemed a little startled at what was happening. "Carter, escort Mrs. Blake to her room and stay with her until you are relieved. I will call headquarters."

Mrs. Blake seemed almost catatonic, staring blankly into space. Constable Carter touched her gently on her shoulder, and she silently turned.

"All is well with Jenkins, Mallow?" asked Frances.

"Sleeping like a baby, my lady."

"Excellent. Please show Constable Carter where Mrs. Blake's room is. Then return here."

"Very good, my lady." And the three of them made their way slowly to the stairs. When they were gone, Constable Dill just grinned.

"You cut it very fine, my lady. I feared that she would harm you, but I did as you said and waited for the whistle. Carter and I heard her confession from the closet."

"Well done, Constable. There was so little proof, I knew an admission would be necessary." Even with Mr. Mehmet's reluctant testimony, it would've been difficult to prosecute Mrs. Blake. A trap was needed, a final chance for Phoebe Blake to get rid of her opponent. "Fortunately, your timing was perfect. Everyone's timing was perfect."

Constable Dill was grinning and shaking his head. "I must say, my lady, you could've knocked me over with a feather when you walked into the village station this afternoon dressed like a farm laborer. I won't forget that quickly."

"A story for your grandchildren someday, constable. Thank you again for trusting me. Now, there's a telephone in a closet just off the foyer, and you can call your chief constable. I think it's best to call him directly, instead of Inspector Bedlow."

"I agree, my lady." He saluted and headed off. But Frances wasn't alone long. On near-silent feet, Mr. Mehmet appeared.

"Did I play my part well?" he asked.

"Perfect, Mr. Mehmet. She was delayed even longer than I needed."

He bowed. "I am pleased I could help. And pleased you could trust me at last. So I take it, then, as you hinted earlier this evening, that she was the author of these tragic deaths? She wasn't just having a liaison with Sir Calleford that night. She was stabbing him?"

"I'm afraid so," said Frances.

"She killed a kinsman, and the owner of the house that gave her shelter, the man who provided her food?" He shook his head as if unable to contemplate such wickedness. "But I was right, despite your mockery. You were chosen for this task and you followed your fate. You no doubt prevented more deaths and assured punishment for the murders already committed. You were the sword and shield of Allah."

"Oh, very well, Mr. Mehmet. I won't dispute your interpretation. However, I will wish you well. What are your plans now?"

He gave her a mysterious smile. "There are some tasks I wanted to complete here, but that won't be possible. My secret is safe—you have kept your word, and I won't have to give evidence to the police or testify in court, which would've been dangerous for me. However, there will be too much publicity for me to remain here any longer. Some will be disappointed, but it cannot be helped." He shrugged. "That's the way of things. My wife and I will be leaving tonight for a place of safety, and that is all I can say."

America, thought Frances. He had been talking with Mr. Hardiman for days, and Frances would be very much surprised if Mr. and Mrs. Mehmet didn't turn up with a letter of introduction on Hardiman lands in the coming weeks.

"I wish you luck," said Frances. "I will pray for you."

He bowed again. "And I will pray for you."

"*As-salamu alaykum*, peace be unto you. Do I have that right, Mr. Mehmet? Isn't that a phrase you use with your own countrymen?"

Frances had the satisfaction of once again seeing how startled he looked. Then he quietly laughed. "You are absolutely right. And now I say, *Wa alaykum as-salam*, and unto you, peace. You are full of surprises, as always. Dare I say you, of all women, were more nearly created the equal of a man?"

"Very funny, Mr. Mehmet."

But then he suddenly looked serious. "But actually, Lady Frances, I shall always associate you with rubies."

"The rubies in that bloody dagger? I don't know if that's a compliment in Istanbul, but in England, that doesn't sound very gallant."

"My turn to surprise you, my lady. No, not those rubies, but rather, the rubies in the Book of Proverbs. There is much wisdom there: 'Who can show me a woman of valor? Her value is far above rubies.' Farewell, Lady Frances." And with that, he left before she could respond.

Frances didn't have long to mull over her amusement and pride at Mr. Mehmet's comments, when Mallow returned.

"All is well, Mallow?"

"Yes, my lady. I did exactly as you said. Distracted Miss Jenkins, put two drops in the glass, and gave it to her with the gin. She was asleep in fifteen minutes. I checked in on her again, my lady: still snoring when I left her."

"Excellent. We needed Jenkins away while I was confronting Mrs. Blake. I couldn't have her blundering in on that. But no one but Mrs. Blake could order her away—not even Gwen."

Mallow nodded, then eyed the chairs by the fire. "I beg your pardon, my lady, do you have another meeting this evening? I didn't mean to interrupt."

"Yes, I do have another meeting this evening. I had Miss Kestrel tell the footmen to set this up tonight in anticipation of a small celebration. Just you and me, Mallow. Sit with me, and I will pour you a glass of what I've been told is the world's best port, and there's some bread and cheese—no dinner tonight I'm afraid."

Port! Mallow drank very little. Perhaps a half-pint of ale or cider when on an evening off with other servants. When she and her ladyship traveled by train, they'd have a glass of wine. But port was for ladies and gentlemen; it was far beyond her experience.

Mallow reluctantly gave in to the luxuriousness of the leather wing chair, sitting with her mistress in this ancient, distinguished room. Frances poured them each a glass.

"To competent women," said Frances, clinking her glass with Mallow's. The maid slowly sipped the fortified wine. *Oh, this was delicious. No wonder gentlemen set such store by it.* She felt a most lovely warmth soothe her nerves, and took another sip. So lost was she in her port, it took her a while to see how sad Lady Frances looked.

"Is something wrong, my lady?"

"The waste, Mallow. A woman of Mrs. Blake's intelligence and ambition, stuck with nothing to do, used and abandoned and slowly going mad. How many other women are like this? It can't go on."

Mallow nodded in agreement, as they just stared into the fire for a few minutes.

"I beg your pardon, my lady, but Mrs. Blake misquoted the Bible. While I was waiting with the constables, I heard her say 'pride goeth before a fall.' But it's 'pride goeth before destruction, and a haughty spirit before a fall.'"

"Good catch. And how appropriate. This house contains centuries of haughty spirits." *Effie Hardiman would be very good for this estate*, she thought.

Frances finished her port and refilled her glass—and then topped off Mallow's. They drank in silence for a while, watching the fire.

"I shouldn't brood, Mallow. We did wonderful work, you and I, and let's look to the future. There is one more mystery for me to solve, one more decision I have to make, something I haven't told anyone else. Mr. Wheaton has asked me to marry him."

"That's wonderful, my lady," cried Mallow. She put her glass down, got up, and gave her mistress a hug.

"Thank you," said Frances, touched by Mallow's reaction. "But as I said, there is still something to solve. I have to find a way to make Mr. Wheaton understand my terms. I think he does, but for marriage, there has to be a certainty."

"You mean the money, my lady? Your dowry?" Mallow knew those arrangements were very important in the upper classes.

"Oh no, Mallow," she said, waving her hand. "I mean the marriage itself. Mr. Wheaton must understand that I will not be changing my life, although we will be married. I will keep up all my activities, especially with the suffrage group. But if I can reach an agreement with him, we'll move into his house after we're married. Of course, you'll have a choice room, as befits a lady's maid."

That would be grand, thought Mallow. *The hotel was nice, but to take her place as a senior servant in a proper house . . .*

The port was really delightful, and she was hardly aware of Lady Frances filling her glass again.

"But wouldn't you want me to marry a duke or earl, Mallow?"

"Well, my lady, since you ask, it's like the poem of Lord Tennyson's you read to me. 'Kind hearts are more than coronets.' And if I may be so bold, I think Mr. Wheaton has a kind heart."

Frances didn't respond, but smiled quietly to herself. *How nicely put!* Mallow continued. "When I let him in by the side entrance, Constable Dill confessed he was somewhat nervous he was following your directions, my lady, but that he was sure he was doing the right thing." She paused. "I think he will go far in the police service, my lady. Intelligent and well-spoken."

"I agree," said Frances, smiling.

They stopped speaking, and continued to drink in companionable silence as the fire crackled. Soon, they fell asleep in their chairs. Two hours later, Pennington gently woke them up. Frances saw confusion, worry, and sadness in his eyes, but his voice was steady.

"I beg your pardon, my lady, but the chief constable of the county is here with his retinue, and is most desirous of an interview with you at your earliest convenience."

CHAPTER 27

It turned out to be almost dawn before Mallow and Frances got to bed, but the next day they were able to leave for London with Gwen, Tommie, and the Hardimans. With Frances's help, Gwen instructed the estate's attorney, the stunned Mr. Small, to keep the servants paid and the household going until more permanent arrangements could be made in the coming weeks.

And a month later, those arrangements were almost complete. Hal had diplomatically worked out everything with the courts—and with Mr. Small, Mr. Hardiman, and Mr. Blake—and they were all once again gathering at the Eyrie. A table had been set up in the great hall, and again a fire warmed the room against the weather that had turned from a cool fall to a windy winter.

Before they all filed in, Mr. Blake asked Frances if he could have a moment of her time.

"If you want to order me out of your house, Mr. Blake, I will understand," she said. "I will take no offense."

He seemed surprised. "Of course not, Lady Frances. Why should I want to? Because you uncovered my mother's crimes? Should I kill the messenger as they did in ancient Greece? No, I thank you stopping her before she did more damage, and the blame must be mine for not realizing how sick she was."

"It was a subtle madness. No one saw it until the end. But I hope some satisfactory arrangements were made?"

"Yes, thanks to your Mr. Wheaton. The man is a wizard. We were able to get her committed to a private facility for the insane, thanks to Mr. Wheaton's shrewd negotiations. No charges were ever leveled against her maid Jenkins, as you may have heard. I doubt if she had the brains to realize what my mother was up to, and she was as loyal as a dog. She was offered a chance to attend my mother in the . . . institution, and accepted it. It appears to be a good place, not too far from here. I saw it—but my mother refuses to see me. The doctors said maybe later . . ." he shook his head.

"I am sorry. I know it sounds trite, but you must look to the future now," said Frances, and he nodded in agreement.

"Before we conclude our business with the solicitors, I wanted to let you know that Gwen had one request—that the ruby dagger never enter the house again. Of course, I never would've considered it. Aside from its immediate use, I know it comes with a grim history. Still, that shouldn't deter a true collector. The police released it last week, and I sent it to Sotheby's for auction by special courier." He produced a piece of paper from his jacket. "Here's the receipt. I told them to fill it in with your name. It's time that dagger did some good in the world. After the sale, the check will be made out to you. Give it to whatever charities you want."

Frances was speechless. The dagger was worth a small fortune. Mr. Blake gave his so-charming smile. "When you find the words, write me a letter." Frances just laughed to herself—Mr. Mehmet, she knew, would've found this most amusing.

And with that, they entered the room.

Hal took his place at the head of the table. Mr. Small sat at his right, in what Frances thought was a resigned acceptance at the way things had turned out. Hal again wore one of his new suits, even as Mr. Small still dressed in his old-fashioned one.

"Thanks to everyone for coming today," Hal said. "First, I offer my hearty congratulations to Mr. and Mrs. Blake on their recent marriage." Effie and Christopher grasped their hands and smiled at each other, as Mr. Hardiman looked on benevolently. They had married quietly in the village church the previous week.

"And congratulations to them on their position as master and mistress of Kestrel's Eyrie, which, I understand, was a wedding gift from the father of the bride." Frances caught Mr. Hardiman's changed expression—a bit rueful. Hal had negotiated the sale on behalf of Gwen, and apparently had put a very high price on Mr. Hardiman's desire to give Effie what she wanted. Christopher would rent out Blake Court and manage both estates' farmlands.

"We're changing the name," said Christopher. "As my cousin Gwen says she doesn't mind, we're reverting to the old name, before the Kestrels took over the house. It will once again be Marchand Towers." *Ah*, thought Frances. *An emphasis on the aristocratic ancestor. Had this been Effie's idea?*

"The monies from the sale of the Eyrie—now Marchand Towers—will be placed under Mr. Small's management for Miss Kestrel's benefit." He nodded to Mr. Small. "I will continue to represent Miss Kestrel's personal interests. Mr. Small, if you have the documents ready, we'll start the signing."

Mr. Small began producing the various deeds and contracts, and while he was doing so, Hal pulled Gwen, Tommie, and Frances aside. "Miss Kestrel. You are now extremely wealthy. Have you given any thought to how you will live?"

"I thought I would continue to live with my great aunt in London," she said. "Can't I do that?"

"Your great aunt is very elderly," said Hal. "And you may find yourself the object of attention—unwanted attention—because of your wealth. Suitors, many of them unsavory, will be very insistent on meeting you. May I suggest you purchase a small house in a fashionable part of London? As mistress of your own house, it will be easier to keep your privacy."

"Oh! I see what you mean. But I never saw myself as running even a small house, although I suppose—"

"But Tommie will move in with you," said Frances. "It's perfectly respectable for two unmarried ladies to share a household. And Tommie will help you run things, and keep you safe from fortune hunters."

Gwen gasped, as Tommie looked back and forth between Frances and Gwen.

"Could we really? Is that possible?" Tommie began to smile, then said, "But my mother, she's so sick, and—"

"For goodness sake, there's nothing wrong with your mother," said Frances. "She just likes making her cook and maid fuss over her. And you can visit her as often as you like. You're staying in London, not moving to China. You'll get a small house and staff it with a cook and houseman. I'll wager we can get a married couple."

"When we're back in London, both of you can call on me at your convenience," said Hal. "I have already convinced Mr. Small to make the necessary funds available. I'll introduce you to house agents and servant agencies and will be happy to take care of the details."

Gwen finally found her voice. "Oh Tommie, that would be wonderful. Do you think we could get a dog? A small one, for the yard?"

Tommie reached over and took Gwen's hand. "Yes. I'm sure we can," she said quietly.

They rejoined Mr. Small, and Hal was showing Gwen where to sign the sales agreement for the Kestrel estate, when Mallow walked into the room.

"I beg your pardon, my lady, but you have a visitor at the servants' entrance. A member of the police, my lady."

She was surprised. *Surely it wasn't Inspector Bedlow coming back to arrest her again?*

"Very well. I think they can run everything without me." She followed Mallow to the servants' hall, where Constable Dill was waiting for her. Only, judging from his uniform, he wasn't Constable Dill anymore.

"Congratulations," said Frances. "I see from the stripes on your tunic that you have been promoted to sergeant. Well deserved, I may say."

"Thank you, my lady. I hope I haven't disturbed you, but I heard you were visiting again, and I wanted to thank you for the recommendation you gave to the chief constable. It was really your work that solved the murders."

"But you had the courage and wit to listen to me. Not every constable would do that. If you want to thank me, when you become chief constable, promise you will use your influence to allow women to join the service."

Sergeant Dill laughed. "I don't know if I will rise to those heights, my lady, but if I do, I certainly will." He cleared his throat. "And just one more thing, if I may. Miss Mallow, there is a party this evening at the local grange hall. May I escort you there? I assure you—and you too, my lady—that it is most respectable. The vicar and his wife attend. Refreshments and local musicians. I will of course see you back to the house afterward."

"If you wish to attend, I owe you a dozen evenings off for your work," said Frances.

"Thank you, my lady." She gave it some thought, as Sergeant Dill looked on hopefully. *It wasn't the cinema in London, and certainly not up to music hall standards, but it might be entertaining.*

"Thank you. I would like to go."

Frances suddenly felt like she was in the way, and left the two of them alone to make arrangements. But as she walked away, she heard Mallow give permission to Sergeant Dill to call her "June." *It must be love*, thought Frances. Mallow invited very few people to use her Christian name. How funny it was: When Mallow had first come to work for her, she had been convinced that respectable people never became involved with the police.

And here she was, allowing a police sergeant to escort her to a party.

And speaking of love and change, Hal was waiting for her outside the great hall. The paperwork had been taken care of. Gwen and Tommie said they would be in the solar working on some suffrage materials, and said Frances could join them there.

"You said you wanted to talk to me," said Hal. "I know we've been so busy in these past days, we haven't had time to really talk since you solved the murders." He looked a little shy. "Shall we find a comfortable place?"

"Yes. There's a pleasant morning room here." They settled down there. Hal looked nervous, and she felt a little bad for keeping him on tenterhooks for so long. He sensed this would be an important talk.

"You've asked me to marry you," she said. "Is that offer still open?"

"Franny, you know it is—"

"I told you that there are some things I wanted to do. I still do, but perhaps we can do them together. I don't see why I can't achieve what I want to achieve as your wife."

He leaned over and kissed her warmly. "What was it?" he whispered in her ear.

"It's what happened here that really made up my mind. It made me think about what women can or should do with their lives. I had always imagined that I would devote my life to my causes, but I've decided I don't want to end up bitter years later because of what I denied myself. Although, I don't want my sister-in-law's life either. As happy as Mary is with her lot in life, I could never live my life through a man."

"And your solution?" asked Hal. He had a half smile. *He's wondering if the conditions will be too impossible to meet*, thought Frances.

"You and I will have a new kind of marriage, one between equals, where the woman's work is just as important as the man's. Equal lives. What I want in life will be no more or less important than what you want. Can you accept that, Hal? You must mean it. You must know it is the only kind of marriage I can accept."

Hal brushed his fingers along her cheek. "How could you think I would accept any other kind of marriage with you? Your charitable work, your suffrage work, even your detective work, are what make you—you."

"So you won't worry about me?"

Hal laughed. "I didn't say that. Of course I'll worry. Can you live with that?"

She considered that. "Yes, Hal. And I will be your wife." And they kissed again. "But the engagement must be of a suitable length, so we can truly know each other. And no public announcements in the *Times*. No . . . fuss."

"I accept your terms, Franny, without reservation. But can you accept one of mine? I know you well enough to know that you won't let me ask your brother for your hand, as is customary. But may I ask for his blessing, for the sake of family harmony?"

"Yes, Hal. That will work nicely."

"Excellent. Because he just arrived."

"What? Did you bring him here expecting this?"

"I had no idea he was coming until the butler announced him, while you were out with Mallow. Is he still furious about your involvement here and your arrest?"

"He's calmed down a little, thanks to Mary's help, although he still brings it up. But what's he doing here?"

"I don't know. He asked for you and was put into the drawing room. Perhaps we should see him together?" He reached for her hand, and they walked to the drawing room, where Charles was pacing, a habit he had when something was weighing on his mind. He looked up as they entered.

"Dear brother, what are you doing here?"

"A little research. Remember that Turkish gentleman you asked me about? Mr. Mehmet? He disappeared the night of Mrs. Blake's arrest. We've had agents trying to find him, unsuccessfully. We had important business with him. So I thought I'd come to have a look myself, speak to a few people. And since you're here, I can ask you. What do you know? It's something of a coincidence that a man I told you to avoid suddenly vanishes the night you solve another mystery." He smiled wryly.

"You told me to avoid him, so I did," said Frances.

"Franny, you of all people should know that I could always tell when you were lying. You were up to something here, and now Mr. Mehmet is gone. He was of great interest to my office and I need to know where he is."

"How should I know?" she asked, with her wide-eyed, innocent look.

"Dear sister. I really don't think I'm being unreasonable. You run charities with great competence, and know that I am not teasing you when I say I don't know half a dozen men in London who could do better. Even your suffrage work—we're a political family and you're doing difficult political work, never mind my personal feelings. But you meddled in Foreign Office affairs. You have no concept of the implications, and as a result of your . . . investigations, we're left with some loose ends. Wheaton, I could use some support here."

"As I serve both you and your sister, my lord, it would be a conflict of interest to offer an opinion."

"Typical lawyer answer," said Charles. "Serves me right."

"Stop being silly, Charles," said Frances. "You're not going to change my mind on appropriate women's work, so save your breath. And I don't see any harm done to the British Isles. I do know I saved my friends and helped catch a murderer. Finally, I cannot say for certain where Mr. Mehmet went, but I have some good ideas, if you ask me nicely. And later. Meanwhile, Mr. Wheaton has something to ask you."

"Oh, very well. What is it, Wheaton?" Charles's shrewd eyes glanced from Hal to Frances. He smiled again. "Or do I already know? You finally got my sister to come around, Henry?"

"Not exactly how I'd put it, Charles, but we have reached an agreement."

"Mary didn't mention anything to me. Surely, Franny, you told her already."

"Oh, I think you'll find she won't be at all surprised," said Frances.

"Meanwhile, it goes against your sister's principles for me to ask you for her hand. But we would very much like your blessing."

Charles said nothing, but reached for a brandy decanter and poured a large glass.

"I wouldn't have thought that the prospect of gaining Hal as a brother-in-law requires your getting drunk," snapped Frances.

"It's not for me, it's for him," said Charles. "If he's going to be your husband, he needs a stiff drink."

"You're so funny. You should be on the music hall stage," said Frances. Charles laughed.

"I daresay I can approach the idea of marriage with Franny with a clear head," said Hal, giving a loving look at his fiancée.

"Then good for you," said Charles. "Of course you have my blessing." He slapped Hal on the back and pumped his hand, before giving Frances a kiss and whispering "well done" in her ear. He proceeded to pour drinks for all of them for a toast.

"Have you given any thought to the wedding?" asked Charles. "St. Margaret's in London? Or our parish church by our country estate—if you want something simpler."

"I haven't given it any thought at all. But you two gentlemen feel free to stay here and discuss it to your heart's content. I have things to do." Gwen and Tommie were waiting for her to work with them on the latest suffrage project. Hal just grinned and cheerfully drank the brandy, but Charles looked annoyed.

"Where are you running off to now?" he asked.

Frances spun around. "Women's work," she said. And strode out the door.

ACKNOWLEDGMENTS

Once again, I was fortunate to work with a great team: Many thanks are due to my indefatigable agent, Cynthia Zigmund, for her perseverance and wise suggestions over the years. And no writer has been luckier with his publisher: thanks to the wonderful people at Crooked Lane Books—Matt Martz, Dan Weiss, Sarah Poppe, Heather Boak, and Lindsey Rose—for their editing acumen, patience, and humor throughout the process. And finally, thanks also to my family for their unwavering support as I sat on the couch night after night writing away. Most of all, thanks to my wife, Elizabeth, for years of support and never doubting that my novel would be published.